CW01660900

AGONY

AGONY

by

FEDERICO DE ROBERTO

Translated by

Andrew Edwards

ITALICA PRESS
NEW YORK & BRISTOL
2021

Italian Original: *Spasimo*

Translation Copyright © 2020 Andrew Edwards

Italica Press Italian Crime Writers Series

ITALICA PRESS, INC.
99 Wall Street, Suite 650
New York, New York 10005

All rights reserved. No part of this publication may be reproduced, stored in a retrieval system, or transmitted, in any form or by any means, electronic, mechanical, photocopying, recording, or otherwise, without prior permission of Italica Press. For permission to reproduce selected portions for courses, or other uses, please contact the Press at inquiries@italicapress.com.

Library of Congress Cataloging-in-Publication Data

Names: De Roberto, Federico, 1861-1927, author. | Edwards, Andrew (Translator), translator.
Title: Agony / by Federico De Roberto ; translated by Andrew Edwards.
Other titles: Spasimo. English

Description: New York : Italica Press, 2021. | Series: Italica Press Italian crime writers series | Italian original: Spasimo. | Summary: "Agony is the first English-language translation of Federico De Roberto's "Spasimo," a psychological-detective novel that marks the first time an author with Sicilian connections penned a detective story in the procedural manner from crime to conclusion. De Roberto brings together a diverse set of characters - including two Russian anarchists and a melancholy young poet - each struggling with a complex moral dilemma. De Roberto uses a multiplicity of techniques to portray their issues. In this complex scenario, the judge called to investigate the death of Countess Fiorenza d'Arda has to determine whether it was murder or suicide. He works on shifting ground as each new revelation uncovers another aspect of the case, another moral quandary shedding new light on the motivations of the central characters"-- Provided by publisher.

Identifiers: LCCN 2020034405 (print) | LCCN 2020034406 (ebook) | ISBN 9781599103938 (hardcover) | ISBN 9781599103945 (trade paperback) | ISBN 9781599103952 (kindle edition) | ISBN 9781599103990 (adobe pdf)

Classification: LCC PQ4839.O3 S6313 2021 (print) | LCC PQ4839.O3 (ebook) | DDC 853/.912--dc23

LC record available at https://lccn.loc.gov/2020034405
LC ebook record available at https://lccn.loc.gov/2020034406

Cover Image: Lausanne, view over Ouchy from Le Colibri Estate, 1868. Photo by Constant-Delessert. Musée historique de Lausanne.

For a Complete List of
Modern Italian Fiction
Visit our Web Site at
http://www.italicapress.com/index011.html

Contents

About the Translator

Andrew Edwards is the co-author of *Sicily: A Literary Guide for Travellers;* and *Andalucía: A Literary Guide for Travellers;* in addition to *His Master's Reflection,* a biography of Lord Byron's doctor, John Polidori; and *Ghosts of the Belle Époque,* a history of the Grand Hotel et des Palmes, Palermo. He is also the translator of the books *Borges in Sicily, The Sicilian Defence,* and various academic treatises. He spends his time between the UK and the north coast of Sicily.

Federico De Roberto: An Introduction

In 1861, Federico De Roberto was born in Naples where his father, Ferdinando, had previously been an officer of the Kingdom of the Two Sicilies ruled by Francesco II. His Sicilian mother, Marianna degli Asmundo, was born in Trapani of an aristocratic family from Catania. The family moved back to Catania when De Roberto was nine after his father's death in a train accident. The subsequent years in post-unification Sicily were to have a significant effect on Federico's life and writing.

De Roberto's secondary schooling took place at the city's Technical Institute, after which he decided to enroll in the Faculty of Sciences at the University of Catania. Discovering that he had no scientific vocation, he independently began to study literature and the Classics, particularly Latin. These more literary interests prompted him to collaborate with publications based in Florence and Milan, notably the *Rassegna settimanale (Weekly Review).* His real debut came with the publication of the essay, *Giosuè Carducci e Mario Rapisardi, Polemica,* which dealt with the on-going literary feud between these two men of Italian letters. Leaving his university studies, in 1881 he took over the direction of *Don Chisciotte*, a journal named after Cervantes' famous character.

He looked to Giovanni Verga and Luigi Capuana, two greats of Italian realist literature, for inspiration. In Milan, he became a literary critic for the daily paper, *Corriere della Sera*, where he deepened his connection with Verga and Capuana, eventually forming lasting friendships with both writers. De Roberto dabbled with the *Scapigliatura* movement, whose name derives from the verb *scapigliare* which refers to disheveled hair – a suitable name for a group of bohemians modelled on the French style. Photographs exist of Federico with abundant locks pushed up from his forehead and flying out over his ears, a world away from later images where he is pictured with a balding pate, slicked back hair and a handlebar moustache.

In truth, De Roberto was never really a bohemian despite his contact with the likes of Emilio Praga and Arrigo Boito, both poets and *scapigliati*. His forays into the field of critical review helped him to pen a series of essays featuring authors of note, including Zola and Flaubert, which were collected together and published under the title, *Arabeschi (Arabesques)*. In addition, he pursued his interest in realist fiction, which led to the publication of his first set of short stories in 1887, *La sorte (Fate)*. The influence of Verga's realist style (known as *verismo* in Italian) can clearly be felt, although many critics have noted De Roberto's more disquieting, harsher focus.

The story, *Ermanno Reali*, was soon to follow. Originally planned as part of his collection, *Documenti umani (Human Documents)*, it became a standalone project. It could be seen as a precursor to *Spasimo (Agony)* as it deals with the eponymous protagonist's angst-ridden struggles. Reali is attracted to two women — Rosalia, the wife of a friend and, Massimiliana, who has come to Palermo with her uncle. He avoids Rosalia out of loyalty to his friend and pursues Massimiliana, who is tormented by an abusive past and feels unworthy of his affection. He proposes marriage, which causes her to faint. The two women comfort each other and decide to visit Ermanno to explain Massimiliana's reaction, only to find that desperation has driven him to suicide.

The tragic nature of male–female relationships explored in *Ermanno Reali* is developed further in *Spasimo*. The critic Carlo Alberto Madrignani, who has written widely on De Roberto, felt that the former text demonstrated a late-romantic autobiographical element together with themes of love and honor similarly explored by the Frenchman Paul Bourget. In fact, Bourget, known for his examination of human emotion and character, was another of De Roberto's literary guides and a major influence on his work, especially after the pair met in Catania during one of De Roberto's trips down from Milan and Florence.

The years following the publication of *Ermanno Reali* (1889), until the turn of the century, were very productive for De Roberto. In 1890, he started work on *L'Illusione (Illusion)*, the first of his three novels to feature the Uzeda family, specifically the aristocratic Teresa Uzeda, who is portrayed from childhood to her death in an intense and narrowly fixated manner. The Nobel Prize nominee, Benedetto Croce, was not enamored of this tightly focused world of highborn passion, where he considered situation and dialogue were destined to repeat on numerable occasions. Although not a critical success, the book did provide De Roberto with the Uzeda dynasty that would populate his masterwork, *I Viceré (The Viceroys)*.

In a letter to his friend Ferdinando Di Giorgi, he explained the layout of his new project: "The first title was *Vecchia razza (An Ancient Breed)*: this shows you the ultimate intention, that it should be the physical and moral decline of an exhausted lineage." Descendants of Spanish viceroys, the Uzedas are wealthy and utterly concerned with the propagation of their riches through inheritance. In a family laced with inter-marriage and internecine conflict, greed and power take the upper hand. *I Viceré* is a text that reeks of corruption, De Roberto's pointed way of representing the family's moral and physical, if not financial, bankruptcy. The family members are compelled to follow their obsessions beyond any other consideration.

The novel is divided into three parts, starting with the funeral of Teresa Uzeda in 1855 and the subsequent machinations leading up to the unification of Italy or *Risorgimento*. Part two features the aftermath of these events and their familial repercussions — marriages are annulled, partners are changed, and stolen monies are invested in treasury bills and dishonest land deals. Political expediency is the catchphrase by which the family continues to live. Consalvo Uzeda takes center stage in part three, and despite being disinherited, rises to the position of mayor. The novel closes with the 1882 elections when the franchise was extended to a larger part of the populace.

Once again, Croce was scathing in his criticism of the book, and in addition, its publication coincided with a general decline in the popularity of realist works. It is fair to say that De Roberto's pessimistic look at the *Risorgimento* would have been quietly forgotten without the success of Giuseppe Tomasi di Lampedusa's book, *Il Gattopardo (The Leopard)*, published posthumously in 1958, which prompted a reassessment of De Roberto's work. Leonardo Sciascia was among those who championed it, considering *I Viceré* to be second only to Manzoni's *I promessi sposi (The Betrothed)* in the canon of Italian letters. His critical hindsight is also crucial to the work's appreciation. De Roberto was too close in time and space to the events he portrayed: a new country, straining to find its feet, did not want to see itself in such an ugly mirror.

De Roberto's disheartening lack of success with a book now considered a masterpiece of *versismo* forced him to turn to other themes. He refocused his attention on strands of thought he had touched upon in *Ermanno Reali*, specifically how the psychological impact of love motivates human action. This is exemplified by the treatise he published in 1895, *L'amore, fisiologia, psicologia, morale (Love, Physiology, Psychology, Morals)*. Although it attracted some interested critics, it was not successful and considered a rather indulgent exercise. If essays proved unfruitful in developing these subjects, he decided that a fictional vehicle designed to engage the reader would be a better approach.

This idea formed the kernel of thought that led to *Spasimo*. He delineated it further in a letter to Domenico Oliva in 1896, declaring that he wanted the text to be "an interesting novel." He goes on to say that, "Too often, if not to say always, our novels are declared boring. I proposed to write one that you couldn't say that about... and it will indeed be a popular serial, whilst also wanting to be a work of art." De Roberto intended to address a widespread audience without abandoning his exploration of those preoccupations prevalent in his recent works. In the same letter, he also mentioned a desire to frame *Spasimo* within a moral rather than immoral context in complete contrast to the Machiavellian maneuverings of the Uzeda family.

Spasimo was released as a serial, which ran from November 1896 to January 1897 in *Corriere della Sera*. It was subsequently issued in book form later in 1897 and has been labelled a *psicologico-poliziesco* (psychological-detective) text. The author had labored over *Spasimo* prior to its release, honing and compressing the story with much care. It is a simplification to say that it marks the first time an author with Sicilian connections decided to pen a detective story in the procedural manner from crime to conclusion. As one of the first of its kind in the country, the book reflects more than a footnote in the annals of Italian crime fiction because it brings together a diverse set of characters, each struggling with a complex moral dilemma. De Roberto uses a multiplicity of techniques to portray their issues, ranging from a diary and letters, to the selective recall of the main protagonists.

Ferpierre, the judge called to investigate, sets to work on shifting ground as each new revelation uncovers another aspect of the case, another moral quandary that sheds new light on the motivations of the central characters. It is Robert Vérod's accusation that Countess Fiorenza d'Arda was murdered and did not commit suicide that initially prompts Ferpierre to delve deeper and to feel his own pangs of self-doubt as he contemplates the stimuli that drive Alexi Zakunin, the countess's Russian lover, a nihilist revolutionary. When the aforementioned Oliva reviewed the book for *Corriere della Sera,* he dismissed these deftly interwoven investigative threads as something for the "common reader," preferring to highlight the emotional depths lucidly explored by De Roberto. With this rather pompous comment, Oliva does, however, indicate that De Roberto was successful in writing a novel to interest both the casual reader and the more devoted admirer of literature.

It has also been pointed out that *Spasimo* contains, like *Ermanno Reali*, some biographical and autobiographical elements. The figure of the accuser, Robert Vérod, is an allusion to Édouard Rod, the Swiss author of *Le Sens de la vie (The Meaning of Life).* Rod and De Roberto were friends who shared an interest in portraying the motives that push characters to act in a moral or immoral manner. As with his literary counterpart, Vérod, Rod was prone to melancholy moods and a negative view of human behavior. Also an incident involving a young Alexi Zakunin, De Roberto's revolutionary, has parallels with the life of the writer, himself. Zakunin places a stone on a track to see if it will derail a train, creating a momentary twist of fate that could have devastating consequences for the passengers. It was the death of De Roberto's father in a train accident that cruelly affected his own childhood.

The author's mother, Marianna degli Asmundo, had a significant impact on her son throughout his life. At the time of *Spasimo*'s publication De Roberto moved back to Catania, motivated both by his brother Diego's wedding and a certain loyalty to Marianna. She was always a presence behind the scenes, manipulating decisions and events. She disapproved of his desire to turn *Spasimo* into a theatre production, suggesting that he would have to invert the book's order to avoid the early death of Countess d'Arda in order to keep the interest of the audience. She praised the text but would have preferred him to adapt *Ermanno Reali*. In this instance, De Roberto ignored her and pressed ahead with a theatre version, which was unfortunately never staged.

Although the countess dies at the beginning of the book, she is a constant presence throughout its pages. The mechanism used by De Roberto to illuminate her thoughts — Ferpierre reading her diary — brings Fiorenza d'Arda fully into focus as a character tortured by the nature of her relationship with Zakunin. Her religious beliefs run contrary to the manner in which they live their lives. Ferpierre's interviews with the main protagonists often reinforce her written viewpoints, but equally as often seem to cloud the facts. One of De Roberto's most innovative ideas was to show the doubts and confusions of the investigating judge, who, although not a morally ambiguous modern hero, is far from the one-dimensional stereotypes of the plodding policeman or the insightful savant.

De Roberto's own emotional life was complicated and often thwarted. When he left Milan at his mother's behest, he left behind Ernesta Valle, who was married to a Messinese lawyer. She styled herself a countess, although her right to such a title has been disputed. De Roberto was thirty-six when they met, she a mere twenty-one. He was utterly struck by her poise and beauty and soon came to call her Renata, a name chosen to symbolize the rebirth of his love. After his move back to Catania, they continued a long-distance relationship via copious correspondence, which languished in the University of Catania archives until it was uncovered and published by the researchers Sarah Zapulla Muscarà and Enzo Zapulla.

Ernesta enjoyed her life as the wife of a lawyer, frequenting the salons of Milan. While De Roberto remained in the city, they were able to arrange furtive encounters at La Scala opera house or in cafés. In Catania, under his mother's imploring influence, De Roberto was reduced to sublimated rose-tinted prose and descriptions of his literary projects. In one letter, he wrote to Ernesta about his mother's request for a copy of *Corriere di Catania*, which had printed a review of *Spasimo*, a review he called *bestiale* (beastly) because of its overly sycophantic praise. Nevertheless, he sent a copy to his 'Renata' because he knew she wanted any news of his work.

He also mentioned to Ernesta that he wanted to finish writing about the Uzedas by following *I Vicerè* with *L'Imperio (The Empire)* and in so doing to complete a trilogy. It is clear from his correspondence that he held little faith in its success. The years at the turn of the century were dark and claustrophobic for De Roberto, his depression compounded by his perceived provincialism of Catanese society. His love for Ernesta was one sustaining force, but even that began to wane, stretched as it was by time and distance. He eventually switched his affections to Pia Vigada, who was based in Rome and also married. Through a long correspondence, history repeated itself.

In these and other writings, some critics have detected a misogynistic streak, most markedly in his treatise, *L'amore, fisiologia, psicologia, morale*. In the book, *Printed Media in Fin-de-siecle Italy: Publishers, Writers, and Readers*, Olivia Santovetti has noted that one of De Roberto's critical targets in the essay was Paolo Mantegazza'a *Fisiologia dell'amore (Physiology of Love)*. Mantegazza thought that feelings of love were more intense in women. This, as Santovetti says, ran contrary to De Roberto's belief in the male's superiority in matters of love, sex and biology. Annamaria Pagliaro, in her work *The Novels of Federico De Roberto: from Naturalism to Modernism*, sees the female characters in *Spasimo* and the subsequent story, *La messa di nozze (The Wedding Service)*, as vehicles to laud the intricacies of the male intellect.

An increasingly embittered De Roberto was right to be pessimistic about *L'Imperio* as it would never be published in his lifetime, but he continued to pursue other ideas, which did reach their intended audience. The trauma of the Great War formed the basis of his 1921 work, *La paura (Fear)*, in which a group of Italian soldiers in a trench in the Valgrebbana are alerted to a change in enemy troop configuration by the loud crack of gunfire — the Bohemians in the opposite trenches have been replaced by Hungarians. Lieutenant Alfani, happy to be stirred from boredom, makes the decision to man an empty lookout post so that the enemy's movements can be observed. To reach the appropriate spot, he orders the troops to run the gamut of a defenseless passage. The designated soldiers are all killed, one after the other, by a Hungarian sniper.

Each remaining soldier knows his time will come, and there will be no escaping the inevitable fate. We learn of their stories and fears, of their beliefs and families. De Roberto chooses to give voice to his characters through regional dialect, affording each individual an immediacy of speech and feeling that reinforces the absurdity of their task. Morana is the soldier who finally refuses to submit to this tacit form of suicide, choosing instead to take his own life rather than be ordered to do so. De Roberto is the witness to their fate, the observer reporting the meaninglessness of war.

The author never experienced the trenches himself since he was fifty-three when the conflict broke out, but he was able to recreate the horrors in a way not achieved by some of the Italian writers who had actually fought in the war. He was only able to conduct research after the censorship of the war years had lapsed and he could access first-hand accounts and conduct correspondence. Despite the praise for his understanding of conflict, there is, as Gabriele Pedullà notes in his introduction to *La paura e altri racconti di Guerra (Fear and Other Stories of War)*, a distinct lack of description regarding the visceral smells of war, the olfactory stimulus of being in such a perilous and sensory position. Regardless of his scrupulous study of the subject, this was something De Roberto could never recreate.

La paura was first printed in the periodical, *Novella*, then re-edited and re-released just after the author's death. It is now often published together with his other stories based on the Great War. Throughout his forties and fifties, De Roberto continued to produce works in various genres, including short stories, but also pieces for the theatre and further essays and treatises. As each saw the light of day, he would return to work on *L'Imperio*. During this period, he was in contact with the playwright and poet, Nino Martoglio, who agreed to stage his 1912 work, *Il rosario (The Rosary)*, which was received with a degree of critical approval.

De Roberto was also appointed chief librarian at Catania's civic library in 1918. In 1922, when Giovanni Verga died, De Roberto occupied himself by organizing Verga's papers and beginning a study of his life and work. By 1923, he decided to re-issue *Ermanno Reali*, some of his early poetry and to publish his translations of French literature. He was, however, primarily preoccupied with his mother's illness and put aside the majority of his endeavors to care for her. In spite of their problematic relationship, her death was a huge blow, and the years spent looking after her were insufficient to prepare him for her loss.

De Roberto's own health was also starting to cause him problems. He suffered his first attack of phlebitis in 1919, which caused inflammation and inhibited his ability to walk unaided. A few short months after his mother's death, he was struck again with a serious attack and collapsed outside his front door in Catania. He died on the same day, 26th July 1927, at the age of sixty-six. De Roberto was never publicly mourned in the city due to a disagreement between his friend Sabatino Lopez and the Fascist authorities in charge of the local government. Nationally, his death was also overshadowed by the demise of Matilde Serao, the journalist, editor and novelist who had been nominated for the Nobel Prize on four occasions.

L'Imperio, although it remained unfinished, was published by Mondadori in 1929. As we have seen, more of De Roberto's writing would also surface posthumously. His work on Giovanni Verga was released as late as 1964 under the title, *Casa Verga e altri saggi verghiani (The House of Verga and Other Vergian Essays)* and it is only thanks to the Zapullas that we know the contents of his detailed correspondence with Ernesta Valle. Federico De Roberto never gained the degree of critical acclaim in his lifetime that he now justly receives, taking his place among the most illustrious figures in the world of fin de siècle realist and modernist literature.

Andrew Edwards

AGONY

I

The Events

All those who spent the fall of 1894 on the shores of Lake Geneva will still recall, without doubt, the tragic incident at Ouchy. It created a great impression, feeding much curiosity, not only in the communities of holidaymakers scattered along the lake, but also among the cosmopolitan general public who read about it in the papers.

On October 5th, a few minutes before midday, the sound of a firearm and confused shouts came from the Villa Cyclamens on the road halfway between Lausanne and Ouchy. They violently interrupted the usual tranquility of the place, attracting neighbors and passers-by. The Villa Cyclamens was rented by a Milanese lady, the Countess d'Arda, who stayed there every year from June to November. The friendship between the countess and Prince Alexi Zakunin had been known for some time. He was a Russian revolutionary originally sentenced in his own country, then expelled from all the states in Europe and finally given refuge in the territories of the Swiss Confederation.

The two lovers were at home in the villa on the day of the tragedy, and it was the shouts of Prince Zakunin, along with the detonation of the firearm, that brought the terrified servants running to the scene. They were confronted with the dreadful spectacle: the countess lying lifeless at the foot of the bed, the right side of her temple pierced by a bullet, a revolver next to her hand. Even though the horrid sight of death, a sudden and violent death, was such that nobody approached the body, it wasn't the corpse that created the strongest emotional impact but the survivor himself. The cold face of the unfortunate woman had the color of wax. Like a pallid azalea crisscrossed with thin red lines, it was partially stained with blood. Nothing in it revealed the constrictions of agony. On the contrary, a confident serenity and something approximating a smile played across it. The woman's violet lips were slightly parted, her beaded line of teeth just visible. With her wide eyes turned upwards, she seemed to be in ecstasy, as if she still hadn't completely let go of life, as if she wanted to prove she was very much part of human existence, in silence and shadow finally finding happiness and wellbeing. Deathly pale, with distorted features, untidy hair tumbling over a forehead soaked with glacial sweat, with a mad look in his eye, his lips, hands and whole body trembling, as if in full fever, Prince Alexi instilled a feeling of fear. After shouting for help in a hoarse voice, he had knelt down next to the corpse; embracing it he had covered himself in blood. Only two brief and monotone words came from his convulsed mouth: "It's over! It's over!" In those words, in the lacerated voice with which he repeated them, there was a grief, a bitterness, a desperation so strong that the dead woman seemed to merit less compassion than the living, than this inconsolable man lost in pain, frantically trying to catch his breath. From time to time, when his hands tired of stroking the dead woman's hair, her hands, her clothing, he would place them around his neck in a violent gesture, as if he wanted to strangle himself. It was then that the servants, the people who had gathered, tried to console him, to drag him away from the cruel spectacle. With a savage kind of energy, he pushed everyone back, spreading out his arms, then he came to a halt, finally crossing the deceased woman's room with an uncertain step, as if drunk, only to come back and collapse next to the corpse.

The villa was open to everyone. Nobody had thought to stop them from entering. Doctor Bérard had quickly arrived from the nearby doctor's office but had only been able to say that it was a swift death. The news spread rapidly among the community of foreign residents, and the curious flocked to the villa, especially those who knew the countess and the prince. Although nobody had any news on what had happened, the servants were the ones on the inside. Zakunin seemed deaf and dumb, he didn't recognize the people who approached him, who tried to hold out their hands, nor did he hear the words of sympathy, the words full of sorrow and kindness directed towards him.

The answers from the serving staff didn't throw much light on the sequence of events. They only mentioned the superficial circumstances of the catastrophe. They all said that the prince had returned to the villa two days before, after an absence of a few weeks; that the countess had got up very early this morning as usual and had spent an hour out on the terrace, while her companion had worked in the study with a lady who had arrived around nine o'clock; that the countess had sent Giulia, her long-standing Italian maid, to town before lunch to pick up a few things; that when lunch was ready to be served, they had heard the shot, which had startled everyone. They then saw the frenzied prince hurtle from the second-floor chambers down to the ground floor, asking them to call for a medic. Everybody had swiftly gone to the countess's room, where the foreign woman had tried in vain to aid her, before, equally in vain, trying to console the desperate prince.

In the middle of all the confusion, few had noticed the foreign woman. She was young, barely twenty years old, with strawberry blond, short hair combed in a masculine manner, clear, cold eyes, rather on the small side and dressed in black from head to foot. She had stayed bolt upright and stationary next to one of the windows, her arms were folded, her head titled forward. She seemed almost unaware of the curiosity her presence was starting to create. Of those present, Baroness Börne was at the heart of a group showing most interest. She was Austrian, overweight and short in stature, the only female bystander who had come up to the villa. She was looking fixedly at the foreign woman, as she overwhelmed the servants with her questions, who, not knowing how to answer, had gathered in groups to explain what had happened.

"Poor woman! My poor friend!" exclaimed the baroness. "But why? How can it be? Did she leave a note? They haven't found anything that she left? There has to be something. Keep looking. She died straightaway? She must have suffered, but nothing she couldn't tolerate! She was strong, a very strong woman, in spite of her thin delicate body. Moral pain.…"

Turning to a young Englishman with a red moustache, blue eyes and a bald head, she lowered her voice and asked in an insinuating manner: "Do you think she was happy?"

He responded with an ambiguous gesture, which could have indicated agreement, doubt or ignorance.

"And the poor prince!…" the baroness continued, still looking out of the corner of her eye at the woman. "It's a shame to see him suffer so. Someone should persuade him to leave the room." These words were directed straight at the unknown young woman, but as she didn't respond, the baroness proposed: "Why don't they at least move the body on to the bed?"

She was part of the group by the corpse, and seeing that those present agreed with her, she asked them to let her pass. She approached the prince, who at that moment was propped against the bed, his arms hanging down, his hands taut and his eyes lost in their gaze, which was still on the dead woman.

"We can't leave her like this.… We think she should be put on the bed. Do you want us to do that?"

But he didn't answer, or even show that he had heard her, and when the baroness put a hand on his shoulder, he trembled as if shaken by a magnetic current: his stare, lost, empty, disconsolate expressed such a dreadful anguish that the talkative lady was temporarily at a loss for words.

"What misfortune! What pain!" she said, disturbed by the scene. "But one must summon enough strength to resign oneself to destiny! Doctor," she added, turning towards Bérard, who at that moment was approaching the prince, "We would like to move the body.... It looks like the poor woman is suffering on the floor! And all these people, can't they be asked to leave?"

"Yes...certainly," answered the doctor rather hesitantly, without knowing what to do. "But before we settle on doing anything, we ought to wait for the magistrates."

"Has somebody told them?"

"They're on their way."

The murmur of voices ceased in the adjoining room just as the Lausanne and District Justice of the Peace entered along with the Police Commissioner, another doctor and two gendarmes.

The first thing the magistrate did was to order the indiscreet bystanders from the deceased's chambers. Once this was completed, the two gendarmes took up position at the door to the adjoining salon in order to prevent them from returning. Only the foreign woman, Doctor Bérard and his police colleague remained next to the corpse. Bérard was explaining the hopelessness of any treatment and the swiftness of her death. Nearby, without being asked, Baroness Börne was telling the magistrate what had happened, while the prince and the commissioner looked on.

"What has prompted such a disastrous turn of events? Was there nothing that could have prevented it?" asked the magistrate. The baroness, still incapable of remaining silent, only shrugged this time and looked at the prince, as if to indicate that he was the only one who could answer.

Zakunin wiped his hand across his brow, appearing to wake from a deep sleep, and said: "Yes, it could have been prevented.... I should have prevented it."

"Did she suffer much?"

"She suffered so much...so much!" the prince responded, sounding such a note of profound sadness that the magistrate, himself, was moved.

"Was she ill?" he asked the doctor after a brief silence.

"Yes, a pulmonary infection."

"Did she know?"

"Definitely, there was no way to hide it. She was so intelligent and courageous, compassionate lies would have been useless with her."

"Was there no hope of a recovery?"

"Her illness had a predestined ending, there was no cheating it, but through an appropriate regime she could have lived for a good few years yet."

"So, it's not only her illness that prompted her to kill herself?"

"It's not the only thing," repeated Prince Alexi like an echo.

During the magistrate's questions, Baroness Börne's attitude was very odd, almost comic. As she couldn't speak, she closed her lips, moved her eyes, shook her head, tilted her entire body, as if repeating the justice's questions and confirming the others' answers in order to prove she had foreseen everything. By signs, she would intimate that she had an observation to make, even, at times, interrupting: "That's it! Exactly so! Precisely! Having the religious sentiments that she did...."

"What were those?" asked the justice.

"Few women I've known had such a strong, devoted faith," answered the doctor.

"Truly," interrupted the baroness once again. "It seems incredible how great her fervor was! I can tell you something about that. She wouldn't go for a walk if she couldn't end up at a church. Her favorite excursions were to the districts of Echallens, Bretigny, Assens, Villars le Terroir, simply because of the Catholic churches she found there. On Sundays and saints days she would spend long hours here, at Saint Louis, kneeling until she had no strength left. I must say to you that I find it incredible that with such a great faith she could do what she did."

The prince didn't speak. The nervous tremors shaking his body were beginning to subside. The violent convulsions, the dreadful expression on his washed-out face and his reddened eyes were changing. Pale, exhausted, with no strength, he seemed on the point of collapse.

"Was she alone when she killed herself?"

"Yes, alone."

"Did you speak with her this morning?"

"Yes, I spoke with her."

"Was she depressed, sad?"

"Fatally."

"We ought to see if she's left anything written down."

The baroness clapped and exclaimed: "That's what I've been saying since the start!"

On a signal from the magistrate, the commissioner began his search.

There were only a few pieces of furniture in the dead woman's room. The bed, a wardrobe with a mirror, a chest of drawers, an escritoire in the full sunlight of a nearby window and a small table in the corner were the full complement of furnishings. On the escritoire, there were two piles of English books with white covers, a drawer with writing paper, an old sweet tin and a travel bag. There were more books on the small table and the night-stand next to the bed. The commissioner went through them one by one, he opened the drawers, none of which were under lock and key, and after checking the toiletries and perfumes, all full, he closed them again. The deceased's correspondence was on the escritoire in old pasteboard boxes along with a purse full of Italian and French notes as well as gold and silver coins. At the back of the right-hand desk drawer the commissioner found a boxed book in a black case, locked with a very small key. He was about to open it when the prince took a step forward and said: "It's a memoir, the diary of her life."

By the tone of his voice, by his whole attitude, it looked as if he wanted to defend the intimate thoughts of his poor lover from any prying eyes. Baroness Börne approached the justice to protest that "it was precisely here you could find something!" The book, however, extracted from its velvet case by the commissioner, was already in the magistrate's hands.

The cover was also black with silver fasteners, like a book of remembrance, its very appearance expressing the sadness and pain that must have embittered the poor woman's life. The magistrate quickly leafed through it. The writing was rather large, thin, lightly pressed, elegant and admirably clear. She had written in approximately three quarters of the book. The magistrate focused his attention on the last pages, but after reading them, he let his head drop.

"It's difficult to understand," he said. "It's not a confession...."

Meanwhile, the commissioner continued his investigations in a small area next to the dressing room, where another wardrobe, a washbasin and clothes chests took up all the space available. He found no letter there either. He came back into the bedroom, crossing it to enter the salon: the search was even briefer and as unsuccessful, apart from the divan and armchairs, there was only a table full of trifling knick-knacks and a piano with a score by Pessard. The commissioner was already retracing his steps when a rumble of voices, shouts of anguish, made him turn back. The gendarmes, obeying his orders, had greeted a women dressed in black but stopped her from entering. She was wearing the black veil so common to women of Lombard origin.

"Ah, *Signor*! Ah, *Signor*!" exclaimed the woman, pressing her hands together, her drawn face furrowed with tears. "I want to see her! To see her one more time! My lady! My good lady! Ah, *Signor*, to see her!..."

It was Giulia, recently returned from the town. Petite and thin, somewhat advanced in years, she seemed bewildered with grief.

"Let her pass," ordered the magistrate, on hearing the baroness's explanation that she was the countess's serving woman and had enjoyed her complete confidence.

She entered, sobbing and tearful, hands together, and as she moved towards the body, the same nervous trembling took over the prince's body once more. His face had that look of terrible dismay, of dreadful pain, as if the presence of someone dear to the dead woman would intensify his torment. He was no longer looking at the body, but at the disconsolate woman. He seemed to want to approach her, to be next to her so that he could unite their pain, so he could talk about her and hear her talked about. Everyone, the law officers, the doctors, even the baroness herself felt moved by the anguished attitude of the unfortunate soul. Only the foreign woman remained still, rigid and impassive, avoiding almost everyone's gaze.

"She said she would, and she's done it now! She's done what she said she would!" cried the woman next to the body. "She wished for death, she called for it.... The poor woman! Ah, *signori*! She sent me away, she sent me away, so she was alone.... So, I couldn't read it in her face! If only I'd been here with her! How many times, the poor woman, how many times had she prayed to God that she'd die! And she's killed herself!" She repeated herself, sounding increasingly heartbroken, as if up until that moment she had been able to doubt the events and to hope, but that now she had suddenly received undisputed confirmation of the disastrous news. "She's killed herself! She's dead! *Signor! Signor!*"

The baroness passed her hand in front of her eyes, sighed and took the serving woman in her arms.

"Enough now, you poor woman. There's nothing for it but to resign yourself to what's happened. Calm yourself! Enough now! The best thing is to tell these gentlemen of the law about where she sent you. Where did she send you? And why?"

"To the town, to pay some bills...to buy some things.... I don't know anything else. Originally, when she got up, I thought she wanted to come with me, then she changed her mind, and she sent me."

"Did she give you a letter? Do you know if she wrote a letter, last night or this morning?"

"Last night, no. This morning, yes. This morning she wrote a letter."

"Who was it addressed to?"

"To Sister Anna."

"Who is Sister Anna?" asked the magistrate, who had patiently left the garrulous baroness to ask the questions.

"Sister Anna Brighton, the English lady who used to teach her."

"Where does she live?"

"I don't know. There was a foreign place name on the envelope."

"You don't know the address either?" the justice asked, turning towards Prince Alexi.

"I don't know, but…"

His anxiety appeared to lessen. He was on the point of saying something, when there was a noise in the background. The police were preventing somebody from entering the room. This time, however, the unexpected visitor in question wasn't grieving or crying. With a resounding, irritated, almost imperious voice, he said: "Let me pass. I must come in, I tell you!"

As the commissioner went to see who it was, Bérard and Baroness Börne also approached the door.

"Vérod!" exclaimed the baroness when she saw the tall, corpulent, young man with dark hair and a lighter moustache trying to force his way through. He quickly entered when the guards, receiving a sign from their superior, stepped to one side. But once he gained entry and had taken a few rapid steps, the newcomer appeared to hesitate, undecided: the irritation creasing his face was subsiding amid the confusion and distress. Passing the threshold and seeing the body, he put his hand to his heart and leaned back against the door, the color fading from his cheeks. He was near to collapse.

"Our poor dear friend!" the baroness said once again, holding out her right hand in an effort to comfort him, to give him courage. "Who would have thought it! Doesn't it look like she's asleep? Our poor dear friend! Killing herself in this way…"

The young man recovered his posture, and taking a step further, said in a firm voice: "No."

Anxiety and astonishment quickly flashed across those present.

"What do you mean?" asked the magistrate, going up to Vérod and looking him straight in the eye.

"I'm saying that the lady didn't kill herself. I'm saying that she was killed."

His voiced echoed strangely, as if he was speaking in an empty space, so glacial was the silence surrounding him, so surprised were the minds of those present, hanging on his every word. Prince Alexi, upright, stock still, his head held high, also looked fixedly at his unexpected accuser.

"How can you be sure?" asked the magistrate.

"I know it."

"Do you have any proof?"

"No material proof, but moral certainty."

"Who do you think killed her?"

The young man raised his arm. Signaling the prince and the foreign woman with his index finger, he said: "Them."

Everyone turned their astounded gaze towards the accused.

At first Prince Zakunin's expression didn't change. He seemed not to have heard, or at least, not to have understood. Little by little, his lips twisted, bitter and ironic, his brows raised over his suddenly sunken, almost bright eyes, animated by a painful smile. His features revealed the feelings of surprise, incredulity and even amusement prompted by such an unforeseen charge. The unknown woman remained with her arms folded, looking at her accuser, her mask-like face showing neither disdain nor surprise.

"If I wasn't certain, I wouldn't have spoken out."

"What interest would these two have in such an outcome?"

The young man spoke with a violence he struggled to contain.

"The evil in their souls, their savage pleasure at doing harm, destroying a life, spilling blood. The voluptuousness with which they put an end to the long martyrdom of that poor unfortunate woman by killing her."

His voice trembled, his hands were also shaking, his eyes full of tears. In the circumstances, the emotions generated by his words unexpectedly gave way to feelings of real fear, when the prince, approaching his accuser, fist in readiness, features contorted, stared bitterly at Vérod and began to insult him: "Madman! What are you saying?"

The two men were face to face, their eyes sharpened steel, sparks ready to fly, their looks trying to penetrate each other's soul.

The magistrate and commissioner were forced to intervene.

"Tell us where your certainty comes from?" said the former.

"From everything, everything. From the lady herself, whom I knew and was very fond of. From the Christian resignation and angelic kindness of her soul. From the actions of these two, their bloody instincts and shared evil nature. Nobody who knew her will believe she has killed herself. Ask whomever you want, ask everyone.... Tell them," he added turning towards the servants, who looked embarrassed. He was trying to provoke an immediate testimony from those present: "...Tell them that you knew her, that she was fond of you, tell them if it's possible, if it's believable."

The magistrate interrupted him, fixing him once again with a scrutinizing gaze: "This woman has said the opposite: she has stated that the lady of the house intended to kill herself on other occasions, that she sent her away deliberately this morning and that today she did nothing more than put into practice a firm, long-held plan."

"Do you believe that?" exclaimed the young man disconcerted. "Did you say that?"

The woman didn't answer. She looked around, lost, almost vacant: she didn't seem to understand or even see.

"Whose firearm is this?" the magistrate asked her.

"Hers."

"Could someone have taken it? Where did she keep it?"

"Locked. Hidden."

"You see," said the magistrate, facing towards the young man. "Nobody confirms your accusations. Do you insist on them?"

The magistrate spoke in a serious manner, almost in a tone of disdainful reproach given the way the young man had skated over his lack of proof. He looked around, doubtful, passing his hand over his forehead. He once more saw the lifeless body sprawled on the floor, the rigid form of the dead woman, the face even whiter than before with the blood stains losing their purplish color as they were beginning to dry, the mouth still half-open, the eyes fixed, terrible, no longer in ecstasy. After a moment's silence, he extended his arm and repeated in a barely audible agitated voice: "I swear that this woman has been murdered. Please allow me to speak to the senior examining magistrate."

II

The First Investigations

Judge François Ferpierre, the senior examining magistrate assigned to Lausanne's central court, was very young: still less than forty years old. He had a solid legal background, much knowledge of life and the human heart, plus a natural aptitude for observation, which in the exercise of his profession had turned into an inspired clairvoyance, an almost fateful prescience. This made him one of the best magistrates in the Swiss judiciary, although his first vocation had been different.

A lover of letters, he had started by cultivating a literary path, initially dismissing his legal studies as unnecessary and thankless. He harbored a kind of rancor towards his family who had exhorted him to follow them. Writing romantic verses and novelistic prose, he trained the divinely creative muse of imagination, intending to reach the heights of fame and scornful of the need for more real forms of remuneration. The death of his father, the financial support behind his large family, woke him from such dreams. He then understood that it was his duty to take over his father's role, and in a blink of an eye, he said goodbye to the splendid fantasy and directed his activities towards a more positive path. His first steps, however, hadn't been altogether useless: the habit of psychological investigation picked up during his fictional reflections had set him in good stead when it came to unravelling the mysteries of judicial inquiry. He had started by studying life through books, and thanks to this, he was soon able to understand what it was really like.

Politics and the law are perhaps the two professions that afford the best way to gain knowledge of fellow humans. Politics, though, is prone to the very passions that a politician claims he can judge in others, whereas the magistrate, aloof, dispassionate, a stranger to the interests that surround him, is better placed than anyone else to read the human heart. And Ferpierre, after giving free rein to the lively passions of his youthful artistic leanings, had in time understood the exaggerated, fake and unhealthy nature of an overly assiduous adherence to a poetic interpretation of life and had also realized as his feelings had become more austere that his judgments had become equally severe. The long-standing moral background of the Swiss — their seriousness, bordering on sadness, accumulated by a people in deep contemplation of the gigantic Alps; the almost thankless rigidity of a Protestantism that saw Geneva ban music for a time as an overtly sensual art — was eventually awakened in Ferpierre after his early daring, and the somewhat intentional froth of the young poet gave way to the inflexible integrity of the mature man.

Consequently, Ferpierre felt moved by a secret distrust of the characters involved in the drama at Ouchy as it was told to him by the Justice of the Peace after his summons to the Villa Cyclamens. Of course, the dead woman stirred a great deal of pity, but if it ended up being true that she had indeed wanted to abandon this life, she would be as deserving of reproach as of compassion. Furthermore, the ties that had bound her to Prince Zakunin were outside of the law. Her friendship with Vérod was also tainted. Without seeing the accuser, from just the mere mention of his name, the judge thought he recognized Robert Vérod, the Genevan writer who had lived for many years in Paris, where he published books full of life's bitter teachings. If he wasn't very much mistaken he had known him well: fifteen years earlier Vérod had entered the University of Geneva when Ferpierre was taking his final course in Law, and a circle of students had counted them both among their number over a period of two years. But why did the younger man see the countess's death as a murder and why was he bent on revenge, if not for the fact that he was the prince's rival and a lover of the deceased? The foreign woman's haughty and challenging attitude, her harsh glances, the certainty that she also had some affiliation to nihilism, were enough to turn the Justice of the Peace against her; however, all of Ferpierre's severity was directed towards the prince.

He had long been aware of his reputation. He knew that, although he belonged to one of the most distinguished families in his homeland and was the owner of a considerable fortune, he had been exiled for his complicity in a plot to assassinate a general. He knew that while in exile he had continued to increase his conspiratorial activities, that he had ended up as one of the most feared leaders in European revolutionary politics and that a death sentence was hanging over him. He also knew that, notwithstanding appearances, his radical political activities didn't take up all his time, since Zakunin still managed to find enough hours in the day to live the life of a lothario, passing from one love affair to another, repaying the poor wretches unable to resist his seduction with desertion and betrayal. And the Countess d'Arda had let herself be seduced by this blood-thirsty rebel, by this unworthy Don Juan! Had she wanted to die in order to avoid the destruction of her dream of a faithful loving relationship or had she been killed by the prince and the nihilist?

Ferpierre, uncertain and confused by the mystery, spent the evening of the catastrophe discussing these and other questions with the Justice of the Peace at the villa, after ordering the removal of the body to the autopsy room and a complete seizure of all the papers to be found in the Villa Cyclamens. Given the assumption that the prince's love or fickle attraction for the countess had ended, was boredom and inconvenience, or for that matter, misunderstanding and disagreement, enough to explain the homicide, if, indeed, it was a homicide. The rationale suggested by the accuser and relayed to Ferpierre by the Justice of the Peace, in other words, the wickedness of the nihilists, lacked any sense unless it was accompanied by a concrete, real motive. To destroy a life for the sole pleasure of destroying it belonged more to the beliefs of a madman rather than any nihilistic creed. The murderers had to be driven by a passion or some kind of interest. Perhaps the cruel schemes hatched by the prince, the conspiracies in which she knew he was entangled, the blood of others she had heard them say he had split, perhaps it had all just terrified the countess. Wishing to stop his involvement, could she have stumbled across some secret of his or one belonging to someone else: a secret that could have invoked the rigid discipline of the mysterious sect, thereby arming Zakunin and his accomplice? The Justice of the Peace saw some foundation to this argument, but Ferpierre saw it, at the very least, as fairly unlikely, although not totally inadmissible.

It was more likely that, if there was a crime, it was a crime of passion. Did the prince fall out of love with the countess, then rekindle his passion, only to kill her out of jealousy? Who would he have been jealous of, if not Vérod, who was so disturbed by her death that he had taken on the role of accuser and avenger without anyone asking him to do so? Or maybe it had been the foreign woman who had committed the misdeed because she loved Zakunin and was jealous of the love he showed towards the Italian? The crime, whoever was to blame and whatever the motive, could never have happened without a fight between the murderer and the victim, however brief, but there was no trace to be found in the actual room or on the body of the deceased. From the position of the firearm, which had the hilt pointing outwards and the barrel towards the body, the doctors had deduced that the countess, if it was suicide, must have shot herself standing. The firearm then falling from her grip had twisted in the air, accounting for its location on the floor. Although it didn't seem very natural for the poor woman, contrary to most suicides, to have ended her life in such a position, the fact that the revolver was hers and she had hidden it would appear to exclude its use as a murder weapon. In addition, the revolver was partially cocked, and a bullet had slipped from the chamber, which would be consistent with its use by a woman in the throes of suicide, little experienced in weaponry, whose hands must have been trembling for those reasons, whereas in the hands of a killer it would be less explicable.

In order to fix on a particular hypothesis, it was necessary to wait for the results of the autopsy. In the meantime, Ferpierre, who had set up his center of investigations in the dining room to be at the heart of events, ordered Vérod brought to him.

When the younger man appeared, Ferpierre noticed the pallor of his face, the anguish in his looks, the bewilderment in his attitude, all of which clearly confirmed that he must have been linked to the dead woman by feelings of a powerful yet delicate nature. Nonetheless, Ferpierre instantly recognized in him the former literature student, irrespective of the number of years that had flowed under the bridge. On seeing him, he recalled the many times they had met during those two years at the University of Geneva, occasions when they never exchanged any words of friendship. Even in those days, Vérod's melancholy and bitter character had been apparent during discussions with fellow students: none of the sentiments that Ferpierre had subsequently adhered to, neither his poetic enthusiasm, nor his strict sense of duty seemed detectable in such a closed soul. He wondered if Vérod also remembered him from these previous encounters. Had he asked to see the judge knowing who he was? Would he make himself known?

"You wanted to speak to me?" said Ferpierre as he rolled these questions around his head and sorted out the confiscated papers. "Well, here I am, but first your name and age?"

"Robert Vérod, thirty-four years old."

"Are you Vérod, the writer?"

"Yes."

"Born in Geneva, living in Paris?"

"Yes."

Either he didn't recognize him, or he didn't want to say that he recognized him.

"Right, what proof do you have?"

Not only was Vérod, contrary to his earlier display, now unsure of himself, he also appeared to behave as if he had been accused, such was his confusion when asked what must have been a foreseeable question. He stayed silent for a while, began to say something then stopped himself, remaining hesitant. Finally, he approached Ferpierre offering him his hand.

"If only you knew, sir," he said with a subdued and shaky voice, "how my heart is full of tumultuous feelings, how scared I am to talk, how I must beg your indulgence and discretion in order to say what I have to tell you."

The senior magistrate felt moved by the sincerity and delicacy of his entreaty. But he still didn't want to provoke him into revealing their previous connection, hoping that Vérod, himself, would allude to their former acquaintance. He pushed the papers to one side and shook the hand that the young man had so anxiously offered, as if wishing to cling to Ferpierre. He replied: "In agreeing, I would simply abide by the rules of my office, but let's go one better: forget our respective positions and confide in another man, not to a judge."

"Thank you, sir! I thank you for these kind words. In fact, I wouldn't have much to say to the judge and perhaps I wouldn't be able to communicate my moral certainty, lacking any real proof..."

"And to the man?"

"To the man...to the man I would pose these questions: the person who has put up with life when it was so full of shadows, do you really think she would shun it now when she finally saw it sparkle with light? The person who has suffered silently in such a resigned manner, would she be so regretful, would she rebel against such an unexpected hope?"

The judge listened with his head tilted, not looking at him. He didn't answer immediately.

He then raised his eyes to look at Vérod and finally began to question him: "Were you very close to the deceased?"

The young man fell silent. His eyes started to fill with tears.

"I shouldn't, no, I mustn't talk about this,..." he murmured in a broken voice. "I'm not going to reveal to anybody a secret that isn't mine, a secret that isn't completely mine. Look, I think it would hurt her, that she would have forbidden me from adding anything else."

"Did you love her?"

"Yes!"

His tears had been held back, his face now showed a sense of joyful pride and happiness.

"Yes, with a love I'm happy to declare, head held high, to anyone. Why should I deny it?"

"And did she love you?"

"Yes! And no one knows, will never know, the depth of our love. The world is a sad place, and life soon becomes embittered, but nothing, neither acts, nor words, not even a thought, ever contaminated the feelings we shared."

"Nevertheless, the prince must have had reason to be jealous?"

The blissfully proud expression on Vérod's face gave way to a bitter grimace of disdain.

"Jealous? To be jealous he would have needed to be in love first. And if he had loved her, truly, faithfully, would she have fallen in love with me?"

Ferpierre was amazed at the way in which he demonstrated these feelings. Had he incorrectly recalled the brutal and unrewarding truths that Vérod had espoused in his younger days or had the pessimist, the sceptic, been converted?

"Ok then, how was the relationship between the prince and the countess?" he asked, continuing with the questioning. "Is there any doubt that they were once in love?"

"You know very well, sir, that love can mean many different things with regard to our illusions, our whims, our greed.... Indeed, her love for him was cheated by illusion and deceit. She loved him because she believed he loved her; he, who only knew how to hate!"

"Why did they never separate then?"

"Well, he certainly wanted to separate. He told her, he threw her loyalty in her face and left her more than once. However, she didn't want to acknowledge that she had been deceived, or she only felt it deep inside. Thinking that such deception would ultimately have to be paid for and these errors would lead to suffering, she accepted her agony."

"Can you tell me how she was badly treated?"

"It would be impossible to go through it all. Everything he did, every one of his words was an affront, an insult."

"Who told you all this?"

Although the magistrate had hidden his doubt under an ambiguous expression, the young man protested: "Never from her, sir! I never heard her utter a bad word against that man. I knew it. I saw it myself. I knew him in Paris many years ago, before he was with her. I know what he's like, and not just me, everyone knows."

"Did you meet up with him after he knew the countess?"

"Never. Last year it seemed that he had left her for good. Then, after he came back, I saw him a couple of times from a distance."

"What do you know about his political activity?"

"That it wasn't the least of the poor woman's worries."

"When she first met him, was she unaware of the goals he was pursuing?"

"I don't know, I don't think that.... But she did know he had been exiled from his country and condemned to death. Kind and sensitive as she was, she must have felt such compassion for him. If he had told her that his blood lust was nothing more than a love of liberty and justice, charity towards the oppressed and the dream of a better world, her naïve soul, so unaware of evil, must surely have burned with enthusiasm and admiration!"

"Do you think that disillusion set in very soon?"

"Too soon...and too late! Yes!"

"When did you first meet her?"

"Last year."

"Where?"

"Here, at the Beau Séjour."

"She still hadn't rented the villa?"

"Yes, but she was spending a few weeks in the hotel."

"Where did she live during the winter?"

"In Nice."

"So last year they weren't together?"

"No."

"And how long have they been back together?"

"For the last few months."

"The woman, the young woman, can you tell me who she is?"

"A compatriot of his with the same ideological beliefs"

"Do you know the nature of their relationship?"

"No, but it's not difficult to work it out."

"Could she also be his lover?"

"Would it shock you? Don't you realize that these avengers of oppressed humanity love pleasure, they seek it out, they're more than happy to link it with duty."

The young man's tone got more and more bitter as he spoke of those he supposed had wanted the death of his beloved.

"Assuming that the young woman was the prince's lover, could she have killed the countess out of jealousy? But who was she jealous of? Surely not the countess, as she was loved by you and not the prince. Nor could she have been jealous of the prince, who no longer loved the countess but her instead! Given the state of affairs, what motive would she have for committing the crime? On the other hand, you mentioned the maid's testimony in order to confirm your accusation. How do you explain that the woman, having hardly seen the body, was saying that her mistress had carried out her stated resolution to kill herself?"

"Doesn't this prove to you,..." said the younger man, without directly answering the question, yet forming another, "doesn't this prove to you the depths to which she had fallen? Isn't it obvious that, sustained and inspired by a faith like hers, life must have become totally unpleasant and intolerable for her to talk of suicide? There was a time when she wanted to die. I, myself, heard the words from her own lips. Maybe once, but not now. I have to say that, between us, we now had a real hope of happiness."

Soon drowned by tears, he couldn't go on any further. Increasingly impressed by a moral fiber contrary to his own recollections and Vérod's reputation, Ferpierre mentally began to consider the effectiveness of the moral proof finally pinpointed by the accuser.

What he said was true, if the dead woman had loved him, the accusation of suicide would appear to be less plausible. The fact that otherworldly feelings had intervened to prevent the woman from killing herself was something that the judge believed to a point, yet it was human sentiments, completely human sentiments, that he thought far from improbable in dissuading her from the fatal course. The types of motive that drive people are very diverse, and in any hierarchy of feelings faith is ranked very highly, but in practice sentiments don't always match this ideal scale, and on many occasions, inferior passions, or even base instincts, are stronger. Religious feeling, which forbids a voluntary death, is often ineffective in the face of intolerable pain and the need for tranquility or rest. Love, the chance of satisfying an essentially vital passion, is more quickly reconciled with life.

But what was such a presumption worth? How would it be of use in blaming these two individuals?

"You will understand," stated the judge, once he had calmed Vérod, "that I must ask you certain questions that you'll find painful. I think I have understood the reason why the countess, in your opinion, would have stayed with a man who was no longer tied to her. She wanted to accept and almost suffer the consequences of her mistake, as if it were a well-deserved punishment, am I right? However, this was only possible before she met you. On that day, when another ray of hope shone down on her, how was she then going to regain her freedom?"

"Yes, why didn't she ever get it back?" said Vérod, as if talking to himself.

"Did you know the reason why?"

"She told me herself."

But instead of revealing it, the young man fell silent. Looking fixedly ahead with an expression of bitterness, he shook his head.

"And it was?…"

"She didn't believe in herself. She didn't feel free. The commitment that she had undertaken when agreeing to live with that man was, to her, a sacred commitment. She didn't want to pass from one man to another, and I didn't want her in such a manner."

Were Vérod's scruples believable? Does a man in love who also feels loved really recognize any obstacles in the way of his desires? Certainly, in those souls capable of harboring generous thoughts and a delicate conscience, they have a great deal of force, especially at the onset of an affair. It was obvious the young man was in the early stages given his own declarations, and he appeared to be so different from his reputation. He spoke in a voice laden with sadness and still so close to tears that Ferpierre didn't want to doubt his sincerity.

"But then," he replied, "if the lady loved you and didn't think she was free, if she wanted to, but also felt incapable of breaking the tortuous link, if her new love, her reason for living, was off limits owing to her moral scruples, don't you think this refutes rather than reinforces your accusation? The hope that must have sustained the countess would have become another reason for desperation."

"How?… Why?…" stammered Vérod somewhat dazed.

"I suggest that in wanting to love you and in not feeling able to love you without losing her self-respect, she didn't find the comfort you speak of but, on the contrary, an extreme pain and the definitive reason to end her life."

The young man, as if he hadn't understood at first, or had seemingly misunderstood, now looked at his interrogator with frightened eyes. From his entire demeanor, his half-open lips, to his shortened rapid breathing and the trembling arm guiding his hand to his chest, he seemed to have been stabbed through with a sharp blade.

"Me.... Me.... You're saying that because of me?... I have killed her? Oh!"

Hiding his face in his hands, he smothered an animalistic cry of pain.

Ferpierre was forced into silence, rather through an unprecedented trepidation than any form of discretion. He had come to prepare a case and was now in the middle of a drama. He was used to a show of raw passion, but chance had now put him in front of a tortured soul who took him back to the memories of an unexpectedly awakened youth. The man before him was not only an old acquaintance he had frequently conversed with in the past but was also one of the evident talents of his day. Owing to the nature of his talent, he hadn't always felt kindly towards Vérod, but he hadn't realized, as he now did, how little the man resembled the author. Yet the same intellectual rivalry between them disturbed him, it took him away from his accustomed indifference and a necessary serenity. In addition, witnessing such pain, he was moved at the very time he needed all his clarity of thought to study the accusation.

If the young man was groaning because of the suspicion that he was the unwitting cause of the countess's suicide, one had to believe that, not only was such a suspicion far from unlikely, it also made him feel a kind of remorse. However, the judge didn't want to attribute any more force to the idea. Lacking material proof, he wasn't able to form an opinion about anything except mere speculation. Between the two hypotheses, which was worth more attention: Vérod's assurance that the countess wouldn't have been able to commit suicide while the light of a new love was brightening her shadow-filled life, or the opposing idea, that the very impossibility of following her feelings had revealed the irredeemable misery of her own existence?

Accustomed to exercising his powers of analysis in doubtful and tangled cases, the judge was increasingly hesitant. Yet, instead of mulling over the various hypotheses, he made every attempt to distract himself by stopping any particular notion from taking root against his will and assuming the mantle of truth. He knew that the growth of ideas is much more rapid than the growth of plants that sprout leafy branches in all directions and that opinions, however much they seem to depend on the will or to bend under the weight of contrary views, are, nevertheless, tenacious and at times, resistant to the greatest forces.

Even, Vérod, who seemed so confused and despondent, rose up in quick reply.

"No!" he said brusquely, lifting his head and shaking it in protest. "No!... It's not possible! It can't be true! If she had killed herself because of me, wouldn't she have told me, wouldn't she have left me her final words, the words of her pain, a farewell, a goodbye? I only spoke to her yesterday, and nothing, nothing would have made me suspect that she had that idea in mind, on the contrary! No!" he repeated in an increasingly firm voice as his conviction became stronger. "She didn't kill herself. She was murdered! You don't believe it because you don't know, because you didn't know her! You needed to touch her hands in order to believe. But I'm sure a wicked crime has been committed here today. I promise to confound the murderers, to avenge her death. At the moment, your task is to believe nothing, to investigate, to help me look for the missing proof. It's out there, and I will find it!"

"So much the better!" replied Ferpierre. "And you can also be sure that I'll be looking for it, that I am looking for it!"

And so, before being persuaded by the force of Vérod's argument, he asked him to take his leave and gave the order to bring in the young woman.

"Your name?" he asked

"Alexandra Paskovna Natzichev."

"Where were you born?"

"Krakow."

"How old are you?"

"Twenty-two."

"What's your profession?"

"Medical student."

"Where are you living?"

"Zurich."

She answered with a short, dry tone, almost impatient with the questioning.

"How did you come to find yourself in this house?"

"I came to speak with Alexi Petrovich."

"About what?"

"Things that wouldn't interest the judiciary."

"Or perhaps they would be of great interest!"

The young woman didn't answer.

"Do you share the same ideological beliefs?"

"Yes."

"Did you come to speak to him about political matters?"

Another silence.

The judge briefly waited for an answer then continued in a measured tone: "I must tell you that such reticence could harm you. Do you know what you're being accused of?"

She shrugged her shoulders with indifference.

"Who are you accusing? Me, Alexi Petrovich, or both of us?"

"You're trying to switch roles. It's your turn to answer. Is it only his beliefs that you share?"

"I don't understand."

"Aren't you also his lover?"

The young woman looked at her interrogator with an inflamed angry expression yet said nothing.

"You still don't want to answer me. Ok, I'll ask you another question. Where were you at the moment the countess died?"

"In the prince's study."

"And where was he?"

"With me."

"Did you know the deceased?"

"I never spoke with her."

"Did you see her today?"

"No."

"Did you know that she had lived with your friend for years, that she loved him, that they loved each other?"

The judge, spinning out the question in order to make an effort to read her thoughts, didn't take his eyes from hers, but her response was impassive: "Yes."

"Did you know if they were jealous of each other?"

"I don't know."

"Were you aware of their disputes after the initial period of happiness?"

"No."

"What did you do when you heard the gunshot?"

"I came running."

Ferpierre hadn't expected that answer. If she was truly with the prince, wouldn't she have said: "We came running"?

"Alone?" he continued.

"With him."

"Was she already dead?"

"She was."

"Why would someone kill her?"

"No idea."

"What did the prince say?"

"He cried."

"How many times have you been to this house?"

"Two or three."

"Did your visits upset the countess?"

"I don't know."

"Do you know Vérod?"

"I've no clue who he is."

"He's the person who made the accusation of murder."

"I don't know him."

The judge stopped the questioning.

"Your ignorance of the matter is somewhat too great. Let's see if we can help you remember. In the meantime, remain at our disposal."

She left with her head held high, just as impassive as she had remained throughout the interview. Ferpierre watched her go, reflecting that he would be unlikely to get any information from that source. He had already had occasion to meet more than one of these slaves to a mysterious soul, these young women in the flower of youth, in the midst of a rigid study regime, who had followed a tragic ideal with an iron heart. In order to triumph, they didn't only know how to defy or to overcome all manner of obstacles and resistance, but they were even willing to sacrifice their lives. The fog surrounding these events was far from clearing. In fact, it was getting thicker. The judge was becoming impatient to meet face to face with the man who must surely be the principal actor in these proceedings.

When the prince was brought into the room, Ferpierre closely observed the figure before him. He was, without doubt, one of the most handsome men he had ever seen: tall, strong, agile, his cheeks framed by a silken blond beard, his brown hair thinning towards his forehead, giving it a wider appearance. His complexion was rather pallid, almost ghostly, as can be found in those of aristocratic blood, his eyes a deep blue under the clear arc of his brows, his aquiline nose twitching with nervous nostrils, his dress elegant, his bearing very princely.

In seeing him, anyone would have recognized a noble, gallant gentleman and nothing of the revolutionary. His face, previously broken by his desperation on seeing the corpse, and then his anger at Vérod's accusation, had now calmed, and he wore an expression of profound sadness.

"You are Prince Alexi Petrovich Zakunin? Where were you born?"

"In Chernigov, in 1855."

"Have you ever been sentenced?"

"I was banished to Siberia for conspiracy, then pardoned but exiled from Russia."

"Wasn't there a more severe punishment?"

"All successive penalties against me have been merged into a death sentence for high treason and regicide."

"Do you know of Vérod's accusation?"

At the mention of these words, he flushed red, and his eyes lit up once more.

"And your answer?…"

Zakunin rubbed his forehead, almost in an attempt to restrain his anger, then said, "It's true."

Was he confessing, was he declaring his guilt? Was he admitting to the killing? The judge almost doubted hearing correctly, so unlikely did it seem for the prince to contradict himself from one moment to the next, but his doubts didn't last long as Zakunin soon clarified his thoughts: "It's true.… I killed her.… She's dead because of me.…"

He was speaking slowly, stock still, with such a muted voice that Ferpierre could hardly hear him.

"She's dead because of you, by your hand?"

"What does it matter? I'm responsible."

"On the contrary, it matters a great deal, and I'm sure I don't have to explain to you the difference! Are you confessing to driving her to suicide rather than actually killing her? How did you drive her to suicide?"

"Because I was unworthy of her, because I ignored her, because I hurt her."

"You didn't love her anymore?"

"I didn't love her."

"And yet you cry for her so much?"

There were, indeed, tears in his voice. As he left the question unanswered, the judge continued: "Did you want to leave her?"

"I did leave her."

"Why did you return? Was there any affection remaining? Did you pity her?"

"So much."

"Was she deeply in love with you?"

"As I was with her, once."

"Were you ever happy?"

The prince's eyes reddened.

"Did she still love you?"

By way of an answer the prince slowly, desperately shook his head.

"Did she give you any reason to be jealous?"

He answered this new question with a hesitant gesture.

"Were you aware of a new love in her life?"

"I guessed it."

"Did you ever challenge her on her friendship with Vérod?"

At the mention of this name, the prince screwed up his eyebrows and began to shake.

"No," he replied in a low voice.

"What would motivate him to accuse you?"

"I've no idea."

"Pain? Jealousy?"

"Perhaps."

"How long had you been in a relationship with the countess?"

"Five years."

"Was she single when you met her?"

"Single, yes, a widow."

"Where did you meet?"

"In Aberdeen, in Scotland."

"How old was she?"

"Twenty-nine."

"Then or now?"

"Now."

"Did you never think, even in the early days, of getting legally married?"

"I don't hold with such a practice."

"Given her Christian beliefs, didn't she suffer from a situation she would have seen as immoral and punishable?"

"She had taken up that particular compromise with her God."

"Living with her, sleeping under the same roof, knowing her intimately, it's impossible that you didn't see this catastrophe coming."

"I wasn't living with her anymore. I came to see her once in a while."

"In that case, where do you live now?"

"In Zurich."

"When did you get here?"

"The day before yesterday."

"Nothing made you suspect her desperate intentions?"

"I noticed that she was suffering more than usual."

"Did you ever suggest to her that you might finally go your separate ways?"

"Never."

"What did she think of your political ideas, of your actions?"

"She was inspired by the idea of humanity's redemption. She was disgusted by the acts."

"Did she ever intervene and stop you from committing such acts. Did she try to dissuade you from your work?"

"Often."

"In what way?"

"By telling me that love, not hate, was the remedy."

"Did you keep her up to speed with your political secrets?"

"Once."

"And now? Did she ever try to catch you out?"

"Oh no! Never!"

"What is your relationship with Alexandra Natzichev?"

"We share the same train of thought."

"Do you work on propaganda together?"

"Yes."

"Would the deceased have had any motive to be jealous of the woman?"

"None whatsoever."

"You aren't connected to her by anything other than a common ideal? Don't lie about this, so we can be clear about the truth."

"I swear there is nothing else between us."

He seemed sincere.

"Without your knowledge, could the young woman have fallen in love with you, a fact which could have prompted her secret jealousy of the countess?"

The prince delayed for a moment before answering.

"No," he finally replied.

"Where were you when you heard the shot?"

"In my room."

"In your bedroom?"

"In the study."

"When, precisely, did the suicide take place?"

"At a quarter to twelve."

"What did you do on hearing the shot?"

"I came to the room."

"Did your young companion arrive after you?" asked the judge trying to give his voice an air of tiredness, by way of hiding the importance of the question, making it sound an inconvenience to ask such a thing.

"She came with me."

Straight away they had both answered this question in the singular, when it would have been more natural to have said: "We came." Ferpierre attributed a certain importance to this fact, seemingly from which one could deduce that they hadn't been together, contrary to their assurances. But who found the countess? Who was lying? Who should fall under suspicion?

"Do you remember when the deceased bought the firearm?"

"She won it in a raffle a while ago."

"And the bullets?"

"She bought them when she wanted to practice her shooting."

"So, in summary, she must have killed herself because of the pain you caused, because being your de-facto spouse without having undertaken any actual ceremony, she couldn't stand her abandonment. However, she was in love with someone else. You've admitted you suspected as much.... So why would she have killed herself if she loved another? Where did they come from, these obstacles and hindrances to her new-found happiness?"

"From the lady herself."

"What are you trying to say?"

"Her ideas of duty, of respect and honesty, were very great."

"If you suspected that she wanted to kill herself, why did you never take the weapon from her?"

"I didn't suspect it."

"Her maid, on the contrary, has said that such a thing was foreseeable."

"She was party to her confidences. I wasn't."

"Understandable, given you were the cause of her pain! But, didn't the woman ever forewarn you? Didn't she ever tell you to watch over her?"

"No."

"Right. Let's hear what she's got to say."

The judge suddenly decided to bring the two of them together in the same room.

Ferpierre had remembered the Justice of the Peace's words regarding the prince's worried reaction when Giulia Pico had made her appearance, the fact that he had started to shake nervously once more and to breathe anxiously. He thought that perhaps Alexi Zakunin saw her in the role of accuser and that she had been responsible for his agitation. Yet now, being warned of the forthcoming confrontation, nothing in his expression indicated fear.

The maid was in the room with the deceased offering her final compassionate services to the countess's body before they took her away. She washed the blood from her forehead and cheek, rearranged her hair, crossed her hands over her chest and placed a rosary between them. The poor woman couldn't see what she was doing so thick was the veil of tears covering her eyes. To one side was the Baroness Börne, still trying to busy herself: over-zealous and talkative. It didn't take much for her to follow the maid when she was called.

Ferpierre had to repeat his question two or three times to the poor woman, given the extent to which she was dazed with grief. Giulia Pico, forty-five years old, born in Bellano, on Lake Como, had been in the service of the countess since her lady's childhood years in Milan.

"You said that your mistress had shown a desire to die on more than one occasion?"

"Yes."

"Since when?"

"For quite a while...more than a year."

"You never spoke of this danger to the countess's friend?"

"Yes."

As if he hadn't heard her assertion and as if the prince wasn't present, the judge continued to question the maid without turning to face the accused.

"When did you tell him and under what circumstances? Try to be precise."

"Last year, one day when the *signore* was about to depart.... The countess had really begged him not to leave her alone. He left, and then she cried a lot. She spoke about dying.... When he returned, I told him to look out for her."

"What was his reply?" said Ferpierre coldly, turning towards the prince and looking at him fixedly.

"I don't remember what she's talking about," he replied, maintaining the judge's gaze. "I have confessed my faults. At times this woman has spoken to me about them. Perhaps she intended to make me realize the danger, but she never clearly mentioned why there was a reason to be fearful."

"In recent days," said the judge, redirecting himself to the maid, "was she still talking about her intention?"

"No."

"How do you explain this? Didn't she still have the same reasons to complain about him?"

"The *signore* had been more considerate towards her for some time."

"Is it true what she says?"

"No, it's not. If I had recognized my faults, if I had made amends for them, she would still be alive."

Lowering his gaze, he spoke with such a sincere tone that Ferpierre was impressed. Given the maid had said that he had started to treat her mistress better and that he had remained silent at first then denied the fact, insisting on his guilt, the accusation now appeared to have less force. Therefore, if one wanted to believe Vérod's arguments, shouldn't suspicion fall once more on the young female student? Did the prince want to press the case for suicide in order to save his political compatriot?

"What did your mistress think of the woman who was here, the Natzichev woman?"

"I don't know. She didn't see her."

"But she knew of her visits? Did they upset her?"

"I don't know...."

The judge noticed that the presence of the accused now seemed to stop her from talking openly.

"Leave us alone," he said to Zakunin. Once the prince, bowing his head, had disappeared through the exit guarded by the gendarmes, Ferpierre approached the woman.

"Listen," he said quietly, yet in a lively, persuasively confidential tone, "we're faced here with a serious doubt. While appearances show that the lady has killed herself, someone is sure that she has been murdered. There is no one better placed than you to help the authorities discover the truth. Do you really think that she killed herself? Now you have heard the accusation, do you have any doubts?"

The woman put her hands together, indecisive, confused.

"What can I say, *signore*! This is dreadful! I don't know."

"What do you think of the master? Do you believe he is capable of committing such a crime?"

After a moment's reflection, she answered resolutely: "No."

"Why do you say no?"

"He loved the *signora* a great deal when they first met. He was madly in love with her. He cheered her from her sorrows."

"What sorrows?"

"She was suffering, she was laden with grief. In the space of a few months she had lost her father and her husband and remained alone in the world. The count died in a ghastly manner, flattened by a train."

"But afterwards, did the prince mistreat her?"

"Yes, she disrespected his beliefs, and he abandoned her; but that's no reason to suspect him of such a horrible thing."

"Do you remember when, how and why the mistreatment started?"

"In Italy, when the *signore* was expelled from our country."

"How long ago was this?"

"The year before last. My mistress had long hoped that down there things would be better, more in her control!"

"Did you notice quarrels between them?"

"Not exactly quarrels. The *signora* always begged when she wanted something. He let her speak, he didn't answer and then he did whatever he wanted."

"Did he betray her with others?"

"I don't know. Who could say what he got up to during the long periods when he was away."

"You said that things had improved recently. When did this start?"

"Three or four months ago."

"How did you come to notice this change?"

"He came to look for her after a long period away, just as I thought he was never coming back."

"He came from Zurich?"

"Yes, I think it was from Zurich."

"Did he stay long?"

"A few days, but afterwards he came back many times, staying with us in Nice and here. He seemed a different person, he seemed worried about her."

"How would you explain such a change."

"I couldn't say. Perhaps on seeing her so sad and sorrowful, he realized he had behaved badly."

"Pay good attention to the question I'm going to ask you now. What was Monsieur Vérod to your mistress? Tell me what you know. We need to uncover the truth, punish the culprits if there are any and avenge the death of the poor woman if she was murdered. You wouldn't want the killers to go unpunished?"

"I'll tell you what I think is true. The countess never spoke to me about him. Just once she said to me: 'Signor Vérod is very nice, don't you think?' I understood that his company, his friendship was very welcome to her, although sometimes she avoided him."

"Why on earth was that?"

"I don't know. In fact, at times he appeared to displease her so much that she disliked him. But that soon passed...."

"Perhaps she feared that Monsieur Vérod, like all men, would end up treating her without the thoughtfulness he had shown at the beginning."

"I don't think so. Signor Vérod is so pleasant! Maybe she was afraid, yes, but..."

"Of what?"

"Of herself."

"Ok, if the countess harbored such a liking, and if the prince noticed just as you did, don't you think that when he started to treat her better it was due to a fear of losing her and jealousy of Vérod?"

The woman opened her arms and shook her head.

"I couldn't say, *signore*."

"And the Russian woman, the young student, what do you think? Why was she here?"

"She was always shut up in the study with the prince. I wouldn't know."

"How many times has she been here?"

"Three or four."

"Did you ever suspect that they had an intimate relationship...that they were lovers?"

"I can't say. One day..."

"What?"

"I saw her kiss the prince's hand."

"Did you hear what they were saying?"

"They were talking in Russian. I couldn't understand."

"Let's make an assumption. Let's say that the woman loved the prince. Isn't it then true that she would have been jealous of the countess?"

The maid answered with an ambiguous expression, which could just as easily have meant her lack of knowledge as it could her agreement.

"Yet, if she knew of their troubles, her jealousy wouldn't have been so justified," suggested Ferpierre in opposition to his own argument and in an effort to see clearly through this mystery, thus giving voice to all the ideas before him. "Did she know they were having problems?"

"I couldn't say."

"Had she noticed that the prince was treating the countess in a better manner?"

"I don't know, *signore*."

"If she had and she loved him, jealousy could have strengthened her resolve?"

The maid said nothing, almost understanding that, more than questioning her, the judge was really talking to himself, that he was thinking aloud.

III

Robert Vérod's Memories

The sun was setting. Behind the Jura mountains, the golden rays that were slicing through the clouds massing on the summits resembled an enormous cabinet of swords. The western shore of the lake was a slate board, green like a mill pond around the lower forested shores of Saint Suplice, regaining its blue color in the high basin enclosed by the Alps where the snows were flamed by the last remaining vestiges of light. Two stationary sailing boats, juxtaposed like two wings on the motionless water. A fragile line of smoke from the Collenges direction. These were the only signs of life. Breaking the infinite silence were the slow chimes from a bell announcing that a life had just come to an end.

Robert Vérod turned to the heavens, the earth and the light of day, wanting to hold them all to account for such a death. At times he lost consciousness of the terrible truth. Before the natural spectacle he had admired so often with her, she still seemed to be at his side. Then he shifted his anxious gaze, and the solitude terrified him, the horror weighed increasingly heavy upon him. In order to breathe, he walked and walked, with no particular destination. Remaining in one place would have suffocated him. On a hill neighboring Lausanne, beyond Croix, a carriage approached. He halted his stride and began to shake.

On this road, at this very point, at this same time, he had seen her for the first time. A year before when he was wandering along this street, she had passed him in a carriage, maybe even this one. Her image vividly surged to his mind with startling clarity.

What was he doing in those days? What was he thinking about? What were his hopes? His life was empty back then, grey, useless. His thirty-four years had produced no wrinkles on his forehead, but so many on his soul! His closed thoughts, the assiduous self-absorption, ingrained instincts and a stubborn need for self-analysis had poisoned him. Water droplets would never again seem liquid pearls when, equipped with jaundiced lenses, he had seen a horrid world within.

Vérod had spent too long contemplating his own motivations, and the beauty of things had lost all its charm. He had known the cost of joy, and deep down, he knew all hope had been consumed. Once, at a younger age, he had been proud of his capacity to examine life, seeing it as a force and a source of power. With the years, he had come to see it as his downfall. In the world of ideas, extreme horizons and dizzying heights were familiar to him. In real life, his footsteps were less certain than those of a child. And when he attempted to react against this powerlessness, he realized that his will was ineffective, that he would remain condemned to a barren existence. Born where three cultures met, from a strain with too many confused identities, attracted in different ways by hereditary instincts and acquired concepts, he felt sure that he wouldn't be able to enjoy other pleasures apart from these arid thoughts.

He had lived, but how? Like the visitor to a *cosmorama* who, at any given moment, sees himself inside the events being portrayed, knowing that they are all painted on cardboard. He didn't believe in life. The unfeeling object, the inanimate work of art could be illuminated, but they would always remain as they are: cold, mute, inert. In just such a way, he had loved the living. But what of feelings, not that he had dreamed of changing the nature of things, that would be impossible, but he had once thought he could be understood by like-minded souls.

This dream had never come to fruition, and his own pride had persuaded him that he had a soul somewhat out of the ordinary, worth rather more than others'. His pride had been punished by the frightening solitude that surrounded him. Sadder still than the solitude was the subsequent idea that, although humans valued each other to a lesser or greater extent, they were condemned to misunderstand each other.

For years he lived with this desperate belief, with the bitter complacency of knowing the sterile truth. His works reflected rather too closely these opinions, this negative, cold, bitterness. He said that life was a trick, that there was no distinction between sentient man and the blind power of nature, that everything in the world was reduced to an impassive mechanism. He had no reason to live, and his life was one continuous death. He put a brake on any temptations, starting with the desire to die. With the fury of an iconoclast, he destroyed all those images of beings and things he held within. This was his life, when she first appeared.

He saw her in the carriage coming slowly down the hill, accompanied by another woman: they briefly exchanged glances. Her appearance dazed him, her white, pallid complexion, her air of tiredness. What was she trying to say with those eyes?

He had seen her again the same evening, around an hour later, at the medical center, where a friendly doctor had persuaded him to take the waters in order to ease his state of mind. He needed another remedy altogether! Neither showers, nor fresh air, nor exercise were able to do anything against his pain. They passed each other once more on the terrace of the center, this time at close quarters, and although this encounter had been as rapid as the first, he had time to note that her faded beauty had been unexpectedly revitalized, illuminated, even though he had only looked at her once. What was she trying to say with those eyes?

Now the shadows surged more thickly from the lake's basin. The golden clouds had turned grey, and there was only light enough in a few isolated violet strips to stave off the dying day. The reflection of this color gave the still waters an iridescent metallic sheen. The denuded foothills of the Savoyard mountains seemed to fall vertically over the lake, and the summits stuck out darkly as if incised through the cloud cover. Yearning for the recent past, Vérod started to walk again.

The approaching night overcame him. What was he going to do during the night? At least during the day, wherever he looked, he saw something they had talked about together. He could see her once more, as he had so many times before, bathed in the last rays of the sun, quietly contemplating the silent spectacle of the sunset. He contained his breathing and his stride as if in the presence of a living being, fearing her disappearance, her dispersal, her loss. And she had disappeared, she had been dispersed, he had lost her! How many times this feeling of fear had tightened his stomach! Had she really been made for a life on this earth? How many times he had heard her say, when talking about the future and the things she had to do: "If I'm still in this world!" He stopped, unable to see anything, his eyes full of tears. His pain was so acute, so indescribable, that he seemed to wallow in a mortal sensuality. As he wept, the tears reflected the sensuality of his love, of his joy, hope, compassion, fear, his pain.

His first impression on seeing her had been so strong that he hadn't completely understood her beauty. Was the languid, almost hesitant grace of such a tall, slender figure her greatest attraction? Or was it in the purity of her features, her delicate face, her smooth forehead reminiscent of a work of sculpture, crowned by her abundantly shimmering black hair, which cascaded in two bands over her temples, giving her a resemblance to portraits of the Virgin Mary? Or was it in the painful sweetness of her gaze, the deep-seated expression of an anxious soul?

Calmer contemplation had later led him to understand that it was all of these things together that produced her complex charm, but he had then realized that such a beauty wasn't made to last. There were days or hours when her cheeks seemed too drawn, when the outline of her face was altered, somewhat close to disfiguration, when her complexion, unlit by the fire within, took on a wan appearance, and her gaze seemed veiled, almost blind. Yet these sudden darker moments appeared to be nothing more than the consequences of too great a beauty, an uncommon, otherworldly beauty. They had sent shivers of fear through him, revealing a latent threat hanging over her life. The feelings of admiration that such an impressive creature inspired in moments of splendor, suddenly changed to moments of pity. The pity felt for such a fragile and fleeting beauty had caught hold of Vérod's heart so firmly that he couldn't then feel admiration for any other woman endowed with haughty, triumphant attractions.

He still remembered the words heard one distant night when, in an all too rare moment of peace and spurred on by the cheerful crowd, she had agreed to play the piano. A heady music came from the sonorous instrument, and the mysterious power of the melody was, to the young man's soul, an explanation of why the sudden energy made a supernatural beauty shine in her features. Faced by such a phenomenon, he felt rather humiliated, almost hurt: the more beautiful she appeared, the more he felt she was out of reach, the more mediocre and unworthy he considered himself to be. However, at the height of his anguish, as he realized the distance between them, he unexpectedly saw, without any interruption in her performance of one of Bach's *largos*, that her rosy cheeks were fading, and the marvelous purity of her features was altering, dissolving. At that moment, one of the spectators, whom Vérod believed was imbued with feelings resembling his own, approached him and pointed towards her, saying: "Look! Isn't it a shame? If it wasn't for these sudden weaknesses, what a perfect beauty! She'd be truly wonderful, if she wasn't overcome in such a way from one moment to the next!"

And then, just as rapidly, her anguish and sadness dispersed. He no longer felt a distance from her but a closeness — not owing to the other man's comments, but to a rush of tenderness when he thought about her, a feeling of compassion, a need to lavish his jealous care on that vulnerable creature, a vigil-like affection, to make up for her former troubles, to spare her future misfortunes.

Had he been successful in his aims?

Once more, his attention wandered from these lofty thoughts to the spectacle before him. The first lights were now illuminated against the remaining twilight, the banks of the lake and the base of the Savoyard mountains. The lamp from a small boat, like a burning star, ploughed the lake. To leave, to flee, to disappear: this was the only way they could have both avoided further pain. He had been tempted to flee. When anxiety took hold of him looking at her from a distance, he realized the fire that would burn when she was close by. He remembered the letters he had written during those days that announced his departure, letters in which the resigned sadness of giving up on a love he understood would be all-encompassing was hidden by insinuations regarding the vulgarity of the location and its inhabitants. Although once intent on leaving he had nevertheless remained, continually postponing his retreat for one last sweet glance in her direction, until, finally, he got to speak to her. He had been able to listen to her voice: a subdued voice of slow harmonies, of veiled music, the echo of a profound soul. There was such subtle virtue in her words, as if each of them seemed unprecedented, opportunely created to express her hidden thoughts. And he had stayed to hear her.

From then on, his heart had been filled with the utmost admiration. He hadn't believed it possible to be so dependent on another human being. Replaying previous loves in his memory, he found nothing that matched his present reality. These loves were dead, completely, not that this deprived them of their power over him, nor that they seemed paled by the natural state of affairs, which gave precedence to actual events: this new manifestation simply overcame all others by its sheer virtue; it overshadowed all the other ghosts and their images by the purity of its light.

His veneration grew still further owing to the sudden faith he had placed in a heart then unknown to him. Ideas of beauty are naturally associated with those of goodness and virtue, so it becomes nothing short of easy to attribute them to the beautiful. However, hadn't he been used to fending off such overtly obvious and unchecked assumptions, to observe others, himself, and life in general with an equal degree of penetration, to deny any credence or prestige to all of this? With this unexpected devotion, was he, perhaps, now paying for his long, tireless and desperate resistance to all flattery? But the biggest proof of the change in his mind-set had been that he no longer continued, as in the past, to embroiled himself in the exhausting and barren task of self-analysis, in the ongoing recourse to doubt. Instead without discussion, he had virtually obeyed an extraneous, imperious will. The expression of this will was found in her eyes that said: "Love and live, believe and live, hope and live." And he had conformed to these commandments.

The act of faith that he had made by attributing such worth to his beloved was strengthened on a daily basis by numerous proofs. How could he have fallen into a trap if all around him held similar feelings? Words of admiration were to be heard on many lips, and her appearance was matched by her actions: a kindness, gentleness and compassion, full of charm and grace. She didn't look as if she were made for this world, her gaze and her thoughts seemed to be constantly fixed on the heavens. When he went to look for her, when he needed to see her, he was sure he would find her in a church, crossing herself before God in a humble manner. The times, unseen, he had crept into these hushed locales to see her! How many indescribable hours had she spent there! How he had cried with a bittersweet sadness and nervous amusement on recalling that he had also once believed, on remembering the naïve soul that had died within him, in the hope of still being able to believe in order to feel closer to her, to communicate with her!

One day in Evian, he had accompanied her to a church where they were celebrating a festival that attracted believers from far and wide. He had similarly tilted his non-believer's head like the other humble celebrants, just as she had, not only to follow the example of the faithful, but also to hide for a while the tears that blinded him. On another occasion, she had stopped on a mountainside in front of a little chapel whose grilled door still had the rusty key in the lock. With her delicate white hands, she had tried to unlock the door without any success. He had managed to do it, and on gaining access for his devout companion, he thought of the secret strength behind her apparent weakness. Her poor hand had been exhausted in vain, and it seemed to have given up trying, but a muscular arm coming to her aid had surmounted the obstacle for her. It was at this moment that he had been overcome by the desire to kiss the distressed hand, to kiss the back of it devotedly, to kiss the palm avidly. He sensed the need to feel it on his burning brow. Wasn't her hand kind and helpful? Hadn't he once seen it compassionately treat a wounded man, a poor madman whose insanity had been mocked by all, who only received sympathy from her. The man had fallen. He was bleeding. At the sight of such a spectacle, as his words became even less coherent than usual, and the cruel laughter grew, she alone, like a sister of mercy, knew how to treat him and heal him. Her hand was gentle and nimble, dexterous in the act of charity, seemingly animated by a vibrant life of its own. It was a broad hand, flexible, veined and fresh like a leaf. When he held it tight, he truly felt the freshness of a healthy leaf.

The memories, the sweet, luminous, everlasting memories pursued him through the serene evening, under that green-tinged sky, like the hope she had awoken in his heart. She had breathed life into his dead soul. She had been the life in his soul. Everything that she believed, the simple things, the good things, the eternal things, had ended up as articles of faith for him. She had managed to accomplish all this quite naturally, without knowing it, with the sole virtue of her presence, just as the sight of the sun makes one believe in light. She did kind things because she was born to do them. This lead to a new feeling, unprecedented and unbelievable, taking hold of his heart, a feeling that ought to have been the cause of intolerable pain, but which he bore resignedly, almost with joy. He greedily wanted to take possession of her miraculous heart to ensure that he had her all to himself, yet reason dictated that she couldn't be parted from her vocation of kindness simply by the love of one person. What madman would dream that every ounce of available air was exclusively his?

Therefore, he hadn't felt jealous on finding out that she belonged to another. He reasoned that, if there was another, it must have been due to her kindly feelings.

Nobody could blame her in this regard. Nobody could distract her from her mission. She knew the secret tracks of the heart, she was aware of the words that soothed and healed, gentle words like a balm. The man she had formed a relationship with would have needed help; wasn't he therefore pursuing an unreachable goal with hot blooded intent? Wasn't he pushing timid souls into a terrible struggle by virtue of his own desperate example?

Yet, she had found her place at the side of that man so full of hate, for whom life had no worth and whose path was littered with corpses. The ideals of justice and peace were nothing new to her, ideals that had prompted him to rise up in arms. However, she must have had to defend those sacred ideals, to protect the beauty of ideas from bloody contamination, to convert the fanatics and to comfort the desperate. She represented reason as opposed to sophistry, humility rather than pride, love against hate. She was the counterbalance to evil, a glance from her a consolation to the world.

Looking around, Vérod no longer knew where he was. He needed to rub his eyes before he was able to recognize the Rue de Belmont. He fell against the road-side parapet, crying out: "Soul! Soul! Soul!"

His desperation made him shake silently given the belief summoned up by this invocation. He didn't want to resign himself, nor could he, to the monstrous reality, and a violent scorn-laden energy roused him. Cloudy images and cruel resolutions darkened his expression as he clenched his fists. Desperate words came from his lips: "There is nothing! It's all a lie! There's nothing out there except evil!"

If love was repaid by hate, if someone who knew the kindness of her heart had cruelly destroyed the poor fleeting life of that woman inspired by love, a woman who was due attentive and concerned care, then there was nothing, nothing other than evil.

Yet Robert Vérod suppressed his words. Since the day that he had glimpsed the all-encompassing beauty of this believer in God, he had been dazzled and converted. A judge and a guardian had kept vigil within. They defended him against any troublesome thoughts, against any undeserving proposals, against any impure images. Through his actions and frame of mind he had wanted to be worthy of her. Such a work of self-preservation had been easy until this day. If doubt had occasionally bitten home, when bad omens had become cruelly apparent, he had only to think about his beloved to reignite his faith.

And now she was dead! She was dead! He saw her before him, stretched out on the floor, motionless, frozen, with that hideous bloodstain on her pale temple. A mortal anxiety suffocated him. He wanted to believe that death hadn't destroyed her completely, that her miraculous soul was still alive, watching over him, repeating words of faith and pardon. But it couldn't be. Even her charming voice, which he still had in his ears, couldn't persuade him of it. The otherworldly life of her soul wasn't enough to comfort his miserable existence. His mortal eyes needed to see, his ears to hear, his hands needed to stretch out and touch hers, to touch the hem of her clothes: a desire that would remain unfulfilled forever. To pardon the killers? It was his job to avenge her!

The last rays of twilight were still glinting out, but the light of the moon had already cleared the eastern horizon. There was a heavenly tranquility. Amid that tranquility, amid the imposing silence, Robert Vérod put his head in his hands to try and calm the storm of emotion assailing him. He hesitated over the thought that he hadn't sufficiently inspired the judge with his certainty. Why hadn't he been more effective? Given that coincidence had already ensured the judge was one of his old colleagues, why hadn't he let him know it? Why hadn't he been able to convince him of his sincerity? It wasn't only discretion that had prevented him from evoking their old acquaintance, it was also fear, knowing that Ferpierre was different: rigid and severe. Had the judge seen things with more clarity? Had he deceived himself? Had she really wanted to die?

Vérod's train of thought shifted to the past. He remembered the disturbing surprise he had felt on discovering the damaging secret troubling her poor soul. While she saved others, she considered herself lost. These words she had once uttered returned to Vérod. One day, at the news of a desperate suicide and in the face of general condemnation, she expressed a feeling unheard of among believers: she said that it was by no means certain quitting this life would carry inevitable damnation; that faith doesn't always condemn a voluntary death. One's conscience had to evaluate freely the motives as with any other human action and accept the consequences of the will. If deception, fear and cowardice merited disapproval, there might be other reasons that should inspire a greater degree of clemency in judgment.

In order to come up with these ideas and express them, surely she had to be at the low ebb of considering suicide? On realizing that the facts corresponded to these arguments more than Vérod had thought possible, his heart was filled with a great compassion.

Yet she hadn't thought about death so she could flee from pain. She used to say that pain was the very condition of life, and that far from fleeing it, one had to embrace duty and be glad to endure it calmly. What she had wanted was to escape from evil influences. She had confronted them in order to destroy them and had descended to these levels in an act of redemption. She had placed an unfailing faith in the power of love to triumph. Skating over human laws, and what greater proof, over divine commandments, she had hoped to get the man, who had denied and fought against them all, to come to a form of acceptance. But she had stumbled by failing to persuade him in this realization, to make him believe in something good. And she had awoken feeling impotent, wounded and discouraged in the face of such a lofty dream. Her love had been scorned, her prayers mocked, her faith offended. His destructive ways had continued more eagerly than before, and she, who had wanted to stop them, now considered herself an accomplice. She had then realized too late that the path she was following would inevitably end only one way. She saw his deception as unpardonable, leading her to thoughts of death. Robert had found her at that very moment, when the last glimmers of hope had flickered out, when the consequences of Zakunin's inevitable deceit had seemed ever more serious. He had seen his own deliverance in her, and she had felt the renewed vibrancy of life. Blinded, she had been his eyes; wounded, he had supported her. Their mutual salvation had gone unrecognized for many days. Each feeling reborn because of the other's presence, neither of them had thought their respective qualities could produce such a miracle. In the beginning he had been happy to glance in her direction, he had bathed in her light, never before imagining the joy. When he had finally understood things, when another kind of happiness became a little clearer, he had fled.

Turning his gaze to the mountains, grey under the glimmer of the moon, he now remembered the day he had left. It had been a cold, pale dawn, the leaden lake whipped by the wind, bristling with waves. He had escaped without a moment's hesitation. The hope and certainty of seeing her again were enough to sustain him. When? Where? He didn't know, but he knew he would. And he carried her in his soul. He hadn't cried, knowing she was in his heart. On seeing the grey boat on the grey waters, while waiting at the lakeside, out of breath, he had felt a tightening of the heartstrings. While the shores of Ouchy and the heights of Lausanne had still been in view, he hadn't taken his eyes from them.

He remembered nothing of the voyage, except a few passing images. The night prior to leaving, he had spent the whole time writing. He had known that he wouldn't have been able to send more than a word of farewell, but he had still written through the night. Once aboard, he had been assailed by fitful sleep and a distressing nightmare. There was the constant roar of the waves breaking against the powerful hull and the sound of his own labored breathing. With the shore slipping away, he had lost all perception of where he was and where he was going.

He had gone to Italy to look at the beautiful countryside, the perfect sun, the sweet skies that had made her who she was. He had gone to Milan with the aim of seeing her birthplace: a tall, severe house built like a tower, located in a remote and silent street, in front of a little church adorned with flowers. He had visited the small provincial town where she had spent her adolescent years in school, then travelled to Brianza, famed for its roses, where she had passed such a large part of her youth and where her family was buried. His mind had been occupied with cheerful thoughts, imagining the youthful years of his beloved and the naïve hopes that she had harbored and the pure happiness that must have been spread by her kindness. He had cried grateful tears. The turbulent tears would be waiting for him elsewhere.

After this long pilgrimage, as the good weather was beginning to fade, he had gone to Nice, his usual stop before Paris. He had lost his sister in Nice, his only companion from his orphaned childhood. Before her grave, he always meditated on the terrible enigmas of life and death. On this occasion, he had approached the grave feeling less sure of himself than usual, full of new thoughts to confide to her cherished memory, looking forward to the inspiration she would give him. He had once told the countess about his dead sister on a trip to Chillon. He had mentioned his tender feelings for her and the loss he had felt; the sensation that part of himself had been shut inside that coffin. She had asked him to keep talking about her, repeating her plea more than once. She had wanted to know all about her life and to picture her likeness. With words whose secret only she possessed, she had expressed the tender strength of brotherly love.

Hastily walking to the grave so he could conjure up the guardian angel-like images of the deceased and those of his absent love in one thought, his eyes had been struck by something glinting. On the memorial wall, next to the skeletal wreaths gathered in votive offering, a large white crown shone like a halo. It wasn't interwoven with flowers, but with white fabric and silver thread: an expert hand had folded the white satin, the white lace, the white voile, in order to form snow-like petals and foamy leaves.

His confusion before the spectacle lasted for a few seconds, as he thought about the fact that he was the only one who had loved his deceased sister. He was astonished and unaware of the origins of such an offering. Its appearance here left him perplexed and worried. Then, in a flash, he understood. Surely nobody except someone so full of compassion would have bothered to come and place that votive crown. Tears started to well unstoppably in his eyes. The secret benefactress, the compassionate consoling soul. He recognized the sentiments that had guided her to this memorial, the sentiments that she had hidden behind the weaving of the garland. Thoughts of his sister's remains would have made her tremble while positioning the white wreath. Trembling too, he cried with secret joy, with boundless gratitude, with timid hope.

So, he was alive in her memory, in her heart! At a time when he questioned what she would think of him during his absence, when he doubted if she would even recall him at all, he had found her sharing in his private ritual. Veiled by the tears, he fixed his gaze on the luminous crown. It seemed that his dead sister could now miraculously express the feelings overwhelming him — as if through time and space her thoughts came to him, that from beyond this life her soul began to speak, repeating the advice he had heard before: "Love and live, believe and live, hope and live."

Imagining them joined in the same picture, he saw them holding hands, beaming as they met each other. The distant countess had taken the deceased from her tomb, the two ghosts living the same intangibly superhuman existence. Yet over and above the marvelously blissful thoughts, the anxious ecstasy and a comforting faith, a secret feeling of distress gripped his heart as he mused on the lack of words to express the force of his devotion for his absent love. The need to bow before her overwhelmed him. To kiss the hand that had threaded the virginal crown was the only thing he could do. But would this be enough for him? Wouldn't he be suffocated by all the sweet thoughts spinning around his brain? He could only answer such a pure love, one that had guided her to this tomb, with the demanding and damaging variety. Wasn't it true that he now wanted her all to himself, now that they shared this life from beyond the grave? Had his flight really been useless? What was he to do now?

The memory of these moments of great anxiety prompted him to stand up. He turned towards the lake, stretching out his arm as if looking for support, like a drunkard. The sweetness of these thoughts was intoxicating, taking away his present torment. However, the bloody image reappeared, leaving his heart broken once again. Iniquitous destiny had destroyed the only creatures worthy of this life: one after the other he had lost his sisters.

"Sister! Sister!"

Indeed, she had been a sister to him. A sister's love, the word *sister,* they were the only two things that acted as a salve to his heart. All his other loves had been treacherous, poisonous, they hadn't left one decent memory: nothing but disdain for the deceit, for himself. He had once gloried in his passions, he had been arrogantly proud of them, as if each had been fortunate. So maliciously conceived as they were, they carried with them the seeds of their own destruction. Nothing but rot had remained, leaving him infected, but that was no more than his deserved punishment.

Not wanting to fall into the same trap, when he felt the resurgent need, long unfulfilled and suppressed, of an intimate relationship, and not wanting to live alone, he had, in her, found a sister. To go and look for her, to tell her in person the joy that she given him, had been his first impulse, but he hadn't acted on it. The hesitation in his soul had still been too forceful, and his solitude had been consoled by constant thoughts of her. He could wait, and indeed, he wanted to wait. Jealous of himself, almost afraid of damaging his feelings by investigating them, he had lived his secret happiness while almost forgetting its origin. As if waking from a pleasant dream, when latent and unknown energies are let loose, his senses had been multiplied. He had found a new virtue in everything around him.

Finally one day, he wrote to her. Overly lively verbal expression would not have suited such a sensitive soul or his own secret feelings. In writing to her he could contain the full force of his passion. Quieting his hopes, moderating his joy, he wrote only of his gratitude.

She answered him. She mentioned his dead sister. What other memories could have the effect of these sisterly words?

"I surely knew and loved your sister. When you spoke to me about her, when you told me of her precious, special gifts as a person and a kind soul, I felt that she embodied the aspirations of my youth, that she was the sister I never had, who could have been at my side in moments of joy and sadness. When you detailed the torment of her death, it seemed as if such beauty and kindness had been lost to me as well. I decided to pray at her grave, when I found out that she was buried in the city where I spend part of my time. I gladly did this, and I'm pleased that my idea was so gratefully received. . . ."

And now she was also dead!

On the day she died, joy had died with her. The moon hung over the landscape with a deathly light. The whitewashed walls seemed like memorial stones. A dead silence and stillness took hold of everything, of the waters, the land, the sky. Now he had another grave before which he had to kneel and place votive offerings. The blood-stained body would have remained on the autopsy table during the afternoon, in the hands of the anatomy experts. At this time of night, it would be in the church.

Vérod looked around to determine where he was, so he could head for the church. He was on the road to Lucerne. With a firm step, he set out in the Jurigoz direction. In the very same house of worship where they had met on the first few occasions, they were going to have their final reunion!

Far from her, his gaze and thoughts had been directed to the heavens in an effort to seek her out. After the first letter, he had intended to write to her once more, but the words had escaped him. Back then his life had been full of anxiety. He saw her wherever he looked, believing she was present in all that was beautiful. At times he felt jolted to his core when he caught a glimpse of someone in the distance who bore a passing resemblance to her. Yet after these flights of fancy had passed, his pain was all the more acute. His nights were filled with terrible dreams, during which he was sure he had already lost her and that he would never see her again. One, in particular, returned regularly: he was standing before her with his heart full of tumultuous feelings, with his hands trembling, and he couldn't say a word to her. After waiting for his words, she just left, disappeared, leaving him motionless, leaden.

This feeling of anxious inaction also affected him while awake, it stopped him from running to her side. When he went to Nice and didn't find her there, he was almost relieved. On seeing her again at Ouchy, at the start of summer, he had trembled. With time and distance, he had believed, and indeed, almost hoped to have escaped her charms, but her presence had renewed the wonderment. However, the anguish, the fear and all his unworthy feelings suddenly subsided when he was by her side. Could he remain silent about the fact that he lived for her favor? Even before he had spoken, she had understood him. She wasn't offended by his confession of love, nor had she doubted it. She was a stranger to false modesty and hypocritical feelings.

"As I believe in you, could you believe in me?" he had said to her. They were on the mountain, in the Comte woods. Away from the luxuriant foliage, the lake, the mountains, the entire countryside seemed limpid and clear in the dazzling light. There was also a real gleam in her words: "Truth is like light, it can't be hidden. Memories of you accompany me everywhere. The hope of seeing you again makes me smile. I knew this day would come. But there are other truths in life, although what I have said to you is completely true, it's also a moral certainty that our love can't last. Love must be satisfied. It dies while in the full bloom of life. Staying alive for fear of dying is the same as killing yourself because we all must die. But the course of love depends on one condition: abiding by the rules. Think about your deceased sister. What would you have wanted for her had she lived? That she would have fallen in love with a man and been loved in return. You wouldn't have gone into that man's past in too much detail, you wouldn't have worried about his first and less dignified passions. This is all part of nature's law, which makes men more lustful and impatient. Yet that man would have scorned his own past and would have trembled with delight and pride at giving his heart to that virgin. This would have united them forever, but they wouldn't have been happy with a tacit compromise. They would have asked for divine and social approval, because morals dictate that love forms the basis of the family, so it doesn't die or end in transformation. We have met each other too late. I don't deny that one can love more than once, especially a man. For us women the experience is more prone to risk. In general, the more one tries, the less one is believed. I have lived outside the rules for so long that I can hardly now expect to return to the fold. You don't want to believe it now, and you're sincere, but you'll be equally sincere later on when you will believe it. I don't make myself out to be worse than I am, but even if everyone else isn't aware of my decadence, I am, indestructibly so. This feeling makes life compete with faith. Before your sister's grave, when you were far away, when I wasn't completely sure of what would happen between us, I thought we could be linked by a kind of familial bond. Now I realize that even this will be forbidden territory for us. You must be ashamed of me. If your compassion was stronger, you wouldn't be able to overcome the temptation to change the nature of our relationship, or by overcoming it you would suffer too much. All these things are outside the laws I've mentioned, they're naturally destined to perish or cause hurt...."

He had tried to object to this brilliant demonstration, still not knowing what lay behind such a firm belief. She had simply stretched out her hand towards the distant mountains: "See those slopes? Some are in the sunlight, some remain in shadow. But as the sun continues its journey, the moment arrives when they are lit up, and the others become veiled. The truth is in the whole, just as with the light: it goes nowhere without shadow. If at the moment you believe that some mysterious, opportune shadows allow an escape, just wait for the advance of time and the harsh light will show you the deception. . . ."

He didn't let her finish: "And I'm going to tell you some other truths that you don't know or don't want to know. You, who judge yourself so, you who have such a clairvoyant vision, don't know that for all your rectitude, all your sincerity, all your humility, you are still a creature of choice, worthy of reverence. Don't you know that life poisons everything? Who among us is free from mistakes? And do you really think that the difference between little errors and big ones matters so much? What matters is to nourish ideals of decency. Isn't the person who loses the way and finds the road back more worthy of praise than someone who has always followed the straight and narrow? There was a time when I thought this was an injustice of the Christian church, but you, yourself, made me return to my beliefs. If you have erred, the intentions that were guiding you make you more worthy of pardon than anyone else. You, who scorn forgiveness, are hoping for it, are waiting for it. . . ."

"Not right now," was her answer. And she burst into tears. No, not her!

Time passed without these shadows disappearing. He had told her that love had turned him into a different man, a man capable of new things. Pride like this would have displeased her, the presumption would have wounded her. Without saying anything else, he had continued to live under her spell. The certainty of his love being felt in return filled him with pure delight, leaving him little energy for further goals. Hope flowered in the shade, hidden away. Words hadn't been necessary because there was no need: instead they were jealously guarded. Her strength was so fragile that he had resisted the least shock. Left to her own devices, she had kept on going naturally, little by little; she drew her vitality from everything around, she was everyone's vitality.

All of a sudden Robert Vérod stopped, shuddering.

He was in front of Saint Louis. The windows were outlined against the walls of the church, illuminated by the interior light. The lamps were watching over her.

He fell against the gate.

The day before he had listened to her voice! The day before he had opened his heart! The day before she had let him kiss her hand!

Now she was dead, killed, and the judge didn't believe there was a crime, and he was still alive!

IV

A Soul's Story

Judge Ferpierre's uncertainty regarding the events in Ouchy was growing. The results of the autopsy had thrown no light on the subject. The examination of the round entry wound, blackened by the smoke of the firearm, demonstrated that the bullet had been fired from a distance of around half a meter, and if this corroborated the suicide hypothesis, it didn't discard murder, as the murderer could have fired from close range. The internal injuries were equally inconclusive: the route taken by the projectile went along an upward route. There was no sign of violence on the deceased, neither on the hands, the wrist nor the neck.

As a consequence, lacking the necessary proof to confirm one of the two suppositions, Ferpierre was hoping to find some form of moral proof in the memoirs taken from the villa along with the other papers. On the same night as the autopsy, with a feverish curiosity prompted by the mystery, he set about reading them.

The first pages had no date, but they obviously referred to the countess's adolescence. They started with her impressions of coming home from school, her expression of joy on seeing her house and meeting up with her father once more. However, her time spent away wasn't forgotten. In the pages where she detailed the pleasures of her new life, there were still many memories of the old one.

"At this time of day my friends are in the garden. Sister Anna strolls along the path by the fountain, reading from that book that never ends, the poor woman, looking after her little dears. The inseparable ones get lost, arm in arm, among the lime trees. Rosa Bianca remains alone with her thoughts. The crazy ones run around shouting and playing. Who will remember me like I remember them?"

The predominant feeling was the adoration she felt for her father.

"Now I realize that Papa sent me away to school because he believed, as a man, that he couldn't sufficiently attend to my education and my hobbies. But we always understand each other. He says that I'm too serious when we agree on serious matters, and I say, instead, that he is too kind when he takes part in my trivial thoughts or daft ideas. The truth is simpler, and tomorrow I'm going to tell him. Why didn't I think of it before? I'm his daughter. What's so surprising if I'm like him?

"I so like to take his arm when we go out! But, of course it's much better when he takes mine. Then I'm almost proud that my Papa, such a strong, tall man, is relying on me. It seems that I'm of some good to him, but then I get really worried that I'm not of any use at all....

"I must tell Papa something I noticed a few days ago. He worries that I'm bored when he sees me alone in this enormous house. He sees it as his job to amuse me, to find me hobbies and things to enjoy. Today he scolded Giovanni because he was late in getting to the theatre and when he arrived there wasn't a box available. He had become annoyed because he couldn't take me to the performance, not because he wanted to go. Giulia told me that he never goes to the theatre when he is alone. Poor Papa, how it hurts to see him make sacrifices for me! Before he used to go to the club every night, now he never goes anymore. I must beg him not to abandon his friends for me!

"I have said the wrong thing: Papa doesn't make sacrifices for me, as I don't for him. To please those whom one loves is the greatest pleasure. But I would like to persuade him that he is wrong in thinking that I'm bored. I have never been bored. Paola Leroni always repeats this pet phrase: 'My girl, what a big nuisance!' She calls us all 'girls,' although we are older than her, and she is always bored with everything. She gets bored playing, studying, strolling, working, going out, staying in: she doesn't know what to do to stave off her boredom. She must suffer from some illness the poor girl. Perhaps Papa thinks I'm ill as well?"

Suddenly she was talking about her physical ailments, of her father's fears about her health. She thought he was more capable than a nun in his ability to cure the sick.

"I almost wish that I could be unwell in order to see him seated by my bedside, so I could hear him tell me the stories I enjoy so much, so I could see him walking to and fro, preparing the medicine, bringing the table near to the bed, taking over all the tasks from Giulia and doing them himself, better than Sister Anna!

"Oh no! Poor Papa, I don't want to stay in bed anymore. I want to feel healthy, to have a happy demeanor, and to make a lot of noise around the house so it reassures you, and you don't get too distressed because of me. The other day while the doctors were examining me, I saw him in the mirror. He didn't notice I was looking at him. He was wringing his hands with his head bowed towards us, breathing heavily, as if he was the person waiting for the medics' opinion!

"At times, when I have a headache, a cold, or I can't even taste anything, it seems that Papa has my ailment or feels my nausea. If I cough, he seems to get a pain in his chest, if I'm cold, he is too. It is so good to be loved like this!"

She was so tall and her father so young, they were sometimes mistaken for brother and sister. Such an error pleased her a great deal, and she even thought that it wasn't as big a mistake as it seemed: "Could he be a brother to me? Virginia's brother is nothing but annoying to her and the whole family. Men, even when they are good, don't appear to understand such things, the things that we don't enjoy, but my Papa, however!"

And he also found an explanation for this: "He loved my poor Mama so much that he took on her tastes, all her habits, her way of thinking and feeling. And all the love that she had for me when I was a young child was all inherited by him. He knew how to protect it and is now giving it to me. My Mama's death was a great misfortune. We always talk about her. She is always present. If only I could see her one day! But when Papa laments at not sufficiently paying attention to my needs, he isn't right. I thank the Lord for giving me a father like him, who loves me so much, who makes me want for nothing."

She also worried about not being enough for her father; not so much for herself but for him — she thought that if only she had had a sister, between the two of them they would have managed to make him happy. She was jealous of large united families: "When one is in company, everyone says their own thing, everyone thinks about something, different characters react with each other and alter their opinions, whereas can a person on their own be serious and happy at the same time? Can he or she think about everything, foresee and do it all? When I feel bad, I notice more keenly my lack of a sister, a sister who could make Papa happy, who could distract him from his worries and negative thoughts.... I told Papa about this and he said that he was happy with just me, that he didn't want to divide the love he felt. No, Papa, in such a case affection isn't split in two but built upon...."

Yet, however much her love for her father dominated things, she felt that there was a place in her heart for a different object of affection. She confessed this feeling for the first time, on noting the secret shame she would have if her father were to read her diary: "Papa doesn't know that in the evening, before going to bed, I set about writing in this diary on occasion. Yesterday, at eleven o'clock, when he thought I was in bed, the rain fell really heavily. He knew that I would be awake and came to ask if I felt ok. I easily reassured him, but I didn't add that I had felt fine enough to stay up and write in this book. I was wrong in hiding it from him. Sometimes, I feel like telling him, letting him read what I have written. Aren't they the same type of things I say to him out loud every day? But I don't know. I'm ashamed, almost afraid. There are even moments when I feel I'm wrong in writing my thoughts here. At school, Camilla Sergondi was the first to make me think about the idea of a diary, about writing our lives, but we never started. Every night, after thanking God for having a happy day, I thought about the things that had happened, what I had done, what I had said, what I had thought. As for writing, I didn't know where to start, because every day was the same. Then I decided to wait until I was at home, and finally I started. Now I regret it, because I didn't tell Papa about it. What is more, sometimes, like now, it seems useless to write these things: thoughts don't always need to be written down, and there are certain others I don't even know how to write, I can't.... Why are there certain things that can't be written, or even said? But if only I had a sister! I would tell her everything. I know it!"

Finally, unable to keep the secret any longer, she revealed to her father that she had been writing a diary. To sharpen her memory, she used to copy out the poetry that she found most pleasing. there were verses from Prati, Aleardi, Manzoni, Shelley, Byron and, one day, reciting a Victor Hugo poem to him, which she had copied from a newspaper, she forgot bits of it and went in search of her journal.

"I told Papa that I copy out beautiful poetry and write down my impressions. I was resolved to tell him everything but was hoping that he wouldn't show an inclination to read it. When he asked me: 'Will you let me read it?' I gave it to him, but I think I went rather red. He read a few lines, only from two or three pages, then he closed the book and hugged me tightly. He kissed me on the forehead. His eyes were red around the edges. I then felt really brave, almost regretting feeling afraid beforehand, and I begged him to read it all, but he didn't want to. I had to read it all myself, thus making the shame go away, and now I feel free from a great weight and very happy."

She first spoke of Count Luigi d'Arda when talking about poetry and art, with his name becoming more frequent after that, almost always in relation to books and the literary world. A close friend of her father since his youth, the count was one of the few to frequent the Albizzoni home. The young lady judged him very favorably.

"How fond Papa and the count are of each other. How alike they seem. He is kind like Papa, almost having the same manner about him....

"Today the count sent me the novels of Walter Scott.... Today I received from our good friend a copy of Metastasio's dramas....

"The count still practices his fencing, whereas Papa stopped it a long while ago. They talked about it with regard to the duel Tasso describes in *Jerusalem Delivered*. The count jokingly challenged Papa, but he refused, shaking his head: 'We're too old for that sort of thing!' I didn't like that answer much at all! Does he really believe he is old? He is hardly forty-nine! The answer must have also upset his friend, because he said nothing and left earlier than usual....

"Today our friend has sent so many English books to our house that I don't know where to put them. I have noticed that we almost always have the same feelings about the books we read. He has read and studied so much that I don't dare offer my opinion when he asks me, then he tells me his, and there is nothing left for me to do except agree....

"Now I am starting to be braver and give my thoughts from time to time and he praises my taste....

"Still more books! Papa joked that the count is my book supplier.

"Now that he knows that he's my book supplier, he asked if he can put the Albizzoni shield above his book shop, and I agreed. He found it really funny!

"How I like to see Papa and his friend laugh. When people are normally serious, laughter takes on a different meaning, it's more moving than cheering.

"Today the count drew our coat of arms for the space above the book shop: he sketches well with a swift touch. He explained to me that the shield for damsels is different to that of lords and ladies. He talked all night of heraldry and nobility, and I learnt many things that I didn't know previously.

"Papa, who always takes scrupulous care of my clothes, doesn't do the same with his own. I had to beg his friend to persuade him to think a little more about himself.

"Joking among themselves regarding sartorial elegance, Papa observed, as did I, because it's true, that the count has long dressed immaculately. He always says to me regarding the cut of the count's jacket or the folds of his cravat: 'This is the lastest word in Gironi. This is the lastest word in Vassier....' Gironi is the tailor, Vassier the cravat maker.

"More books today, but this time they are accompanied by a business card like the ones that companies use to publicize their address details. At the top is our crest, drawn to perfection, followed by these words: The Luigi d'Arda International Bookstore, Supplier to her Grace, the Marchesina Fiorenza Albizzoni-Vivaldi. . . ." How Papa laughed! 'Let's wait for the bill!' he said to me, continuing the joke, and the count, very serious, answered: 'Our house will present the bill at the end of the year.'

"Now even Papa calls me 'Your Grace,' and when they talk about me together, they always say: 'Her Grace the Marchesina'. Her Grace is very thankful for so much favor!

"The count, I found out today, is younger than Papa. He is forty-four years old. I don't know if I am happy or not about that. . . ."

A blank page interrupted the diary at this point. The manuscript then restarted, with different ink and a slightly modified hand: "We leave today. It has been six months since I have written anything. So many things during this time! It doesn't matter that I haven't written anything on these pages. It's all written here in the memory, in the heart. Luigi cried, Papa tried to keep a stiff upper lip, but he didn't manage to contain his emotion. When I saw them hug with smiling tearful eyes, I also began to cry. Her Grace the Marchesina Fiorenza Albizzoni-Vivaldi is no more. . . ."

And Judge Ferpierre, stopping, thanks to another break in the manuscript, reconstructed in his imagination the things skated over by the narrator.

Count d'Arda, who had seen his friend's daughter born and who had loved the girl like a second father, must have been conquered, in the presence of the young woman, by a different set of emotions, somewhat more tortuous, more sweet. Surely he had tried to resist at first, thinking about the large age gap, suffering in secret, almost ashamed every time that his friend, still unaware of his feelings, alluded to their lost youth. Yet love must have been stronger, imposing its persuasive reasoning. At forty-four years of age, could he be considered old? If his looks and character weren't displeasing to the young woman, what did their age difference matter? Didn't the experience he had gained with the years make him a more suitable match? But above all, didn't his friendship with her father offer a guarantee that he would dedicate his entire life to making her happy? Thanks to his regular visits and close relationship with the family, wasn't it as if he was already part of it?

This argument must have persuaded the would-be countess. Amazed at realizing his friend's wishes, there is little doubt the marquis must have hesitated before giving his blessing. In any case, he had left his daughter free to accept or decline the proposal, with the equal certainty that in considering her match to a man of proven worth like his friend, he would be happy with such an outcome. The young woman read her father's thoughts as if they were her own. Thus, understanding his secret wish and being sure of the count's affection, she must have considered the idea that their familiarity could one day end, which would have led her to feel sorry for these two people closest to her heart, and indeed, for herself. And so, she accepted the idea of making it everlasting, not knowing other men, nor even establishing the differences between one love and another, she had given her consent.

Ferpierre saw his deductions confirmed in the following pages. Although they weren't dated, they must have been written after the honeymoon: "Nothing has changed: we are together as before. Luigi used to come to our house, now Papa comes to see us. He didn't want us all to live in the same house. I would have been delighted if this were the case and so would Luigi. Everything I like also pleases Luigi. Our agreements about art and thought are continuing with regard to more mundane matters.

"Papa asks me if I'm happy. I thank the Lord for the happiness he has granted me, that he has granted us. He doesn't seem to believe what has happened. The idea that my marriage could be a misfortune torments him. Luigi asks me if I love him. It seems that both are doubtful, one of my happiness, the other of my love. They don't insist on wanting assurances, but I can read a secret anxiety in their eyes, almost as if I am hiding something from them. All because my husband is forty-four! If he was thirty-four there would be no doubts!

"What a pleasure! What a pleasure! Finally, I have been able to persuade Luigi of the truth. I told him, while we were traveling that I have been writing down my thoughts in this book since leaving school, and I promised to give it to him so he can read it. He wanted to know if I had mentioned him, what I had said about him and what opinions I had formed. When we returned home, he no longer asked for the book. The other day I brought up the subject myself, but he replied that he didn't want to read it. I didn't think much of his reason: he said that the things I had confided to the page shouldn't be revealed. In truth, he was still fearful of discovering that I thought he wasn't young enough, that I hadn't found him pleasant enough. I then begged him to sit down and listen while I read to him. When I reached the last lines, he asked me, with red eyes, to explain them to him. The last lines, before our marriage, were the following: 'The count is younger than Papa: he is forty-four years old. I don't know if I am happy or not about that. . . .'

"I have explained it to them as best I can. When I knew he was younger than Papa, I felt sorry for my poor father, because I would have liked time to stop passing by for him, indeed for it to go in reverse. Then, realizing that Papa had me, but that his friend was alone, as a consolation I thought it only just that he was younger, so he could marry and have a family. How Luigi hugged me! What smiling eyes! What words of love! I have never seen him so happy, not even on the day I said yes! Now he no longer worries that his forty-four years are too many. On the contrary he's persuaded that the idea of marrying him wasn't as strange to me as he and Papa had feared. I thought it quite natural. I considered for a moment: it's true that Luigi was double my age, but a man's age doesn't count like a woman's. And what is more, who would think my husband was forty-four? Age isn't important, the quality of one's soul is what matters, and as proof of Luigi's kindness, I have the fact that he's Papa's friend. Everything I have heard him say in two years of friendship has shown me that his way of thinking and feeling is considerate, kind, delightful, that he has a noble and heightened intelligence, that he is a deeply cultured man.

"And now I understand that his question had a different angle: Luigi wasn't afraid that he didn't appear young enough, rather that his looks or personality didn't appeal to me.

"Well then, if at times I have wondered why I write these lines, and at others I have thought them worthy, today I think it really has been fortunate to have written them. Through them I have been able to convince Luigi of my thoughts at the time. Oh, how I wish I had written down my precise impressions when he challenged Papa as a joke. He removed a foil from the arms cabinet and took his guard! He looked so good with the shining sword in hand and his gaze flashing like the foil. He was so strong and agile that he truly seemed a character straight from one of those Walter Scott novels that I liked so much. I hadn't then thought about being able to marry him, but I did gladly think that I could be the lady for whom such a knight would take the field. And if he had known the altogether different emotions, until then little felt, when he sent me that small card that jokingly said: 'Supplier to Her Grace the Marchesina Fiorenza.' Our names were together on that card, as on a wedding invite: it was written! Not even then did I really dream we would one day be joined together like we are now, but I certainly took note of our names on the same paper. I thought that it must have been Luigi who had copied them out, that it was him who called me 'Her Grace' and I felt my heart race....

"Ah, if I had only written these things, there would be no doubt in Luigi's mind. I was on the point of telling him, but I stopped myself, in part because he was in one of his doubting moods, in part because I thought it better to write them down in this book, which he'll read one day. Given that he doesn't believe me, it's not worth saying anything to him: better that I confide it to these pages, which are destined to reveal the truth. The fact that I'm writing after the event doesn't make my impressions are any less true!"

And underneath was written in thicker more irregular letters, traced by a trembling hand, these words: "He has read it! He believes!"

So, the memories continued, filled with expressions of happy intimacy, revealing an affectionate soul, innocent and sincere, for whom Judge Ferpierre knew he could feel a kind of love.

Married under these circumstances, to a man who could have been her father, it would have been easy to predict that on giving up passionate happiness for, at most, a certain tranquility, she would, sooner or later, feel snared by the need for something more.

The deceased's confessions destroyed that suspicion. Ferpierre wanted to think that if the writer of these lines hadn't been happy, if she had felt cheated by marrying Count d'Arda, she would have confessed it to the page, frankly, completely. However, she had already noted that she felt things she couldn't write down. Perhaps she couldn't fully acknowledge her deception. Perhaps, instead of veiling things, she had written nothing, leaving an eloquent silence. Yet, far from being quiet, far from alluding to her disillusion, she often insisted on displays of naive, even warm affection, so much so that the judge didn't doubt her sincerity. On the other hand, was the love of a twenty-year-old for a man of over forty really so unbelievable? In order to explain it, Ferpierre focused more on his physical attributes than his moral fiber. Among the papers found in the deceased's house, he had seen some photographs of relatives and friends, two of which, according to Giulia Pico's testimony, were of the count: a handsome figure, strong, noble and expressive, to a degree that would explain the young woman's love. For page after page she had done nothing but talk about him, referring with pride to all her husband's demonstrations of affection. She had transcribed his words of love. She was both delighted on seeing that he now believed in her feelings and on knowing that her father was sure of her happiness.

Another blank page suddenly interrupted the journal. On the following pages there was only one line written: "Father, dear father, pull through! Stay alive for me!"

There was nothing else. Ferpierre almost heard the desperate entreaties convulsing the devoted daughter as she sat by his bedside. But it was all in vain. There followed a lock of graying hair held by two cuts in the paper, with a date in the margin: 3rd June 1886. After this, the book was full of memories of the deceased. The countess confided her dearest recollections as a daughter to these pages with searing grief, yet she remained comforted by her Christian faith to such a degree that, in certain passages, she seemed to talk of him as if he were still alive, in a way that resembled her earlier entries. However, the judge flicked through these pages rapidly, impatient to get to the next inescapable drama.

With time, with the aging of her husband, wasn't it inevitable that the woman's tranquility would come to an end? How would she refer to it?

She didn't. The journal had, though, an even bigger gap than before. The writing appeared, after such an interruption, to be changed still further, and the meaning of the new passages was incomprehensible.

"...Now I'm sure of it. All his words have come back to me. I was smiling then. I was proud of them. Today I'm paying for my pride. At times I doubt the fault is mine. What would someone else have done in my place? The blame certainly lies with my ignorance, my inexperience.

"Why didn't he want to talk about it, or couldn't he? I guess he didn't want to or couldn't. I once asked him: 'But how? How was it?...' I can still hear his answer, as he turned his gaze away: 'Later....'

"In his opinion, killing yourself wasn't an unforgivable sin. To kill yourself because you can't cope with life was in his judgment an act of cowardice, but in other cases, a voluntary death wasn't so open to censure. We discussed this issue many times, and he showed me that the world justly honors those who by death withdraw from servitude, shame, dishonor, who by killing themselves save or help their fellow man. He also said that to die in order in order to punish yourself was an act of justice."

Ferpierre's uncertainty about the meaning of these words didn't last long: the narrator's thoughts were becoming clearer page by page. The countess believed that her husband hadn't died by accident but deliberately, that he had sought out a terrible death under the wheels of a train.

"The people present said, indeed they still say, that they couldn't understand how he had never heard their shouts of warning and hadn't seen their desperate gestures. One of those dizzy spells that he had suffered in the last year could explain it, if I didn't know better.

"He was suffering from a fatal sadness. When I asked him why, he looked at me with such anguish, as if he was on the point of losing me right there. Once, now a long while ago, when he spoke to me for the first time about his bachelor life, there was much disdain in his voice. He had gained a lot of comfort from the certainty of having left behind his errant ways, his guilt!

"In spite of his kindness, he was severe, implacable, when dealing with passionate misadventures. The ruination of a friend of his who had abandoned his family was merited in his view. Not even his death in solitude and poverty persuaded the count to be indulgent.

"I realized what was happening. I didn't talk about it. I was scared, scared even to think about it.

"I'm not being true. I'm not saying everything...."

Ferpierre, seeing that she hadn't written about the drama in the forthcoming pages, stopped once more to think about what he had read.

Between the two of them, certain temptations had begun to appear, but it was the man, not the woman, who had welcomed them! Those last words: "I'm not being true, I'm not saying everything..." did they perhaps mean she hadn't accused her husband because she, herself, didn't feel free of sin? However much the judge's experience made few things seem impossible, however much he had already foreseen the day that the calming effect of an aging husband wouldn't be enough for a young wife, the idea that the countess had fallen repelled him. Ferpierre had come to feel so much affection for her on reading her story, seeing her nobility and purity and sensing a naive sincerity in the pages of her confessions, that her feelings of reticence appeared to be only natural. "I was scared, scared even to think about it. I'm not being true. I'm not saying everything...." When writing these words wasn't she thinking that her betrayal by a husband she loved so much, who doubted her love, who had promised to dedicate his life to being worthy of it, was a guilty blow to him and an unmerited punishment for her? Surely she wasn't thinking that the man had lied or that he had boasted about a prowess he lacked? If disturbing currents of seduction were whirling around her, and she had been able to subdue and dispel them, when, in the eyes of the world, it would have been more excusable if she had succumbed to them, wouldn't it be natural to judge this man's weakness severely? All the pain that disillusion and intrigue, until then unsuspected, had unleashed in her heart was expressed in the words: "I was scared, scared even to think about it...." Ferpierre, rereading them, had his suspicions confirmed. He recognized that the unexpected solution was logical: that's to say illogical or at least overly faithful to the ideas the count had expounded to preclude another conclusion.

Was it natural to assume that Count d'Arda, a rich, dissolute bachelor into his forties, who had felt no need for a legitimate relationship, would be permanently reduced to an exemplary husband who would be happy with the love of that naive young woman? And was it unnatural or inadmissible that the loving wife, ignorant of the ways of the world, would define her happiness by her new married status?

The details of the drama escaped Ferpierre, but he reconstructed them in his imagination. Another woman, a woman totally different from the countess, had seduced Luigi d'Arda. He had tried to resist, convinced that he would be betraying the young woman, showing her a bad example — he to whom not only duty but also interest advised the correct path, the one he had followed at the beginning, but he had been beaten by temptation. What should one think of the countess's suspicion that he had killed himself, that her noble soul could think her husband had made the decision to kill himself, given that he had been incapable of avoiding a mistake? Or was it her romantic imagination seeing a suicide where there was nothing more than an unfortunate accident? Mystery upon mystery; but it would remain impenetrable, as the seal of death had already closed the mouths of the two actors in the drama. The temptress, if she was still alive, was the only person who could clarify things. In truth it mattered little now if the count, succumbing to guilt against his will, had wanted to punish himself by death, thus avoiding the worse punishment of seeing the fall of a wife to whom he had shown the wrong path, or if the death was, for that matter, simple chance. Ferpierre continued the memoirs with renewed energy, in search of more pressing items.

After these swift allusions to the catastrophe, the judge found nothing but geographical description. The young widow took her grief from place to place, along the Rhine, to Holland, to Scotland, and only in this last country did her memoir carry a date. It seemed that, as her experience had prematurely matured her, her thought and style had strengthened in equal proportion: certain landscapes were portrayed with a somber yet vigorous touch, the images sharp and clear. Here and there, among the descriptions, there were pencil and ink sketches, views of places, character drawings — the artist's hand was both graceful and firm. Every so often a few moralizing phrases appeared with no apparent relation to the surrounding notes, demonstrating that beneath the tranquil exterior a secret uneasiness was tormenting the writer — as with this example: "It's not enough to know how to regulate our external actions: we ought to be able to guide our intimate thoughts."

What did she mean by these words? Free and alone, was she was reluctantly feeling besieged by temptations that, no doubt, she knew how to resist? And wasn't it extremely natural that she should be feeling this way?

"The law of forgiveness is necessary, because evil is universal. Without it nobody would have hope of salvation."

Was this idea derived from abstract thought, or rather, from her conscience, which felt some personal blame?

Little by little, other themes came into play. On some pages there was nothing other than digressions about life's problems.

"Injustice is great in the world: nobody is more worthy of praise than he who tries to combat it.

"There are two types of law, that of nature and that of the soul, and often the ideal law works against natural impulses. There was a time when this astonished me, but not any longer. To free oneself of the laws of nature is the most lofty of necessities and the most noble of efforts. The merit is derived from overcoming the difficulties.

"There is always conflict between the two types of law, not just occasionally, and in this life it's not possible to eliminate that, because without the effort nothing good would exist. It is the greatest of tests.

"Those that say it's stupid to advocate equality between men because they are naturally unequal, don't know they are spouting a moral heresy. It would be the equivalent of saying that it's stupid to advocate sacrifice because egotism is a natural law. If loving ourselves is our first real need, to repress it and postpone it for the love of others must be our first ideal need. Men are born different: this hard truth suggests the idea of equalization. These are simple sounding ideas to me, but he says they aren't common."

The judge's attention pricked up at this point. Was the "he" Prince Alexi Petrovich? Didn't these thoughts on social matters date from the time the two lovers had met? The narrator appeared to answer the question Ferpierre had mentally made, as the theme of the memoir varied from one page to the next: from abstract speculations she passed to more intimate confessions.

"No, I hadn't experienced a similar turmoil. I would like to deny it, but I can't. This anxiety, this fever, unknown to me.... I once read that there was more than one kind of love, and I thought that the writer had lied or was wrong. I had thought that there was no more than one way to love. No, he was right. My previous feelings don't resemble today's tumult: Luigi, who had more experience than me, knew it and didn't settle for what I was offering him. He doubted my love because it wasn't impetuous and overwhelming. Given that, my father also doubted my happiness. Perhaps even I doubt it now?

"The clouds advance on the mountain summits. They take capricious form, interlacing like ribbons, extending like veils. One side of the lake has disappeared behind them. The waters have no limit now; they form an open gulf in a mysterious ocean. I still hear his voice. I'm happy....

"I am happy. The flame leaps from soul to soul as from face to face. Its words are like the breath of an internal fire. Can I hide my thoughts from him? And had I wanted to be quiet, wouldn't he have read it in my eyes?

"When we believe in something, we deny everything else. When we experience a feeling, we disregard opposing ones and those that are simply different. This is my first instinct. I think that I've only started to live in the past month or so. Reason provides a warning, the heart remembers. It's another thing altogether....

"If there are various ways to love, is one better, more desirable, truer? Is it the case that the voice of reason isn't heard any more, that all memories are forgotten, that just one idea beats all the others, and one need breaks all obstacles?

"His laughter hurt me today. I didn't want him to laugh when he heard about that act of heroism. How deep his confidence is and bitter his skepticism. Who made him that way? Life. At least that's what he says.

"The pain is greater, though, when I hear him laugh at himself. When he laughs with that false tone, I think there is something broken in his voice, in his heart.

"If it's true that we feel things consecutively, and if we, ourselves, deny those feelings that have died, our current emotional state must believe itself eternal. That's the mistake. The happiness that I've been feeling in the last few days seemed indestructible. Today it's not destroyed, but troubled.

"Such pain! Such pain! I would have never anticipated such misery and pain! This is the first time that I've confided it to anyone. And he laughed! I don't want…

"His letter today made me tremble with magnificent contentment. If it were true! If I were to truly possess such power!"

With this expression of doubt the diary broke off once more, as if the narrator had wanted, before continuing, to try something out. But in the following pages, the confessions were no more ordered than before.

"Life is more difficult than I had thought."

This reflection was the only thing on one page. A little further on, another doubt surfaced:

"Would it be presumptions to believe that one is right?"

Then there were some sentences with obscured meanings.

"In no way, but it's good to hope….

"It's not weakness, it isn't a surprise: I have thought for a long time, faith smiles on me, I see the aim….

"I now lack the words…."

Under the date: "18th June 1890" the following was written:

"Before God, for ever and ever."

Ferpierre tried to disentangle the meaning of these words, thereby reconstructing her personal history.

What Vérod had said was confirmed: the idea of trying to heal Zakunin's damaged soul was uppermost in the countess's thoughts. With her mild manner, due to the attraction of opposites, she had appreciated his impetuous force, the indomitable ardor of the rebel, as if it contained unrefined riches from which one could extract some pure value. It was certain that something simpler, just love, could explain the close relationship that had developed between them. She gave an eloquent testimony of her love when she confessed that she understood her husband's doubts and those of her father regarding her former happiness. Her husband's affection had been enough for her. She hadn't made a sacrifice in marrying him, given the big gap in their ages, and although the possibility of marriage had belatedly appeared, she had been truly happy with him. The doubt was posthumous, but it clearly demonstrated how much stronger and more exciting her new feelings were. Furthermore, the emotions she felt regarding the evils afflicting the prince and the hope that she could be useful to him, bordering on duty, meant that she had given in to affection.

"If it were true! If I were to truly possess such power!"

Certainly, the prince had told her that her love had been a comfort, a joy, a boon to his health. Was he sincere, or was he faking, calculating the effect of his words? It was obvious that the effect had not been insignificant on her loving heart. Both being free, nothing would have prohibited them from a legitimate union, if the rebel hadn't disregarded and hated the law, indeed, directing his every effort to destroying it. Marrying her would have been the biggest proof of his conversion, but he probably wasn't serious in saying he had been converted. It was most likely that they hadn't made any allusion to the future, that the prince hadn't explicitly promised to think about marriage, or that the countess hadn't rigorously pressed for legitimacy. For a while they must have loved each other in a chaste manner, she in the hope of calming and redeeming him; he, no doubt, smiling at such a hope. Then, one day, the complicity of circumstance, the sweetness of the hour, the woman's weakness, the man's overpowering nature had forever changed their relationship. She had suffered greatly on seeing that the purity of her intentions weren't enough, but she hadn't expressed her own pain, certain as she was of having made a lifetime commitment to God and confident of making him recognize, sooner or later, the sanctity of duty, even though he was the man he was.

How bitter her disappointment must have been on discovering the uselessness of her mission! Without a doubt, the disappointment hadn't been immediately obvious. While the prince had kept on loving her, she had continued to hope, to believe with all the sincerity of her conscience that at heart he was her husband. She had waited for a long time full of hope. And the moral distrust, had that preceded or followed her disillusioned feelings? Surely both had been born at the same time.

Her memories broke off once again, as evidenced by her handwriting and the trail of ink. The effort of not believing the harsh reality was obvious in the new confessions. The narrator wrote:

"Belief is needed. Hope is needed.... Most of the time we don't know each other, we need to reveal ourselves as we really are...."

Such an idea undoubtedly referred to the man beside her, to his obstinate insistence on the work of destruction, to the hope she still harbored of overcoming this, of making him return to some form of belief. Then she wrote horrified: "Still the hate, the blood, the fire! No, never! This will never be the road! How is it possible that a loving heart can talk like this? He says that love is paid with love, hate with hate. Such a thing may be just, but it isn't generous. And those he wants to combat, do they truly hate? Don't they suffer too, having to resort to violence?..."

It seemed that the discord between the prince's instinct for rebellion and the countess's predilection for peace had come before complete disillusion, but at the moment of recognizing the uselessness of her efforts, wouldn't she have suspected his lack of sincerity in assuring her that he had returned to the fold because of her efforts? And wouldn't such a suspicion have hurt her, not only because of her beliefs, but also her hopes?

She made no mention of the fate that would befall their love. Had she kept this quiet because she prized his pacification over her own happiness? Or was the opposite true. Had she turned her attention to moral disappointment in order to distract herself from a more frightening vision, from an altogether more fatal disappointment? If this man's love was a lie, given her relationship was outside the law, wasn't the intimate sanction permitted by her conscious now missing? For a Christian, who felt any blame was mitigated, if not excused, by sincerity of feeling, by the purity of the commitment, wouldn't the sudden removal of these conditions imply a serious punishment?

Ferpierre saw that these ideas must have worried the countess at the time. He could almost read it in the lines. And just as a musical phrase anticipates the development and cadence of a melody, his anticipatory logic was confirmed by the following paragraphs in the diary:

"I haven't been brave, but I need to be. Again, I'm afraid to examine my conscience, something which has always come easy to me, and I've always found gratifying.

But the fears of old are but nothing compared with those of today.

"Am I cheating myself? And how can I pretend everyone else is sincere? Is arrogance stopping me from confessing that I have been cheated? But God, who can read my heart, knows that I have believed in good. And I still believe in it.

"He doesn't know me. He obeys so many varied impulses. His thoughts are so complex, his experience has been so vast, that he doesn't know his own mind, and therefore, he can't free himself from the fleeting impulse or from acting out of character. I was hoping to put him back on the straight and narrow, but it's more difficult and requires more time than I had imagined. However, I continue to hope. The trust I had still keeps me going.

"There are moments of doubt. I doubt myself more than him. I think that this hope is a fallacy, that trust isn't sincere, that I use both to hide something less worthy, to prop up a less pure desire.

"Isn't this the judgment that everyone will make? Are ambiguous methods any use for those who wish a correct solution? Must I follow such tortuous paths in order to put him on the right path? I, who must give him an example of the virtue in which he doesn't believe, have given him another proof, of the accommodating weakness that he condemns....

"We are now erring by being together. This is serious: when in love a lover isn't only responsible for his or her actions but also those of the partner. It's on this kind of solidarity that I based my decision, when I was waiting to feel the joy of the prize rather than the pain of error.

"I can't even say that I'm surprised I didn't foresee what was going to happen. So much sophistry! In predicting my fall, I said to myself that he couldn't want my debasement, I thought of entrusting myself to him so that I didn't fall prey to pride by exclusively considering myself able to regulate our love!

"And it wouldn't have been pride as such. This ability is ours, we women, we are responsible for good and bad. Our resistance must dictate the law to the exuberant energy and overpowering will of men. But another idea assails me: it's not necessary for a strong soul to have the law written in a book — it's simply enough to understand it. He, who knows none, tells me that it's because of me he understands the law of love: trust. Now I can't, I mustn't, I don't want to suspect that he has even been trampling on that as well. Yet, what use is it thinking such things, saying them out loud, writing them down, if doubt worries and torments me?

"Little by little, but with perfect clarity, I have seen it grow, surge, morph out of proportion. Anguished doubt has at times been converted into desperate certainty. Then I think that I still have one card left to play, an extreme one, that of pardon. I have a feeling that it won't cost me overly much to do it, which is bad, because if it were costly, it would have more merit. But he can do with me what he wishes, as long as he doesn't deny everything and always...

"Ah, that laugh!"

Was it to be hoped that Zakunin had fulfilled the only condition imposed by the unfortunate woman? On reconstructing, with the help of these confessions, the character of the accused, Ferpierre realized that the adverse opinion of the man formulated by Robert Vérod wasn't due to passion. Behind his profession of faith in humanity, with his preaching of justice, equality and love, a skeptical egotism must be hidden, along with base appetites and unhealthy intentions, given that he had been capable of reducing to such a tormented state the creature who had surrendered to his discretion. If the illusion of inducing him to pursue a gentler social reform had failed, had he at least responded to this demonstration of love with acts of kindness?

Ferpierre returned with renewed interest to reading the diary.

"Today, he has said these precise words to me: 'Well now you believe that your love is immortal? You don't understand that you will stop loving me one day, that already you don't love me as you used to do. You judge me unworthy of love, you think you have sacrificed yourself. The sacrifice costs you, and you want to get some form of compensation. You'll find it elsewhere, don't doubt it, a love offered to you by another.... In the beginning you'll blame me. Later on you'll recognize that I'm not the one to blame. Inside you, inside me, in us all, in our every fiber, our flesh and blood, there is a ferment that neither no one nor no thing can calm. When you feel hungry, you eat. Once you have eaten, you're satiated. Beyond this truth, there is no other. It is necessary to say this, to repeat it, to honor it, and to recognize that your laws, your commandments, your scruples are lies and hypocrisy that we must unmask and overwhelm. Your grandiose concepts — Love, Duty, Law — have meaning but not the one you believe. Our duties and our rights are reduced to finding and sustaining pleasure, which is the reason, the origin and the goal of life. While your pleasure is in mine, we will love each other; when we are no longer enough for each other, our love will end. You mentioned another grand concept — Honor. Where would this be found? My honor lies in saying what I think, in matching my actions with my ideas. The whole world is full of iniquitous prejudices, more stupid than evil. Science, which doesn't lie, has expressed this truth, the only law from a pile of secular falsehoods: in other words, the law of the fight for survival.

"'Hide yourself from it, burn the books that teach it, if you want your lies to perpetuate. But once you recognize it, how can you remain serious, hearing the same old deceitful refrains? You have to choose between life and death: to renounce this life is preferable, but you don't want that, and so I have to live, exterminating the entire human race in order to obtain the one thing that to you seems the most futile of my satisfactions. You want us to be an unbreakable family unit, but why aren't you now happy being free? Isn't it good that you can abandon me if, having seen what I'm like, I horrify you? Let the children be ignorant of their parents' nature, if you don't want them to curse those who have given them life! Why do you want us to be joined forever, when each of us is autonomous, when there is no barrier, on the contrary, everything persuades us that anyone can fall in love with someone else and will, one day, actually do so? If you leave me when I no longer love you, I'll thank you for it, if you betray me when I still love you, I'll kill you. Do the same yourself. You have the same rights as I do. All men behave this way, in spite of the foolish codes and hypocritical preachings. The anarchy that we want to establish already exists in certain customs, but it's still no more than the anarchy you ascribe to us, in other words, damage to the law and a repudiation of it. We need, however, to conform to natural law, a conscious standardization of the life force. Beyond that, there is nothing.'

"I have left nothing out: these were his very words. He's right. Beyond that there is nothing."

Ferpierre, despite being long accustomed to the spectacle of pain, felt moved when thinking of the bitterness of such agony to a believer. The copying down of his words, every one of which must have insulted and horrified her as blasphemy and the recognition that Zakunin was right, were enough for her to be condemned with no excuses, a self-judgment of feeling lost without hope. She must now have realized that the illusion of redeeming his soul and the wish to do good had been simple pretexts, that in his love, in all love, in all life, we hear no voice but that of our basest instincts. And this resulted in her, who had wanted to turn Zakunin back to the path of righteousness, being pushed towards doubt and denial. In place of curing the sick, instead of cleansing the fallen, she had become infected.

But could she really deny for long the beliefs she had held for her entire life? To what degree were they ironic, the words that agreed with his reasoning? While she spoke to him of love, he advanced skeptical and cynical arguments, almost foreseeing that he was going to be betrayed — the poor woman must have mocked her own situation. But what was she thinking with regard to the possibility of betrayal? Did she recognize that, by fatal logic, her first error would be followed by a second and then a third, or did she rebel against such logic? Here was the moral problem, the solution to which would clarify the judicial mystery.

Ferpierre's curiosity grew, he redoubled his attention to the dead woman's confessions.

"What a disaster for a mother to scorn her own child, the fruit of her womb, the best part of herself!

"The unhappiness of life is found in the idea of happiness.

"Will the person who follows a beloved soul to the tomb be long-suffering? Is it a crime for a child, a husband, to die with his parent or wife? Is such a beautiful act punishable? If only I had died with my father!

"Praying to God for death, to hope for it as salvation, to wish for it as a recompense, isn't it almost like actually killing yourself? Is the distance separating the burning vocation from the act really so big? If the act is blameworthy, how can the longed-for intention be acceptable?

"I will not have to wait long. The work of destruction is already advanced. Pain bites my chest with increasing cruelty. Every day, every hour that passes, it does me much harm.

"There are certain coincidences that appear to be warnings, advice, destiny's involvement. Why has this weapon come to hand precisely when I needed it?"

All these paragraphs in which the unfortunate woman discussed with herself the problem of suicide demonstrated that she already had little hope of anything except death. A little further on, she had transcribed a sentence from a book: "When I live under the law, I have the obligation to abide by it; but when I live beyond it, can they still bind me to it?" (Montesquieu)

This judgment must have seen singularly applicable to her own situation. Notwithstanding all her contradictory reasoning, she must have felt that killing herself was a bad act and that the moral order of things deemed it right to put up with life patiently until the end of one's days. However, this commandment would be valid for those who had obeyed all the others. She, however, had infringed a much more serious one and must have felt disconnected from this obligation. Furthermore, by thinking of suicide, she was intending to punish herself.

"Is it time?" she asked at one point. "Surely, when all other remedies are impossible, when hope is completely dead, I'll be able to do it. But am I a good judge of the opportune moment? When it seems that a living being is about to fade away under the action of an implacable evil, isn't it the case that nature often finds the strength within to continue living? Can't life, so abundant and fruitful, unexpectedly resolve a situation with seemingly no exit? Shouldn't hope be the last thing to die?"

Persuaded of such an expediency, she had waited. But what had that brought?

After some blank pages, the judge found another thought that drew his attention.

"New suffering is better than joy and pleasure for making one forget previous heartache — the night of 12th August."

By way of a sign, there were some dried flowers, brittle and discolored, between the leaves of paper.

The flowers and the date under these words made Ferpierre think that something had happened worthy of note, something that had been of special importance to the countess. Continuing to read, he encountered another passage over which he paused for some time. The deceased hadn't been expressing her own thoughts. Once again she had transcribed some text from a book: "Nothing quite makes life so disagreeable as a second love. The eternity and infinity that love brings, spreading over everything, vanishes. Love seems ephemeral, like anything that begins again." (Goethe)

Ferpierre recalled the German poet's opinion very well. Was the countess able to quote it without applying it to herself? The doubt he had expressed with regard to Vérod was beginning to take shape. If she had written out this disconsolate sentence after having met Vérod, when she had been upset by a still nascent fondness, it was enough to believe that this new relationship would provide little compensation, only more pain! After waiting, after wanting to wait, what had this brought her? Not help, but the final disaster!

The quote from Goethe meant that this second relationship was irredeemably condemned, since deluding oneself with the depth of a new affection isn't possible for a heart that has already seen the death of the first. The natives of America believed that the Europeans who came to conquer the New World were immortal: they judged them all-powerful until the first Spaniard succumbed, at which point they recognized the deceit and ceased to venerate them.

What could the instinct for life be worth when ranged against the inevitability expressed by Goethe and subsequently affirmed by the Countess d'Arda? To what extent would it impede her loving again, knowing that her new love would finish like the old? Is the certainty of dying a reason to kill yourself? Whoever contemplates the sad truth of things will live badly, but they will live, because instincts are more persuasive than abstract concepts. Only morals provide the ability to stop such instincts. And the countess found herself beyond moral law.

This was the condition she found herself in, lacking any written documentation legally linking her inseparably to the prince. The example provided by her unworthy lover must have, naturally, pushed her to search for comfort and joy with someone else, and the transience, common to all human things, couldn't and shouldn't have stopped her. Although she was free in society's eyes, she was joined in her own conscience, without the necessary rites, but by a sincere heart. She had certainly found herself outside the law, but with the aim of encouraging the prince, who had abandoned and ignored it, to return to the fold. She had received nothing but a bad example from him, but in return had set him a good one. It wasn't possible for her new love to flourish without her renouncing the mitigations which, in her ambiguous state, would take away her punishment or permit her, at least, to harbor the hope of being able to avoid its severity. "This idea has convinced me: it's not necessary for a strong soul to have the law written in a book — it's simply enough to understand it." Was it possible that she had forgotten her own words and the feeling that had dictated them? If such a declaration was sound and sincere; if the woman's soul was as elevated and strong as it appeared to be in witness statements and the pages of this diary, it wasn't only possible that she had killed herself, but it could almost be foreseen as well.

After meeting Vérod, her heart was oppressed, her life full of bitterness, all her hopes broken, but she was still able to respect herself. In the bitterness of disillusion, she had indeed derided herself and lost heart, affirming that she had been joined to Prince Alexi, not for some noble reason, driven by pure sentiments, but simply to satisfy her own cravings, even feeling that her only error had been diminished. Not only was a second slip inexcusable, it would also have confirmed the skeptical judgment passed on her by her first lover.

"The sacrifice costs you, and you want to get some form of compensation. You'll find it elsewhere, don't doubt it, a love offered to you by another. . . ." These words from Zakunin, which had humiliated and offended her when they were no more than a skeptical premonition, would have been confirmed by the facts, would have expressed the reality, if she had succumbed to Vérod's love — if she had, then the skeptic, the denier, the blasphemer would have been right. The faith, which had sustained her against him, would have been reduced, just as he had wanted, to a lie, to hypocrisy.

Ferpierre repeated to himself that suicide, in these circumstances, wasn't only possible, but almost necessary. For other reasons, he had already recognized such a truth in a melancholic and contemplative nature like hers. For a soul accustomed to looking inwards, she contemplated without fear, almost with a kind of satisfaction, the problems of life. And to throw light on these deductions, he found some new clues in the final jottings of the diary, right there, where the Justice of the Peace had looked for the confession of suicide, without finding anything. The unfortunate woman hadn't confessed that she had kill herself, but the meaning of the final words now seemed clearer to Ferpierre: "It's essential that faith is very robust and searches, indeed, finds a way of affirming itself against triumphant doubt. . . .

"The greatest sadness lies in having to give up hope.

"The last hope…

"Now this terrible dilemma: to continue living sinfully or to…"

These were the last words. Wouldn't the phrase have logically finished in the following manner: "or to die thereby avoiding the guilt?"

V

Duel

Reading her memoirs had shown Judge Ferpierre that Countess d'Arda had found herself in the situation of thinking of death as the only way of ending her misadventures. However, this didn't stop him from understanding that he had to consider other aspects of the case and study in more depth the argument against the hypothesis of suicide adopted by Vérod. With regard to her new feelings, which the countess had fought against because she foresaw their transience, and even more so, their impiety, there were abundant opportunities for joy, a great incentive to live. The same commitment with which she contained herself also demonstrated her strength. Given that she made no explicit confession, the possibility always remained that, having avoided suicide at the beginning and allowing for all the time she had known Vérod, she had not killed herself in the end but had been murdered by one of the Russians, who, taking advantage of the semblance of suicide, could escape from the accusation.

In order to clarify the mystery, one needed to know with precision the exact nature of the relationship between the countess and the young man. What demands and what promises had they exchanged? The letters written by Vérod to her, two or three in total, said nothing of importance, they only expressed the young man's gratitude for her visit to his sister's grave and the hope and desire that he would see the countess again. Nothing else had come to light from any of the deceased's other papers, the most important of which were a bundle of letters from Sister Anna Brighton, whom she had written to on the morning of the catastrophe.

Sister Anna really treated her like a daughter in these pages. Anna replied to the countess's letters full of her troubles and desperation with words of comfort and calls to the Christian faith. Ferpierre had already discovered via the British Legation in Bern that he would have to look for the nun in New Orleans, from whence her letters had been dated, if he was to find out what her old disciple had written on the day of her death. He had already requested that the deceased's house in Nice be searched, likewise the nihilist's in Zurich. He had also asked for information about Zakunin from the Russian Legation.

Meanwhile, the judge called for Vérod, so that the writer could explain in detail his situation with respect to the countess. During his first interview he had said that on the eve of the tragedy, he had been with her and that nothing had made him suspect what would happen on the following day. The judge felt that it was urgent he discover what had been said in that evening's conversation.

When Vérod appeared before him, Ferpierre was struck by his pale gauntness, by the decline in his appearance. The fretful night had passed as if it had been a decade, and he looked ten years older.

"Are you of the same opinion as yesterday?" the judge began by asking. "Do you still believe that your friend was killed?"

"I do!" answered Vérod, immediately shaking like an injured man feeling the sword re-enter a wound.

"And have you found any other proof or argument that sustains your accusation?"

"Not as yet."

"Well, let's talk this through a bit ourselves. If we don't find any material demonstration of the truth, which seems probable, we are engaged in a circumstantial process with a solution that depends on a psychological problem. The most important thing is to know the countess's state of mind in the last few days. However, tell me first of all, do you remember all that has happened between you since you first met?"

"Everything. Every one of her words is indelibly impressed on my memory, and nothing will ever make me forget any of them."

"When did you first meet?"

"The 31st of July last year."

"Do you remember any significant date in the history of your friendship? Did anything happen between you on the 12th of August?"

Robert Vérod passed a hand in front of his eyes before answering, and then, in a low voice, he said: "Yes, we were together. I accompanied her to the mountain."

"What did you say to her?"

"Nothing. There were other people with us. I didn't speak very much, and if we'd been alone, I wouldn't have said anything. This doesn't mean that I hadn't wanted to tell her my feelings, but words were more inappropriate on that day than usual. In the Comte forest, under the green light, among the high columns of the trees, she seemed like a remarkable, animated flower. Her beauty flourished like the flower of life. The scent from the cyclamen was sweetening the air. I collected many flowers for her, those on the mountain slopes, and only they were capable of conveying my feelings when I offered them to her with a trembling hand. Her belt was soon covered with flowers. Even her mouth flowered into a smile."

"Hmm, well, here read...."

Ferpierre took the diary, opened it to the page where he had seen the pressed flowers and handed it to the young man.

"New suffering is better than joy and pleasure for making one forget previous heartache — the night of 12th of August."

Robert Vérod stared at the dead flowers, rereading the fatal thought with a dry eye. He couldn't cry anymore.

"Do you understand the meaning of these words?" Ferpierre resumed. "It seems to be all too evident. While she was with you, realizing the homage you were paying her, discovering the love you felt for her, she saw how her oppressed mental state lifted, and by virtue of these pleasurable feelings, she forgot the pain, but later, at night, alone, reflecting upon her condition, she recognized that she wouldn't be able to respond to your passion, that she had to renounce such hoped-for happiness. Even if she saw an end to her suffering, it wouldn't be a joyous thing, but on the contrary, a new, greater agony.

"The sadness of this thought is in truth fatal, and she knew how to express it incisively, in a way that would make any professional writer jealous.

"On reading it I had already suspected that it referred to her relationship with you, and now, after what you have told me, the truth seems evident. You must see, therefore, that this new love wasn't a reason to give the unfortunate woman hope, but a reason for extreme desperation."

Vérod listened, stock still, with the deceased's diary pressed between his hands. He was unable to answer except with these stammered words, confused and almost terrified: "You think so?..."

"How could one doubt it? Read the following pages."

While the young man read to himself, the judge tried in vain to discover the effect of her diary on his face. His composure had been so altered, his gaze so arid, his eyes so sunken, his lips so worn by pain, that any further sadness was incapable of bringing tears to his eyes or adding further wrinkles to his face.

"You see that the deductions I made yesterday are confirmed by these confessions. Your love, far from consoling her, increased the woman's pain. Didn't you suspect this might be the case?"

Vérod, laying down the book, held his head in his hands. He replied as if talking to himself: "I had hope. I believed that she had some too. On one occasion, we spoke about it, and I told her that not all hopes had the same strength. There are some so constant they seem an unfailing certainty: such hopes are lost in pain and misery. But there is also a distant, tenuous, fragile hope that we keep hidden as if a breath of wind would make it disappear. This is the hope that never dies, that nothing stops us from harboring. I told her this. She agreed. By agreeing, didn't she collude with my secret idea, that for us such a hope would shine?"

"You told me yesterday that, although apparently free, the countess had taken upon herself an irrevocable obligation that placed an obstacle before any new relationship. These were, indeed, her feelings. In many passages of this diary one can find the evidence. The strength of her scruples were, without a doubt, much greater than you believed. Listen, rather...."

Ferpierre read aloud the most significant pages. The meaning of the confessions appeared clearer to him this time and the struggle of her conscience more serious. In order to demonstrate her sincerity to Vérod, he read yet more paragraphs, those that described the ingenuous impressions of the adolescent and the wife. Little by little he reconstructed her whole story, as he had recreated it for himself during the first reading.

"You should believe what she's written here. If she didn't say these things to you, if you thought that she wasn't despairing, this explains things compassionately. Neither the mind nor the heart stays fixed on one idea, on one particular feeling, without some change. Moral strength vacillates from one minute to the next. In your presence, the countess felt less equipped against flattery, but alone, face to face with her conscience, she found the strength to resist such illusions. Note the fact that she consigned to these pages all her impressions. She didn't speak directly of her love for you: if it hadn't been for the words written on the night of 12th August and the opinion transcribed from 'Truth and Poetry,' we wouldn't know, guided by this book, what had heightened her condition. This demonstrates with clarity that she feared such passion.

"Doesn't it also show the strength of her passion?"

"That's true, but in order to know which way she had finally decided to go, I need to ask you to be sincere: what did you ask her for, and how far did you push your request?"

Before answering, Vérod rubbed his forehead with his hands. While the judge had been reading to him, he felt he had penetrated his beloved's thoughts, almost reliving her life, a feeling that left him with a bitter delight. His adoration of the woman's beauty, his compassion for her suffering grew to such an extent that other thoughts were pushed to one side. It would not have taken much for him to forget that she was dead. On hearing the claim that he had been somehow responsible for her death, he was brought quickly to his senses.

"What could I ask her? Do you suspect that I was demanding with her, I, who fled when I feared a sole glance would give me away? Do you believe that I tried to rape her and that she killed herself to avoid my violence?"

These were, indeed, the judge's suspicions. The conditions in which the countess and Vérod found themselves could have lasted, in however ambiguous a manner, if the young man's actions hadn't intervened to alter them. It didn't seem credible to the judge that Vérod, realizing his feelings were reciprocated, would have been satisfied with simple friendship. If the man had used the subtle expedient of poetry to seduce her, if he had ennobled his discontent and his desires with the magic of literary expression, Countess d'Arda, awoken from a fraternal reverie, would have inevitably found herself in the dilemma of having to choose between living immorally or dying to avoid the guilt, perhaps seizing the more desperate, but less unworthy, of the two extremes.

"I don't want to imply that you have been violent with her, nor, considering the spirit of a woman like your friend and her distressing sensibility, that violence would have been at all successful in dominating her. The natural exuberance of passion and some of the burning words that love creates, which cost little for you poets to employ, would have been enough to wake the countess from the illusion seducing her, to show her the inevitable transformation of your friendship and to give her, with the foresight of problems to come, the idea of finally ending a life so besieged by pain. Nor, perhaps, would you have been lowered in her estimation: she must have thought that in you, in a man, the impatience of desire was natural and that the error had been hers for not foreseeing it!"

"You're right," answered Vérod, slowing shaking his head. "It was natural. I see you can't believe that such a natural thing wouldn't have become reality. You won't believe that I fled from her, that I respected her, that I obeyed her. You have no idea about the change that woman's virtue instilled in me."

"Tell me about it."

"It's difficult. I have the habit of giving literary form to my thoughts. You probably find an artist's exaggeration in my words. Didn't you just suspect that I would fall back on the artifice of literature to express my feelings?"

It was true. However much Ferpierre was inclined to sympathize sincerely with Vérod's pain, he distrusted him.

The man seemed better than his works, but his art was too bitter and desperate. That most noble and effective instrument, language, had been put to use in serving such a dissipated body of work. How could he believe in his decency?

"I'm not saying," answered the judge, unwillingly surprised by the self-evident fear of the man, "I'm not saying that you deliberately and studiously set out to seduce her. But you know men. . . ."

"Don't think I'm a man who is any different from the rest," interrupted Vérod. "We all have dual natures, and moral strength is latent even in an uncivilized soul. In order for this to come to the fore, such a soul needs to be educated and guided by a stronger, better one. She revealed things that I didn't know. If you believe in truth, this is the truth. . . ."

With a quaking voice, his gaze fixed on the floor, he told the full story of their friendship. Ferpierre listened to him carefully, but remained doubtful, fearing that he would hide some circumstance or give an unrealistic account of himself with the intention of avenging the deceased or damaging his rival.

"You were harboring hopes, however tenuous and remote. But how did you not think that, for her, your hopes were a reason to be fearful. Wasn't another liaison just going to damage her further?"

Robert Vérod looked his questioner in the eye.

"I wanted to make her my wife before God and man."

Ferpierre nodded his head slightly, indicating that, if this were the case, he would withdraw the observation.

"However," he countered, "she wanted to be worthy of your respect and couldn't hope for it without the consent of her own conscience. Remember, what weakened her illicit relations with the prince was precisely what made it certain she would be linked to him permanently. And leaving him, even for a legitimate marriage, would have contradicted such an idea and destroyed any certainty, wouldn't it? The obstacle, if you believe in the countess's moral decency, must have seemed enormous, don't you think?"

Vérod didn't answer. Ferpierre sensed that he had landed a real blow.

"Consider that the road she had taken had no exit," continued the judge after a small pause. "The only legitimate hope for her was that the prince, recognizing his own faults and repudiating the bloody path he had embarked upon, would finally repay her love and faith. Then she would have been able to rescue her passion: however badly it had started, it would have gone on to last, all to good effect. Without a doubt, it was already too late, but although she couldn't love him anymore, she must have believed she would remain by his side, with things improved, living peacefully if not happily. Outside of that, there was nothing good for her. However weak the bond between them was in the eyes of the world, it must have been an even stronger one for her conscience. Given that their union lacked social and religious sanction, her moral sanction would have been greater. Irrespective of the disillusion, the pain and the insults suffered, she had to remain faithful to the man she had accepted as her life partner. Did her partner's stark faults allow the unfortunate woman to search for happiness with another man? If you think that her sense of duty was reinforced by the task of showing the prince the error of his ways, you will recognize that death must have presented itself once again, fatally, as the end to her misadventures. To believe that she would agree to be with you, you would have to admit that her scruples weren't very sincere, but instead, rather weak. I know that passion reasons somewhat differently and that according to popular belief, love conquers all, but if that's true at all, it would be true of a first and only love. The continuous renewal of love's triumphs is at the cost of dignity, respect, honor and many other things, in themselves very important. Your friend had already followed her sideways path, returning to pay further attention to the voice of love. She had, at heart, laudable feelings, which were set on rescuing the prince, but she also felt she had been wrong. Your love must have revealed the abyss she was teetering on. You, yourself, with faith and only the hope of making her yours one day, pushed her towards the abyss. You wanted to make her your wife; but truly, given the conditions in which she found herself and given that you were both driven by passion, what were you expecting? You wanted to put her on the right track, but wouldn't it have been the case that you would have found yourselves irretrievably lost. Hadn't she foreseen that she wouldn't be able to resist? You're a poet, you know life, you have studied the hearts of men: what is your art for, if it's not capable of making you predict all of this?"

The judge had spoken very harshly. Robert Vérod kept quiet, his head bowed towards his chest.

"But let's return to the most pressing issue at hand. Didn't you tell me you saw her on the day before her death?"

"Yes, in the afternoon."

"At her house?"

"Yes."

"What did you say to her? Did you speak of your love for her?"

Seeing that Vérod hesitated in answering, Ferpierre insisted: "I say again, you must be frank. A fact that is seemingly unimportant, a word, a nothing, could put us on the road to the truth. If love pushes you to punish a murderer, your conscience must remember that justice doesn't recognize passion. Did you speak of your love?"

"Yes."

Vérod was now shaking.

The final conversation with his beloved, the most passionate and most intimate, after which he had renewed his eager hopes, was for him the greatest evidence against the murderers. Could he ever think about the death of a woman who had let him talk about a better future? However, he understood that, according to the intuition of the judge, the value of the evidence could be turned on its head; that the contemplation of forthcoming happiness, in which she believed, but felt was out of reach, was exactly the thing that had made her take the last step. And if Ferpierre was right, the severity of his words was justified; but more than the judge's severity, he was tormented by a deep realization of the evil done to a woman he should have been watching over, and indeed, had wanted to watch over with anxious care. He was no longer crying with grief, as yesterday, but he felt oppressed, gripped and twisted by an iron hand. He was suffocating, the words died on his lips, as he felt he had to tell the truth, but that the truth would count against him.

"Yes, I spoke to her of my love. We spoke about the change of season, the cold that would soon drive us from here.... I wanted to know where she was thinking of going, where and when I would be able to see her again. She said to me: 'I'm still not sure where I'll go, perhaps to Nice, perhaps to Biarritz. Wouldn't it be better if you didn't know, for you and for me?'"

"Do you see? And then what?"

"I said to her: 'Be whereever you want. Near, far, remember that I live for you.' She closed her eyes. I continued: 'It's true. Why should I hide it? Haven't you always taught me to tell the truth? Didn't you know this already?' We were both silent. The sky had darkened. She looked at the grey mists swirling around the mountain sides and covering the vegetation, at the grey, ruffled lake, resembling liquefied lead. The trees, bent over by the force of the wind, were losing their first leaves. I followed her mournful thoughts as she contemplated the autumnal vision. I told her that 'the color of the sky is in our eyes: blue turns to black in sadness; in happiness, grey becomes celestial'. A small azure cloud crossed between the mountain mists like a small slice of heaven. She answered: 'Yes, but it's an illusion, the sky is closed in on itself.' I replied that it would soon open again. Little by little the landscape was being veiled, all the colors had disappeared, leaving tones of black and white: the black peaks, the leaden water, the silver foam, the ashen fog, egg-white little clouds, pallid little clouds, clouds of an iron hue. She said: 'Doesn't it look like a watercolor?' I nodded and then added: 'There's as much beauty in this as there is when the sun shines.' I carried on talking. I told her that an interior light was illuminating my entire life, that my eyes saw nothing but beauty everywhere. Her pale beauty was, at that very moment, stunning, she seemed to reflect the paleness of the nature that surrounded us. I took her hand. The heat of life flowed from her hand through my whole body. She withdrew it from me, losing still more color. I said nothing, but tears filled my eyes. She said: 'Understand that we must part.' I replied: 'I'll always respect your wishes. If you want, I'll leave tomorrow. I'll wait for you far from here. And if you don't want me to wait, I'll try to forget you. It'll be difficult to destroy the hope that rules our lives, but you must realize that my pleasure, my pride, my vanity are focused on being what you wish me to be....' Everything had disappeared from sight, the whiteness of the clouds and the darkness of the mountains were smudged and confused into a uniform grey. Rain continued to fall. She shivered. I took her hand again. I wanted to tell her that this was the last goodbye, that she was leaving her hand in mine for one last time.

I couldn't speak. She didn't withdraw her hand. I stayed silent: too many thoughts pressed down on me."

"Didn't you sense the terrible war raging inside her?"

On hearing this interruption, Vérod shook his head concertedly.

"I don't know, I don't know.... Too many thoughts assailed me all at once, but there was one thing that was worrying me more than anything: if I spoke further she would take her hand away. The veil of mist was lifting. When the lake appeared, the foamed-topped waves that surged and fell were rapid, dazzling, little flickers. A slice of sky smiled on us. Finally, I said: 'You see the blue?' She rose to her feet...."

"And then what?" asked the judge on seeing that Vérod had fallen silent. What the young man was about to say must be serious, it had to be contrary to the accusation for him to stop his story in such a manner. "And then what? Tell me everything, you need to say it all!"

"She spoke about him. I knew that it wasn't love, but duty that bound them together. She stood and said these words: 'I'm not worthy of your love. The sincerity that I expect and applaud in others is missing in me. You know, I have told you that I'm not free.... But the man in question had left me, he wasn't at my side and we had both believed that he wouldn't come back. Now...he's here again. If you want me to carry on respecting you, don't say anything more.'"

"Do you see now? Do you see? And then?"

"I answered her: 'Behave as you must, but the man will leave you again.'"

"Do you see now?" repeated the judge. "If you said these words with the harsh edge that you have just used with me, you must realize that the hate you showed for Zakunin had frightened her? She must have understood that, regardless of your respect for her, the realization that she was the prince's would dampen your affection. Isn't that so? How did she answer you?"

Vérod had titled his head forwards. With a slow voice, he replied: "She hid her head in her hands."

"And, at that moment, did you sense that she was right, that the love between you had condemned both of you to a sad life? Didn't you realize that you had to leave the woman to her fate in order to avoid something worse?"

"Don't say such things!" interrupted Vérod, caught between humility and fervor, wringing his hands and fixing his gaze on Ferpierre. "Don't say that! I don't know. I can't tell you what I felt. Yes, perhaps that, and other less definable things, were all running through my mind, but I loved her, I felt that she loved me, I saw that she was worried about me, that she suffered for me. To flee and leave her alone would have been impossible, not to mention the strength of my gratitude, of my tender feelings, of my pity and that I trembled with fear for her, that I wanted to die for her rather than mix my tears with hers!"

"You told her this?"

"I had to tell her. She listened to me. The squall had finished, the sun was shining on the vivid greens. I said that the storms in her life had to calm at some point and that when it happened I would still be hers. She confided softly: 'If only we had met before!' I continued talking. I didn't ask for anything, but I had to tell her that nothing in the world was irreparable, that life would be really too bitter if hope wasn't there to comfort her. I also said something else, something more definite, although perhaps sad: there is more joy in expectation than in reaching a goal and that, therefore, hope is the greater good. I asked if she agreed and she answered with a simple 'Yes.' This one word, this word of agreement, was the last thing she said to me."

Ferpierre waited until the echo of Vérod's impassioned voice had died. He crossed his arms, speaking slowly, after a brief silence: "Well, we still don't have any witnesses to shine a light on the truth, but I want to believe that, at any moment, irrefutable proof of your accusation will be found. I would like to concede that, on reading the letter written to Sister Anna Brighton two hours before her death, we'll find that she didn't speak of dying, but on the contrary, expressed her imminent happiness. However, as day follows night, if logic is worth anything, we have to believe it was suicide."

As Vérod made no attempt to answer and continued to appear rather withdrawn, the judge resumed: "Your last conversation, the importance of which you don't want to recognize, is enough to explain the catastrophe. I had sensed that something must have occurred between you, which she saw as an obstacle in her path. If the unfortunate woman had deluded herself that there was the possibility of a pure friendship between you, your final words must have disillusioned her. All the arguments that you produced are the usual murmurings of passion. You asked nothing of her, but Zakunin, the man responsible for making her lose her way, had said much the same thing. Life's logic did reflect, in reality, the truth he revealed to her with some crudeness: 'When you feel hungry, you have to eat.' If hope really is the greater good, we can't enjoy it without believing that we are continuing to follow our goal: nobody in this world will be comforted by imagining something they can never obtain. Logically, necessarily, the countess had to fall prey to further error. I say error, although perhaps I should also say guilt. I don't doubt the honesty of your intentions, but your weakness and hers would have led to it being forgotten. The strength of your passion pushed you forward to enter into a commitment that you might have regretted later. Even without predicting your repentance, she felt that the way to any new happiness was barred. All these thoughts, which the unfortunate woman had considered carefully, must have come to the surface with greater urgency, greater worry and greater fatalism after your words. When did you choose to speak? At the most critical moment. Her partner had returned to her side, and he was a reformed character. We have Giulia Pico's statement regarding the prince's better behavior towards the countess. Well, if she had been thinking that her ties to the prince had lessened because she had been abandoned, his return would have then taken away this freedom. Continuing to be with a man she had handed herself too forever, who was now showing an appreciation of her love, must have led to more pressing feelings of duty. She could have found some justification for leaving a man who had abandoned her and, what's more, he wouldn't have thought of reproaching her for the volatility of a faith that she had sought to instill in him. On the other hand, if he had wanted to rebuke her, she would have known how to answer, given the circumstances. To abandon him now that he had returned would have made her feel doubly guilty. And yet she wasn't able to stay with him. She didn't love him anymore, she loved you. In your eyes and voice, where she had first recognized love and compassion, she suddenly now noticed hate towards the man who had stepped forward to block your longed-for happiness. Therefore, not only did she think that she was going to lose your esteem, she also feared that she would be the cause of further complications, pushing two men to hate each other, even to kill each other. A few hours after this moral turmoil, the countess, who was incurably sick, her chest stricken by a ceaseless illness, who had nobody in the world, neither a father nor brother, then sent away under a flimsy pretext the woman who watched over her. We subsequently found her with a weapon by her side, a weapon that belonged to her, which she had kept with the thought of seeking eternal rest. I have to say it: you must recognize that the woman killed herself!"

Ferpierre had spoken even more harshly, as if the man standing before him was the accused and not the accuser. Even the attitude of Robert Vérod was that of a guilty man: his head titled forward, a hand on his chest, he seemed to be doubling under the weight of reproach and his own remorse.

"Don't you have anything to say? Do you accept the meticulousness of my reasoning?"

"No!" interrupted the young man, suddenly pulling himself together in an act of semi-defiance. "It's not like that! It can't be like that! I can't believe it. I'll never believe it! These were her thoughts, certainly, but with regard to her thoughts on death, her feelings about life and love must have been and were greater and stronger. Before knowing her, though, it wouldn't have been difficult for me to commit suicide. I had reasons to hate living."

"The same reasons that made you hate it when you were twenty?"

Ferpierre spoke these words moved by a semi-conscious impulse. Although the seriousness of his mission meant he had to stop the influence of any previous memories of the accuser, an instinctive curiosity to know whether the young man still remembered him, made him invoke the past.

"The same," answered Vérod, looking him in the eye; "but more urgent and more disconsolate than you remember. You know me, don't you? I also recognized you straight away. You know that I am too quick to see the misery, emptiness and horror of life."

"For what reasons? Are you poor? Have you suffered any injustice at the hands of man or fate? Yes, I remember you, but I don't know, how could I know, what has happened to you."

The judge felt a degree of pleasure in focusing on Vérod's pessimism, in obliging him to recognize the error of his feelings.

"Nothing has happened to me. But I cried about everything. Perhaps I was unwell, yes, but sick in my soul, not my body. She was my salvation. After seeing her I felt reborn. This is the strength of love: the very fact that your beloved exists is the greatest reason to live."

"And is this true of any love?"

"Don't talk about the obstacles! Yes, I hate and loath him. I wanted, as I've already said, to kill the man who took her from me, and such hate runs through my words. Yes, she told me everything that your deductions have discovered, all you have been thinking. Understanding that Zakunin's presence was an obstacle to our happiness, I told her how I hated him. Love, a mutual love, flourished despite the obstacles, and he tried to break it but failed. Love will wait and hope. It's true, she was trembling when she heard me speak about him, but that didn't stop her recognizing that I had to wait and was able to do so. I still haven't told you everything that passed between us. Two days before our final meeting, I accompanied her to Mont Chesand. We drank from a fountain. She went first, then from the same cup, I drank the water she had left. It was as if we had pressed our lips together. When she subsequently agreed that I should wait, I took her hand again and kissed it fervently. She shuddered but didn't take it away. I felt that she was already mine, that I would have been able to get another kiss, this time from the fullness of her lips. And yet, a matter of hours later, she was to kill herself?"

"But yes, exactly!" the judge quickly interjected, seeing what Vérod was uncovering in the heat of his defense. "Yes, hours later! This demeanor of yours, which you believed to be respectful and obedient, what kind of love must it have felt like to her? Dominant and egotistical! These pleasures you were enjoying, which made you think about other more significant ones, must have terrified her! She was also flesh and blood, and being by your side, she felt unable to resist such demands. Afterwards, alone with her conscience, she listened to her innermost pressing voice. The whole of the final part of her diary is filled with thoughts of dying. Are you that astonished, when seeing all her exits blocked, she put this into practice?"

"She spoke about it, she wrote about it, but when the time came, thoughts of God must have stayed her hand."

"Thoughts of God stopped her many times, but a moment of intolerable pain finally arrived, and she killed herself!"

"Without leaving any message for me? She knew that I had given my life to her. Would she have destroyed, in a single blow, the effect of her teachings? You say that by killing herself, she had wanted to do away with all that was bad, but by doing so, do you really think she was doing something good?"

Ferpierre stayed silent. Vérod, realizing that he had finally gained an advantage in their sparring, continued: "She thought and indeed, wrote that in some cases you could leave this life without any reproach, although anybody doing such a thing ought to be alone and not dependent on someone else. Haven't you just read her words? 'This is serious: when in love, a lover isn't only responsible for his or her actions, but also for those of the partner.' And would she really have given me an example like this? I only believe in the beauty of her soul, and the certainty that she didn't kill herself just increases my faith in her."

"Was her duty a fixation then, not leaving the man she felt married to?"

"She wasn't really married."

"What did their union mean, if the law hadn't sanctioned it?"

"Do you believe in the decency of human laws, in their perfection? Do you think that salvation is to be found in observing them faithfully?"

"Are you in any doubt about that? Are these the principles that you propagate in your books? And yet you feel such an aversion to nihilism believing in these principles? Don't you realize that deniers and pessimists like you are the teachers, the inciters of all those audacious souls who aren't content with abstract speculations but who logically translate into action the rationales that you preach?"

"I don't deny the law, but I do say that it doesn't resolve the difficulties we are condemned to live with. It only gives voice to them. Even if she had been legally joined to that man...."

"Would you have had the right to seduce her and take her from him? Would she have gone against her word?"

"She couldn't swear undying love."

"But you swore that to her."

"She couldn't love someone who didn't love her."

"Would you say the same thing if it were you who was abandoned?"

Before such a solid argument, the young man went quiet and looked confused. The judge resumed with a different tone of voice: "Ah! We're perhaps not as far from the object of our investigations as you might think! These ideas, the contrast of illusion with reality, the fight between duty and pleasure tore the unfortunate woman to pieces. She saw and felt how difficult life could be. That she wanted to leave it behind is all too evident. It only remains for us to demonstrate that she really put her plan into action. There is no direct proof, but all the presumptions point toward you. Coolly consider, if you feel able, the complete set of circumstances that we have before us, and you'll see that I have reason to think like this. You have denounced the two people who were in the house at the time of her death, but against which of the two should we direct our suspicions and investigations? Now is the time to decide! Is the prince guilty? And why would he have killed the unhappy woman? Because of jealousy? However, above all, you should remember that the man, whom you think hateful and evil, had renewed his love for her and had suffered on knowing that she was losing her affection for him. But was the countess already yours? Did she reciprocate your passion? Did she want to leave the prince and go away with you? No, on the contrary! Until the final moment, she declared herself joined to another, she refused to listen to you and implored you to leave! Given the countess's character, the seriousness of her scruples, the sincerity of her regrets, we have to believe that as soon as you had gone, she once again started to blame herself, to deny the hope she had first felt. In such a situation, what motive would the prince have for killing her? He still loved her, or if you prefer, he was jealous, brutally jealous, the kind of jealousy that saw her as his property and nothing more. But what could she be accused of? Not succumbing to you. He must have been sure that the slightest sign of decency, a token of love or a kind word was enough to stop the countess being yours. I want to believe that it isn't jealousy or hate that makes you lack so much respect for this man, although I have to admit that decent feelings seem to be foreign to him and that he is truly capable of some vulgar crime. However, even the most brutal malevolence needs a pretext, if not a reason, to arm itself and strike a blow. And I don't see any of these pretexts or reasons. You probably suppose that, after having gained ambiguous approval, it was the countess who provoked Zakunin by declaring her love for you? Perhaps, subconsciously, your own self-esteem suggested such a rationale, however illogical. If she had really wanted to take up with you, nobody would have stopped her when Zakunin was far away. And more recently, did she truly have to ask permission from such a man? If he had put his foot down, she would have been able to rebel and challenge him. The barrier didn't come from him, but her, from her own intimate conscience. Therefore, the hypothesis is absurd.

"And what about the nihilist, do you want to focus again on Alexandra Natzichev? Because she loved the prince, she was jealous of the countess and, therefore, killed her? On the contrary, the problems with this theory are no less than the previous one! Before anything else, you would have to prove that they were lovers, something that they deny. Then, even if that was confirmed, why would Natzichev have killed the countess? She would have had to present an obstacle to their love. Could the unfortunate woman prevent the prince from going with other women, did she even know how to do it? What shadow could she cast over Natzichev? Weren't the two Russians free to be together in Zurich? And if we can't rationally accuse one or the other of homicide, can we really suppose that they did it together? The absurdity would be double! Now, if your friend had no reason to end her life, we must accept the suspicion of murder, even without good foundation. However, the motives that pushed her to suicide were not only apparent but abundant. You have, though, one argument in your favor, only one...."

The judge stopped for a moment in order to catch his breath. Robert Vérod maintained the same position that he had adopted when first beginning to listen: his head bowed and his hands pressed together as if he were expecting a deadly blow.

"There are hundreds and thousands of women in the countess's situation, caught between their scruples and the temptations of passion, who don't resort to suicide. They wait, and with time, they become accustomed to a life they once believed insufferable. They come to terms with their scruples. They find in the example of others an excuse; they hope for future redemption. This is the way they all behave, well, almost all. You have, from the very beginning, laid out the importance of this reasoning. But after her final conversation with you when she was facing the inevitably of sin, to believe it, to maintain that the countess didn't want to kill herself, you have to concede that your friend, the woman whose great kindness of heart has been praised by the testimonies of others, whose confessions, I believe, show her to be superior to many others...you have to concede, I say again, that she was like everyone else, that she was also capable of the compromised relationships we witness on a daily basis. It's true that someone who commits suicide leaves little trace of a courageous soul or an indestructible faith, but if, because of your maneuvering, the countess found it impossible to choose a third way, I think that of the two existing options, she chose the best one. Is it strange to you that I should support, contrary to your beliefs, the strength of her conscience, the delicacy of her honor?"

Vérod straightened up and, passing his hand across his forehead, exclaimed, somewhat beaten and lost: "Don't say that! Yes, it's true. You're right. You could be right. But don't say it, don't repeat it! Because then I, I, myself, will have killed her! She will be dead because of me.... Because of me! Can't you see that it's destroying me, this suspicion? I feel like I'm going mad!"

VI

The Investigation

When the judge was left alone, the confidence that had sustained him immediately evaporated. Vérod's resistance had spurred him on, suggesting arguments that seemed strongly against the accusation, but in the end, seeing that Vérod agreed he was right, instead of this affirming his opinion, he started to have doubts once more. His reconstruction of the drama held much truth, but nobody could testify that it was true, and was the possibility of murder really that unsustainable? After developing one of the two hypotheses, he had to examine the other. He prepared himself for the task with a growing antipathy towards the accused. Moved by Vérod's grief and deeply interested in the deceased, he distrusted the Russians more than ever.

The day after his interrogation of the young man, he received, together with the various packets of letters confiscated in Nice and Zurich, the information he had requested from the chief of the police department and from the Russian Legation in Berne with regard to the nihilists. What he already knew of Alexi Petrovich's character was confirmed and documented by the extensive and meticulous reports, full of depositions taken during previous political proceedings. However, he also found out some things that he hadn't suspected.

An inheritor of the genius of the Slavic race, moved by impetuous sentiments overly close to primitive instinct, Zakunin also suffered from a form of hysteria which, according to modern scientists who analyze illnesses of the nervous system, is not only the agonizing preserve of the female sex. Several truly incredible events took place in the prince's youth. Growing up without a father, the hatred of his mother's second husband had turned him into a homicidal maniac. Constantly and cruelly hit, punished with a savage severity surpassing anything his faults merited, Zakunin's character had been embittered.

One day, when he was ten, walking with a friend of his own age, he approached a railway station. The friend explained to him that guards patrolled the section of track allotted to them in order to ensure that no obstacle threatened the security of the train. Taking advantage of a moment when his friend's attention was elsewhere, and without any motive other than a perverse evil curiosity, he placed two large stones on the rails and waited until the train arrived in order to enjoy the scale of the catastrophe. The stones were big, but fortunately friable, and the wheels of the engine reduced them to dust without moving an inch from the line. On another occasion, a few years later, his reckless folly showed up in another form, this time directed at himself. Touring his possessions in Ukraine, a young lad, the child of a peasant, was acting as his guide explaining the qualities of the trees and herbs. On passing through some green scrubland, the boy signaled towards a small plant with large, downy leaves and said: "This is henbane, incredibly poisonous." Quickly, before his young guide had the chance to get near him, let alone stop him, Zakunin grabbed a handful of leaves and devoured them. The guide was mistaken, the plant wasn't henbane, but for the entire day everybody believed that Alexi had poisoned himself and were both amazed and horrified on seeing the ironic happiness with which he waited for death. He rebuked those who were anxious.

His entire youth had been stormy. Lacking money, the gambling demon took hold of him. One night, after losing a sum he couldn't afford, he turned a revolver on himself to avoid the shame. The bullet, after getting diverted, broke his humerus. He also fought a duel on some dubious pretext and refused to come to an accommodation with his adversary. Later on, he saved the same man's life, while heroically risking his own.

Up to the age of eighteen, it had been impossible to get him to learn anything, nor to persuade him to listen to a single lesson. Yet, shamed by a French girl who spoke to him, believing he had knowledge of her language, he changed overnight. For the best part of three years he disappeared, giving himself over to study with the same fervor that had sent him on a destructive course. He rapidly made up for lost time.

Nothing was difficult for his sharp and clear intelligence. His will was capable of acts of iron-like firmness, of tireless perseverance, but he didn't always remain level-headed. Periods of tenacious strength were interspersed with frequent crises of nervous weakness and sickly inertia. This side of his moral constitution was less noticeable because of the way he jealously guarded his weaknesses. Nevertheless, people had seen him cry.

Cold and tough with his fellows, he loved animals with a human kindness. Nevertheless, he loved to hunt, but his dogs were his friends: he spoke to them, he kissed them, he looked them firmly in the eyes as if penetrating their dark, brute-like souls. Before such lowly beings he became humble, he was their servant, ignoring his own needs so they would lack for nothing, and if one them took ill, he refused to give himself a moment's rest. When one of his dogs died, cradled on his knees, he looked at him until the final moments with sad and watery eyes. And when he saw that the animal's limbs had stiffened, when he felt the body was cold and inert, when it had once vibrated with life under his delicate touch, when he understood the mystery of death, copious silent tears fell from his eyes. He hadn't been as tender with the female dogs. In moments of anger, the blows from his riding crop fell only on them. He did, though, change his mind after seeing one of them suffering when giving birth to half a dozen pups. She was ill but didn't want her offspring to be taken away. She whined so pitifully that they were eventually returned to her, and she died with all her pups attached to her breast.

Ever since childhood, he had flown from the company of women as if by instinct. However, when he was twenty, his mother died. Now owner of a huge fortune, in one leap he went from a solitary country life, which was interspersed with periods of vigorous exercise and regimented scholarship, to the adoption of elegant and unwholesome big-city pleasures, a lifestyle he gave himself to in a cold, almost studious, manner. He burnt his way through a lot of money and nervous energy; his already unbalanced constitution wilted. His first true love was the daughter of Prince Arkof. Owing to a moral anachronism, which, given his unusual nature, should be no surprise, he loved her in the manner of an adolescent, with naïve and timid feelings that any other man would have left behind. His solitary and wild upbringing hadn't been a place for poetic phantoms. But by those laws of equilibrium and compensation that seem to extend their dominion from the practical world to the spiritual, poetry of the heart, the virtue that was missing from his life, seized him precisely when he was immersed in the most prosaic and damaging love affairs. Just as shame had once driven him to drag his mind from the limbo of ignorance, so the whirlwind of feelings gained control over his soul.

From one day to the next, for no small period of time, he was unrecognizable as the same man. He left behind discreditable company and then his more sordid entertainments. In an unforeseen reaction, he lived not just from dreams but pure contemplation. All of this, an exemplary life, for no other purpose than to become worthy of being loved.

The spell was broken, and the old ways returned when Princess Caterina's parents tyrannically made her marry General Borischoff, the governor of Kiev. Wild impulses and violent convulsions assailed him once again, yet bizarrely, he wasn't overcome by them immediately. The sincerity of his re-evaluation, of his ability to feel were tested and measured by how he was able to stop and resign himself to the fact that his beloved was in the arms of another. Zakunin, content to sigh from afar, had barely spoken to her and wasn't aware of her feelings. He thought, on seeing her accept the general's hand in marriage, that she loved him and would be happy with him. With his heart bleeding and consumed with pain, he remained silent, distancing himself in order not to be an obstacle. However, when he knew that his fortunate rival didn't merit such fortune, that he was making her unhappy by humiliating, mistreating and demeaning the young woman, it wasn't just sorrow, a bothersome thought, but also a fury full of anger, remorse and disdain that threw him into the arms of the nihilists who were preparing to kill the awful governor. When the conspiracy was discovered, his aristocratic status, but perhaps more so his entirely moral motive, saved him from the cruel penalties inflicted on his companions. Nevertheless, radical politics, which had left him indifferent up until now, soon took hold of him.

When he mixed with the revolutionaries during the preparations for the plot, he hadn't been able to put his mind to the rationale guiding them, dominated as he was by another reason. The love of liberty, hatred of tyranny, thirst for justice and the ideal of brotherhood were incomprehensible to the vengeful lover. However, when he was arrested and judged, when he knew the brutality of the police, the blindness of justice, the heroism of those accused; when he was exiled, under surveillance, wandering the world with murderous intent and seeing the painful contrasts between haughty high society and incurable misery, a new ideal took shape before his eyes: the redemption of mankind.

But as could be foreseen, even in this task, he knew little moderation. In France, Holland, Germany, England, he sought out the heads of anarchist and nihilist parties, giving as much as he could of his strength and active involvement to propaganda endeavors. He got mixed up in new plots that produced bloody results and was, once again, tried and condemned to death. With incredible daring, he returned in secret to Russia several times to meet with his compatriots, providing inspiration and direction. In danger of falling into the hands of the law, he was miraculously saved, and afterwards, continued his conspiracies from abroad, always dreaming and preparing the social cataclysm that would return him to his regenerated country.

Reading these documents left a vivid impression on Judge Ferpierre. The instinctive aversion he felt for such rebellion was now secretly tempered by a feeling of compassion. Zakunin's convulsive soul wasn't completely evil: well-guided on another road, he could have shown a good side to the world. Why hadn't the love of a woman like Countess d'Arda cured him?

The police reports did mention something of the influence her love had on him. Five years previously, during his time getting to know the countess, Zakunin's political activity had almost ceased. It seemed that he had forgotten everything — his ideals, his accomplices — in order to live with the woman. The change wasn't only noticeable in the political sphere, but also in his habits. His exuberant and insatiable capacity for life hadn't previously stopped at the assiduous pursuit of social reform. Between conspiracies, he had found time to move from one affair to another. His conquests were innumerable. Due to a kind of strange fascination, he had managed to seduce all the women who had been an object of his desire. He had left this life because of Countess Fiorenza.

Reading the letters found at the deceased's house in Nice, the judge had precise knowledge of the feelings Zakunin had experienced at this time. The majority of the letters were insignificant or contained things Ferpierre already knew. There were some the prince had written to Fiorenza at the start of their love affair. They were fervent and passionate, full of fiery intent: the words whispered, sang and burnt with a living flame.

"Light of the world, life of the soul, smile of grace, door to salvation, do you want to hear what no living soul has heard? Nobody alive knows who I am. I had no mother. I had no sister. I don't lament this. On the contrary, I'm proud, because now to you alone, I can reveal my heart. . . ."

And he confessed it all to her, candidly. He told her that he was a sick soul, a child, a madman needing of care and love; that his apparent bravery hid a childish fear; that his high-mindedness was humble; that he hated loving; that when he was on the brink of tears inspired by pity, a smile of scorn would repress them; that he passed from one extreme to another with painful anxiety, with tortuous worry; that, prompted by nostalgia, he needed unchanging serenity.

"Your love will be my salvation, my peace, the door, the promised land, paradise lost and found. Love me as I need to be loved, as one loves children and animals, a love that is indulgent, compassionate, consoling, full of respite and support. . . ."

If the Countess d'Arda hadn't succeeded in this, was it her fault? Remembering the dead woman's diary and the prince's own confessions, Ferpierre had to admit that the blame didn't lie with her, but with Zakunin himself. Perhaps if she had known him before, when his malevolent ways hadn't taken such deep root, she would have had success. Their meeting had been too late, and although the prince had forgotten his inveterate thoughts and habits for a while, he soon returned to them. When his reactions seemed to grow in violence, he made the countess suffer all manner of insults for believing in his promises of repentance.

Believing in his assurances, the countess had taken him to Italy, to Milan, to the lakes of Lombardy, to her familiar places, to houses where she had lived, hoping that, away from his fellow believers and in a beneficial moral atmosphere, his redemption would come quickly. Far from this, her disillusionment had been rapid. Zakunin had been expelled from Italy, and the event caused furor throughout the peninsula. Even though the mere mention of a revolutionary name like his could justify the measures adopted by the Italian police, Minister Francalanza had been accused of acting for personal reasons because of the involvement of a *grande dame* like the countess. Lively questions were asked in parliament. The scandal deeply affected her, but nevertheless, she followed him into exile.

Outside of Italy, the prince gave himself, body and soul, to new conspiracies and love affairs. A little less than a year ago, a revolution in Russia, proposed and directed by Zakunin, narrowly failed. The boat that should have been carrying the tsar from Saint Petersburg to Kronstadt was blown to bits, two regiments in Moscow joined the uprising, a column of convicts in Siberia rebelled and marched with arms towards the Urals, and a handful of expatriates disembarked in the Crimea, fanning the flames on the empire's southern border. If the tsar had actually been in the boat, his death, along with those audacious revolutionary uprisings, would probably have signaled the beginning of the end. However, owing to an unforeseen change, the court had taken a land-based route, and the partial revolt had been bloodily suppressed.

The only ringleader to survive had been Zakunin, who had remained at a distance.

This was the man whom Robert Vérod had accused of killing Countess d'Arda.

"Is this man capable of committing the murder?" Ferpierre had asked himself, and contrary to the opinion of Giulia Pico, he answer was: "Yes, he is capable!"

But had he really killed the unfortunate countess? The ability to undertake such a criminal enterprise proved nothing without a witness. In her journal, Fiorenza had, indeed, transcribed his threat: "If you leave me when I no longer love you, I'll thank you for it, if you betray me when I still love you, I'll kill you." Yet, as the judge had demonstrated to Vérod, it wasn't the case that the countess had betrayed the prince. If she had still been an object of his affection, she would have found it difficult to leave him. The idea of remaining by his side through duty seemed to dominate her thoughts. These feelings would have been reinforced by foreseeing the hurt she would inflict by leaving him. Above all though, she had to test if he had truly fallen in love with her again!

What had he done in recent months? In some secret location, did he have documents relating to his revolutionary activities? Very few had been found in his Zurich house, although that didn't mean they weren't important. Some letters from his fellow believers, with recent dates, were full of veiled accusations. His companions in Russia all complained of his silence, of his coldness, condemning him for not fulfilling certain promises they had been counting on, almost accusing him of treason. The nihilists had agreed on another attempt immediately after the previous disaster: an attempt that was tentative and useless, but that had demonstrated that not even the most furious reaction would be sufficient to dampen their spirit or dissipate their efforts. And they wrote to Zakunin: "While we are here, ready to lay down our lives, while we are waiting for nothing more than a word, you seem to have abandoned us? Perhaps your courage has run out after Kronstadt? You're not risking much over there! You're staying nice and safe, as others die here!"

How could Zakunin have let himself be reprimanded in such a manner? Were his fellow believers accusing him without reason or had, in reality, his fervor actually cooled? And in that case, how and why had the obstinate rebel been able to distance himself from his life's mission?

On a previous occasion, at the start of his friendship with Countess d'Arda, the prince had almost abandoned propaganda. Before his political engagement, the young man had been transformed by his love for Princess Arkof. Therefore, taking this into consideration, the judge had to suspect that love was once again the reason for the change. Was it his old passion for the countess, suddenly reignited, or some new affair? Ferpierre couldn't reject, a priori, the idea that Zakunin had started to love Fiorenza d'Arda again. Furthermore, in a spirit like his, inclined to extremes and drawn by opposing stimuli, such a resurrection of feeling was possible, even after inflicting so much torment and especially after the countess's attraction to Vérod.

Yet the prince's behavior in the last weeks didn't encourage such a hypothesis. According to Giulia Pico's statement, he had become better in his conduct towards her, however, it was also true that they had continued to live apart. Could a few days visit every two weeks satisfy a man in love who possessed a jealous heart? Could Zakunin, if he loved her, stay away when he knew that someone else was trying to break down her will? If his love, a love so overbearing it could push him to commit a crime, had been reignited, wouldn't he have thrown himself at the countess's feet, thereby showing he was converted and repentant and able to persuade her to flee with him, to hide in some unknown corner of the world? If he had said something like this, the countess would, without doubt, have been fortified in her resistance to Vérod and she would have said something in her diary. Or was it the case that, consumed by love and jealousy, the prince, due to his own self-worth and arrogance, had said nothing? This was difficult to accept in a man like Zakunin, whose thoughts childishly turned to action so rapidly. What motive brought him back to her side and prompted him to treat her better in those brief and scarce visits?

Ferpierre discovered the motive when he read, among other letters, some business correspondence written to Countess d'Arda by the administrator of her affairs in Italy. The letters spoke of the prince's promissory notes, of bills that he had to pay, of sums sent to him by bankers. It was evident that Zakunin, having compromised his fortune with his revolutionary work, needed a lot of money for his dissolute life-style, and he had turned to her. In the beginning, the intimacy of their relationship excused, if not justified, these loans. Later on, when the first flush of love was over and the bad behavior had started, he was not in a position to meet his obligations. Yet in the meantime, his requirements had become more urgent. The last conspiracy in Kronstadt had cost him a lot, so much so he hadn't known what to do. Some Zurich letters, answers to his own, showed that he had approached various parties urgently insisting they help him.

Reading this gave Ferpierre serious pause for thought: had Zakunin and Natzichev killed the countess to get hold of her money?

The suspicion wasn't reasonable without some further examination. There was much of value found in the dead woman's house, but she was so rich that she could well have had a larger amount in her possession on her last day. If theft was the motive for the crime, the two Russians couldn't have stolen everything. However in such a case, it was difficult to explain the noisy manner in which the victim had died and the cutting grief that Zakunin had shown. Nor was it possible to say how and where they had hidden the amount stolen in the brief moments between the shot and the arrival of the servants. Was one of them their accomplice? Or rather, were the Russians waiting to remove the money after successfully spreading the suicide story, not foreseeing Vérod's accusation?

Ferpierre considered asking the d'Arda accountant in Milan if the sums found at the Cyclamens matched his expectations, and at the same time, to interrogate the servants to discover if any of them had, in the confusion, seen the killers take the missing amount. Yet however much the judge believed anything was possible in this world, he couldn't quite force himself to think that Zakunin was perverse enough to kill for money. The supposition that could be made, that one should logically make, was somewhat different: Zakunin had returned to the countess's side, not because of the love he felt, but for the spontaneous help she would be able to provide. Extremely rich, accustomed to spending less than a fourth of her income on herself, she could immediately get her old lover out of the fix he was in. This would be why the prince went to see her once in a while and behaved in a friendly manner. Love, the passion that can't tolerate delay or distance, detained him elsewhere, it made him live in Zurich where Alexandra Natzichev was staying.

Was it believable that a man such as Zakunin, to whom legend ascribed Don Juan status, would have remained in the student's company without their common doctrines and aims pushing them towards a more intimate relationship? And there was no lack of indication supporting such a suspicion. Just as his *compadres* had done in Russia, his fellow believers in England reproached him for abandoning them: "Your presence is needed here," they wrote to him from London. "We've been waiting for you for four months. What's stopping you from coming? You picked a good time to go against your word! Or has some new affair of the heart kept you there?"

Had the letter-writer gotten wind of his relationship with the young refugee?

The judge found nothing of use among Natzichev's letters. They all referred to the nihilist's studies. There were many written about the most debated social questions, drafts of articles destined for the American magazine, *The Rebel*, and pages from Spanish and Dutch people with whom she was in correspondence. However much his antipathy for the young woman refused to fade, the judge had to admit that she was in possession of a cultured mind beyond the common run of the mill. She wrote correct Spanish, English and German; she sent bibliographies to the newspapers in which she noted all manner of scientific and philosophical publications. The information collected by the Zurich police was also in her favor. It had been three years since she had left Russia, alone and without any means of support, after her father and her brother were deported to Siberia for revolutionary activities. In Zurich she had started to study medicine, living from her work of translating scientific articles on behalf of German and French editors. She knew all the political refugees, but she hadn't taken part in any active conspiracies. On the contrary, according to her words and writings, she disapproved of the continuous and useless sacrifice of life. She was inclined towards moral propaganda, to the indoctrination of the conscience. However, she had an ardent, mannish nature and wouldn't have hesitated to lower herself to action if circumstances had dictated.

Although nothing concrete was said about her relations with the prince, the suspicion that he was her lover had been reinforced. If he was in love with her and had stayed in Zurich for her, wouldn't Zakunin have abandoned the impatient agitators as much for the enervating effects of love as for any persuasion exercised by the young woman? Wouldn't she have convinced the prince to reconsider things, have shown him the foolishness of useless slaughter?

These assumptions seemed correct to Ferpierre, and Vérod's accusation continued to appear unfounded. If the prince loved the nihilist, his relationship with the countess wasn't a big enough obstacle to force him to kill her. Could a rebel like him, for whom the coercive nature of the law held no value, feel so tied by such an entirely moral scruple? In reality, hadn't he left his beloved on other occasions to chase new pleasures? What would stop him from doing this again, with greater freedom than before? Certainly he had returned to the countess's side and had treated her with more consideration, but if this consideration demonstrated that he repented his previous bad treatment, the remorse and the presence of these scruples contradicted the hypothesis of murder: he couldn't wish for the death of a woman if he had regretted being the cause of her pain.

If the prince had been married to the deceased; if, growing tired of her, he had wanted to marry the nihilist, and she had wanted to marry him, the drama could be reasonably reconstructed in another manner. Feigning repentance, the husband would have returned to his wife's side and persuaded her and others of his conversion in order to divert suspicion. Then, alone or with the aid of his lover, he would have killed her in order to free himself. However, Zakunin wasn't inextricably linked to the countess, nor is it believable that he wanted to marry his young compatriot. All such suspicions should be discounted. The man's change of heart was sincere, or at least credible, because he had an aim: he needed money. Beyond this, no reason, however subtle, could explain it.

In his long and varied experience, Ferpierre had closely studied human passions. He knew that unfaithful lovers usually feel overwhelmed on the point of betrayal by a sense of compassion towards those they are betraying. Conscious of the harm they are doing, they ease their guilt by displaying a certain pitying behavior to the betrayed, which is designed to prove the kindness of their soul, but, in fact, is an egotistical pleasure, and as such, creates more offence. The prince, who had forgotten and even scorned the countess when he went in search of simple pleasures elsewhere, revealed himself to be open to a renewed relationship and to just such a presumed compassion. To enjoy his own fortune better, perhaps he had come back to contemplate the spectacle of the unhappiness he had occasioned, to comfort her in this hypocritical way.

If this was a reasonable explanation of Zakunin's feelings, what effect had this produced on the countess? Loving another man, could she really have been jealous of the nihilist, and through this impotent jealousy, have killed herself? This just wasn't believable. On the other hand, the certainty that the prince belonged to another must have given her a sense of freedom, irrespective of the serious obligation imposed by her conscience. She must have felt that most people would excuse her if she had gone back on her word. Nonetheless, her principles mitigated against such an arrangement, and indeed, the hypothesis of suicide appeared more likely if the poor woman had been unaware that the prince's compassion was a lie. Believing it to be sincere, oblivious to the prince's new relationship, she must have felt a growing difficulty in responding to Vérod's hopes. However, was she really unaware of the prince's new love? Or rather, did the prince really love the nihilist? Ferpierre understood that, above all, he had to be certain of this point. Although, doubtless true, it was still unproven.

While he travelled to the prison at Evêché where the accused were detained, he mulled over how he should start questioning the young woman. Her contemptuous attitude on the day of the catastrophe had left him with the desire, almost the need, to pit his wits against her proud demeanor, to make her fold, to confuse her. While the guards went to get the accused, the governor of the prison told him that the young woman's behavior during her two days of imprisonment had been not only quiet, but above suspicion. Yes, she had complained about the cell and the food, she had asked to be able to read and write and had, in fact, written an account of Swiss emigration full of figures and statistics. When she was shown into the governor's office, Ferpierre gave her a signal, and she sat down, holding his interrogatory gaze and folding her arms.

"It seems that you have finally recovered your memory!" the judge began. "And if the notes and figures you have set down in this text are accurate, I see that it's a rather impressive one! I would, therefore, hope that it won't fail with regard to the things that press upon us and that we need to know. How long have you known Alexi Petrovich?"

"For many years."

"Since Russia?"

"Yes."

"How did you know him?"

"He was a friend of my brothers."

"Who were naturally his fellow believers? After you left your country, where did you meet him?"

"Here, in Lausanne."

"Was he alone?"

"No."

"Was he with the countess?"

"Yes, with her."

"Did you go to find him? How did you see each other?"

"He knew of my arrival. He looked for me himself."

"Why did he do that? In order to have news from Russia? To drag you into his plots? Answer me!"

After a moment's silence, the young woman answered: "In order to help me."

"In what way?"

"I was alone, without any resources, in an unknown country. He came to offer his help."

"Did he give you money?"

"He offered some to me, but I refused."

"Then how could he be of any use to you?"

"He recommended various people he knew. He found me some students who wanted Russian lessons. He encouraged me to write for newspapers and magazines."

"How long were you together?"

"One day."

"Did you leave or did he?"

"I did."

"Did you go to Zurich? Did you write to each other? And when did you see each other again?"

"A year later, in Lugano."

"Was he alone?"

"Yes."

"Did you know why he was alone? Did you realize that he had already fallen out of love with the countess?"

"I didn't concern myself with these matters."

"Why did you go to Lugano? What was he doing there?"

Natzichev didn't answer.

"Don't you want to tell me?"

"I can't."

"Were you helping the party?

Again, she remained silent.

"How long were you in Lugano?"

"Three days."

"And afterwards?"

"I returned to Zurich."

"When did he come to the city?"

"This April."

"What for?"

As the young woman remained mute, Ferpierre continued slowly: "You're not going to answer anything anymore? I understand your reserve. You can't and mustn't reveal the secrets of your association. Your silence has to mean that the prince came to Zurich expressly to work on propaganda, to conspire, in effect, for political reasons. I advise you, however, that there are some small obscure points to clarify before this seems credible. During the time that you have led me to believe the prince was in Zurich for political motives, they wrote letters to him from Russia, from England, from all over, calling for him, reproaching him for neglecting the cause, accusing him of cooling and almost of cowardice. We have a bundle of letters that are very clear. How do you explain this contradiction?"

Natzichev shook her head without uttering a sound.

"Do you persist in not answering? And how do you explain that when Zakunin left Zurich and came here to Ouchy, you, who hadn't looked for him before, came running to see him, more than once, to a house that wasn't his, and we found you there with him on the day of the catastrophe? You don't want to answer that either? Well, I'll tell you something else: among those letters, where they almost accused him of treason, there was one from a friend who implores him not to fall back into his habitual and weak old ways, seducing women and spending too much of his time on womanizing.... This friend wrote as if he already knew that a new adventure with another woman was distracting him from fulfilling his duties to his brothers in arms.... Why are you now looking away? If I asked you who this woman was, what would you say to me?"

She responded firmly, fixing the judge in the eyes: "It was me."

"Aha! Are you confessing?" exclaimed Ferpierre. "The other day you were offended by my suspicions! Well now, tell me, when did this change in the relationship between the two of you take place?"

"When he came to Zurich."

"Did he come especially because of you?"

"No."

"Why then?"

"For political reasons."

"Explain to me how this change happened. In two years, you hadn't seen each other more than twice. On those occasions, did he say anything affectionate to you?"

"Nothing."

"And what about you?"

"I loved him from the first day he came to help me."

The young woman's voice, however much she tried to contain herself, revealed a secret anxiety.

"In which case, were you the first to speak?"

"No."

"Did he then declare himself, suddenly, after not having thought of you for two years?"

"He stayed for a few months in Zurich, and we saw each other every day."

"Were you aware that, after having abandoned the countess, he came to Zurich specifically to find you?"

"Yes, I knew."

"And didn't it bother you?"

"No."

"Really? A moment ago, when I asked you about his relationship with the Italian woman, you said that you didn't concern yourself with such matters. If you truly loved him, how could you not feel a burning desire to see him free?"

"I knew he was free."

"You mean his understanding with the countess meant little to him?"

"I mean that he didn't love her anymore."

"But didn't you know that she still loved him?"

"Lately, even her affection had waned."

"Then why had he returned to her side?"

"They still had interests in common."

"By common interests, do you mean those loans that he asked her for? But if she was no longer in love, she couldn't have been jealous of you?"

"No."

"Then why would she have killed herself?"

"I don't know, probably because of her scruples."

"Because she loved another who couldn't be hers?"

"I don't know. Perhaps. Suicide, although it seems premeditated over a long period, is always brought to fruition by an unforeseen moment of impulse. Pain is motive enough. She had much of that to deal with."

"Your thinking is sound! Did the prince know that she was in love with someone else?"

"I don't believe so."

"He never spoke to you about it?"

"Never."

"Right then, let's see what the prince has to say?"

Natzichev left the room, and the judge ordered Zakunin to be brought into the office.

His behavior in prison had been completely different from that of his presumed accomplice. He had asked for nothing for himself, no special food, no books, no letters. He hadn't complained about anything. He had hardly spoken a word. The guards said that he spent his time lying on his bed, motionless, as if asleep. From his general appearance, from his reddened eyes, his interior state of mind was apparent, but was it the injustice of being accused or the remorse for his crime that was affecting him? When Ferpierre asked if he stood by his statement, if he had anything to add in his defense, he answered in a somber voice: "Nothing."

"The other day you recognized your faults. You confessed that you hadn't reciprocated the affection shown by Countess d'Arda. If you didn't love her anymore, why didn't you leave her to follow her own destiny?"

"She still wanted me to be hers."

"Even knowing that she didn't matter anymore to you?"

"She thought she was bound to me forever."

"And you occasionally felt, between one tryst and another, something approximating an obligation to return to her side for a while? Well, such feelings honor you greatly!"

The prince looked Ferpierre in the eye, as if to replicate the irony of the observation. Then, he titled his head and in a low voice, with much bitterness, said: "My feelings and behavior were fatal in the extreme! In fact, when she thought she was free of me and able to think of life in another way, I reappeared, reminding her of previous commitments. Such a mistake must have been an irreparable burden for her."

Was he talking in such a way because it was the truth or because, being guilty, he understood the effectiveness of a defense like this?

"And you also came back to her for money?"

On hearing these words, Zakunin lifted his head and swiftly fixed his gaze on the judge. Then, he lowered it again, confused.

"What kept you in Zurich throughout the summer?"

"Propaganda."

"That's not true. The letters from your fellow believers in Russia and England accuse you of betraying them."

For a third time, the accused looked at the judge face to face and shuddered.

"I had to help others. Do you think that I'm going to reveal secrets to you that aren't mine? Do you want to take advantage of my imprisonment to pursue a political prosecution?"

"No, not at all! I'm prepared to admit that you left some of your companions' letters unanswered, not because of a lack of zeal, but in order to help others. Alexandra Natzichev, for example, took up much of your time. . . ."

Zakunin's gaze flickered.

"Don't speak like that," he said almost voiceless.

"And why don't you want me to speak like that? They were all accusing you of letting your enthusiasm wane and even of being afraid. You let your party chiefs meet in London, and you didn't go to see them, just so you could remain in Zurich with Alexandra, the very same woman who was by your side on the day of the tragedy in a house that wasn't yours. . . . Don't you want us to think that your friendship with her and the frequency of your visits were the reason for the change in your habits?"

"There was no change. I'll say again, the aims we pursue are various, their routes numerous. If I didn't go to London, there were other things for me to do that were no less relevant."

"You don't want to tell me what those things were, and perhaps you're right, because it suggests a certain partisan obligation. But another, more generally understood obligation should compel you to confess the nature of your relationship with Natzichev. I have to tell you, however, that any delicacy you feel is superfluous because she has confessed all."

"What?" exclaimed the prince with a note of profound astonishment.

"That you're her lover."

"She told you that?" the accused cried out once again, his voice and eyes expressing the impossibility of believing such a revelation.

Ferpierre kept quiet for a moment while observing him.

The man's shock seemed sincere. Had, perhaps, the nihilist lied? And why? What motive could have pushed her to confess something that had to be damaging to her reputation? If though, rebellious to all convention, she was oblivious to such damage, she still needed some rationale for telling a lie like that! But wasn't it more likely that she had told the truth and the prince had feigned surprise given the harm such a confession could cause them both?

"She, herself, told me!" said Ferpierre. "Are you stunned?"

"It's not true!" the prince answered.

"How long have you known her?"

"Three years."

"How do you know her?"

"I was a friend of her brothers."

"When you moved to Switzerland, did she come to look for you? Did you help her? You see I'm well informed! She told me these things. Firstly, you saw her occasionally, however, since April in Zurich, you have been together. This all forms part of her statement. Do you admit, yes or no, that you're her lover?"

The impatient firmness of the question made the accused looked directly at the judge. The veins in his temples rippled, his teeth were clenched in anger.

"You're right not to answer. It makes me think that you should confront her."

Ferpierre ordered the Russian woman to be brought back into the room.

The mute anger of the prince immediately gave way to visible anxiety. At that very moment, he seemed to feel threatened, scared, unable to find a way of escape. When the young woman arrived, he fixed her with a burning stare.

"I have called you here again," said the judge, "so that you can repeat in the presence of this man what you told me earlier. Are you his lover?"

The prince leaned towards her as if he was anxious to hear the reply or to suggest one himself.

"Yes," she answered decisively.

"You see," replied Ferpierre, signaling towards the prince. "It appears he doesn't believe you."

"I understand the reason that might persuade him to hide the truth. But the truth will come to be known anyway, and I'm not offended."

The nihilist answered without looking at her accomplice. Only when the judge turned to Zakunin to asked if he still denied it, did she shift and look at him.

"Is she your lover?" Ferpierre repeated while the two stared at each other, the woman with an expression of dominant calm, the prince hesitant and bewildered.

Zakunin finally nodded his head in an act of confession.

"So, did you return to the countess and show yourself to be a changed man simply because you needed money?"

"What are you saying?" the prince scornfully uttered.

"Well then, why?" insisted the judge.

"I suggested that he go back to the countess," said the young woman.

As Zakunin went to make a new gesture in protest, she added: "Don't worry about causing me any harm. You need to tell the truth. Tell him that it was me who suggested you return to her side so you could break with her in an honest and frank manner. I'm not sorry I gave you this advice. It's all preferable to misunderstanding and ambiguity. As it wasn't possible to live with her as you had promised, you had to follow your word and ensure she didn't harbor any new illusions. If this hurt her and caused her to kill herself, it would be unpleasant, but we can't be held responsible for it. In similar circumstances, we would still do the same thing, as would anyone else in the same position."

"Let's leave to one side," said Ferpierre, "any judgment about your supposed conduct. Before we judge it, we need to make sure what it was. Right, if you advised your lover to return to the countess to make a candid break with her, it's likely that he misinterpreted the suggestion and instead of telling her frankly that everything had finished, he became close again, acting in a repentant and subdued manner. It seems a strange way to end a relationship by renewing it. . . ."

Ferpierre had been speaking while looking at the prince. He remained silent and confused, as the young woman answered: "Are you surprised that, on the point of leaving someone he had once loved, the memory of time spent together saddened and moved him, making any frankness painful, thereby causing a delay?"

"I spoke about it with him, and it proved difficult for him to answer,..." observed Ferpierre with an ambiguous nod of the head, as if the woman's zeal made him suspicious. "However, as you're so well informed of what happened between them, although you originally denied any involvement in such matters, tell me if he completed his task with due frankness, because I know from other statements that up until the eve of the catastrophe, he hadn't kept his word, which meant she felt more tied to him than ever."

"What happened didn't only happened between them. I was also there."

"When?"

"On the day of her death, that very morning. Given that it's important to tell you everything, I'm going to explain why I was in the house. I knew that the final split had to come, and I was waiting impatiently for the prince to tell me the outcome. Seeing that he wasn't going to come back to me, I came to him. I found him still undecided, fearing that he would cause her harm. Then I advised him to write to her, an idea that he seemed happy with. We were in the study. We thought that nobody could hear us, when the countess appeared. She started to say bitter things to him and to me. He got angry with her. He forgot the pity he felt. He accused her of spying. He told her that he was going to leave and never return. She left us. We began to prepare our things. A short time afterwards, we heard the shot. That's the truth."

"Can you confirm what the young woman is saying?" Ferpierre asked Zakunin.

He answered with a brief nod of the head.

"What were the bitter things that the countess said?"

It was still the woman who answered.

"She said: 'You talk of loyalty? Is it such scrupulous candor that makes you hide here so you can plot against me? Perhaps I have been an obstacle to your love? Was it really necessary to make such a spectacle right here?'"

The judge remained quiet for a moment, contemplating Natzichev, then, without turning away, he said slowly: "And you think, after this tempestuous revelation, with such disdain bubbling up inside the countess's heart, the story of suicide becomes more plausible? Hasn't it occurred to you that this unfortunate and rather unbelievable scenario might have put you on shaky ground?"

The young woman answered harshly, furrowing her brow: "It's your duty to be doubtful. I have told you the truth, even though it reflects badly on me. Have you got nothing else to ask me?"

Instead of waiting for the judge to dismiss her, she dismissed him.

VII

The Confession

The curiosity awakened in the public by the tragedy at Ouchy was growing day by day. The standing of those involved, the strangeness of the case that had brought together people from varied locations, so different by birth and lifestyle: a revolutionary known throughout Europe like Zakunin, a writer such a Robert Vérod, a *grande dame* like the Countess d'Arda and a mysterious creature such as Alexandra Natzichev, would have excited general interest if the judicial intrigue hadn't already been enough.

The news of suicide and the accusation of murder had leaked out at the same time and divided opinion into two, more or less, equal camps. Maybe those who thought it had to be murder were more numerous, but it was only men with a natural tendency towards a belief in evil doing and, in part, an aversion to the political ideas of the prince and the student that had given rise to such suspicions, given that nobody could put forward valid reasons when trying to demonstrate the rationale behind it.

However, the revolutionaries weren't lacking in people prepared to defend them and with some force. Was the fact that they didn't retreat before bullets and fire in the pursuit of their ideals enough to say that they were capable of a common crime? Wasn't there a big distinction between the two things and aren't the most ferocious sectarians usually, in their private life, people of scrupulous honor and naïve decency?

The details of the private lives of Zakunin and Natzichev gave arguments to both their defenders and accusers when it came to backing-up their opinions.

In the complex makeup of Slavs, both impetuous and cold, at times violently dragged by blind instinct, at others rigidly bound to the most iron reason, people alternately found able motive for the crime and an inability to commit it.

Was it so amazing, or rather, wasn't it natural that, in a fit of jealousy, hate and rancor, these people, who believed themselves above the law, could destroyed a life after having given themselves over to destroying so many others?

On the contrary, their defenders observed that it wasn't credible that the revolutionaries, whose aims were condemned by everyone else, but which they, themselves, considered great and almost sacred, could lose their way in such a vulgar adventure, committing a useless crime. How was it possible that two people who had been exiled from their home, family and friends, from the ties that bind people together, because of their world-shattering work, would then have betrayed their cause obeying such a petty passion?

Others replied that those espousing the utmost human ideals weren't prohibited from passion, but quite the contrary. They tried to prove this with the prince's numerous affairs and that because reason cedes to the rule of passion in most men, it must, therefore, give way more easily in them.

The discussions involving who should be accused were long and lively. Was the prince the killer? Was the nihilist innocent or an accomplice? Opinions were divided on this as well: according to some, the man had committed the crime due to jealousy of Vérod; according to others, the woman had done it out of rivalry.

Those who believed in the suicide felt the uncertainty lent their argument some weight. How could one have faith in an accusation that couldn't be pinned down? To propose that the two had killed the countess together didn't seem possible and only the accusers driven by their hate of the revolutionaries said that the two could have collaborated in a murder pact. If Alexi Zakunin had wanted to punish the countess for her love of Vérod and if the nihilist had wanted to punish her for her love of the prince, any perverse complicity could then have been explained.

Some went even further, knowing that the prince had found himself in financial difficulties, they conjectured that the two Russians had killed the countess in order to rob her. But the malevolence attributable to the perpetrators in such a hypothesis meant that few believed in it. Most accusers recognized that they had to direct their ire at one or the other, but not both. Lacking proof for the accusation or the defense, each of the camps didn't so much insist on demonstrating their own theory as on combatting the opposing position. Those who blamed the prince or the nihilist, saw a lack of truth in the suicide. To affirm the latter, others saw no truth in the crime and thought it impossible.

Judge Ferpierre was attentive to all these voices as he looked to shed light on the discovery of the truth. The last interrogation had left him more hesitant than ever. Why had the accused answered in different ways when asked to reveal the nature of their relationship? Natzichev had certainly not been obliged to confess beyond doubt that she was the prince's lover and, furthermore, she had almost forced him to avoid any contradictions. If she had wanted to deny it, she could have done so, just as he had. It wasn't only a love of the truth that had pushed her to do this. She must have thought that her confession would benefit the prince. Nor was it only politesse that had persuaded the prince to deny his relationship with the young woman; it was also, particularly, a fear that telling the truth would go against him. The more the judge thought about their answers, the more he recognized a secret interest that had pushed them to reply in different ways. However, the issue still remained unsolved: was it two accomplices trying to save themselves or two innocent people who were scared of defending themselves badly?

Doubt consumed Ferpierre once more. There were moments when he thought it was his duty to let them go; then a suspicion, which he couldn't even explain to himself, something ambiguous about their behavior or rather their speech, made him wait and continue searching.

With regard to the worst of the suspicions, that of homicide because of robbery, the judge had received some news from Milan which seemed unfavorable to the accused. According to a deposition from the d'Arda accountant, the sums of money that the countess must have had were much greater than those found in the villa. However, Ferpierre had firm proof that robbery hadn't been committed. Giulia Pico, when interrogated about the honesty of the other servants and the possibility that one of them could have been working with the Russians, gave answers that precluded any suspicion. She said that her employer was full of charity, that she gave and sent much money to the poor and charitable organizations in Lausanne, Nice and Milan, something confirmed by Baroness Börne and all the foreigners from Beau-Séjour. Surely that was the explanation for the difference between the sums that should have been found at the house and those that were actually found?

A new, more in-depth, search of the Villa Cyclamens uncovered no hidden money. The interrogation of the servants and a search of their quarters also dampened further suspicion.

Nothing remained but the mere hypothesis that theft had been intended and Ferpierre didn't give that any credence. He believed that, if there had been a crime, it was one determined by passion. It was, therefore, important to ascertain the nature of the relationship between the two Russians, but no light had fallen on that from the testimonies of those who knew Zakunin and Natzichev in Zurich. Those interviewed didn't know if they were really lovers; some suspected it, and some disregarded the idea. Similarly, opinion was divided on their capacity to commit the crime.

The letter sent by the countess to Sister Anna Brighton would have revealed the mystery, but Sister Anna couldn't be found. She was no longer in New Orleans, where her last letters to the countess had been sent from, and nobody knew where she had gone. Ferpierre was hoping, however, that at some point she would hand over the requested document to the forces of law and order. All of the world's newspapers were talking about the drama at Ouchy and they were saying that only the Countess d'Arda's last letter could clarify matters. They thought it would catch out the accused if it didn't announce her imminent suicide or would save two innocent people if it revealed such an extreme proposition. It was impossible that, in the end, Sister Anna wouldn't receive news that people were anxiously waiting and feel compelled to hand the document to the authorities.

While waiting, Ferpierre had no choice but to delve deeper into the mysterious drama and its protagonists. After getting to know the lives of the two Russians, he could see they had a decent side, but it remained hidden and diminished by hardness, violence and a gloomy ferocity. Perhaps, had they been treated in a different way and experienced better circumstances in life, they would have been better? Yet, the humble, devoted and imploring love of Countess Fiorenza hadn't been enough to redeem Zakunin and, thinking about the agony of the unhappy woman, the judge dispensed with any indulgence, recognizing that a violent man like the prince who wanted the humiliation of such a delicate soul, could have also wanted her dead.

As regards the nihilist, her life, unlike Zakunin's, wasn't full of atrocities. The hard luck that had left her alone at the age of twenty, the courage with which she had fought against the difficulties of life, plus her assiduous study and sharpness of mind, all spoke in her favor. But the judge couldn't pardon a woman, such a young woman, who held to a bloody and destructive ideology and, if he was occasionally inclined to excuse her, her links to the prince seemed without excuse.

How was it that she had thrown herself into the arms of a man who had never been steadfast in his affections? To ignore laws, conventions and social concerns was all too natural in certain mental states, under the influence of particular examples and owing to the effectiveness of frequent proselytization. Ferpierre admitted that Natzichev supported free love, but that her love had to be reciprocated, it had to be founded on sincerity, on fidelity, however temporary, and he believed that Zakunin's life demonstrated that he was incapable of this. Therefore, Ferpierre thought that the two of them were united by mere instinctive impulse, without any refinement of feeling, by a hunger for pleasure. The crime could have sprung from such an unworthy union.

Did the young woman's confession of her relationship, confirmed by the prince, really worsen or improve their predicament? Among the public, opinion continued to be divided. If the countess, no longer in love with Zakunin, but hoping to remain with him, respected and protected, had to give up this last illusion, it could have been the *fait accompli* that determined the suicide. But her new love for Vérod worked against this supposition. If she loved another, wouldn't she have been cheered up by the prince's affection for someone else? This seemed all the more certain, as much as the fact that the friendship between the countess and Vérod couldn't have remained innocent, something much commented on by people. Few believed the purity of their intentions. The young man had to be the happy lover of the Italian aristocrat. Otherwise why would he have been interested in making an accusation? Was it credible that, being in love and with the freedom they both enjoyed, they would have been content to yearn for each other? How could anyone believe that Vérod would have settled for brotherly affection? And what would have compelled the countess to resist him? If she had transgressed the law once, it was inevitable that she would continue to do so. Furthermore, would her respect and fear of Zakunin have been able to stop her, given that he wasn't bothered about her, or rather, he was totally neglecting her?

These presumptions passed from mouth to mouth, becoming, in the minds of some, undeniable truths: that Vérod had been the deceased's lover was now not in doubt. It was this certainty, along with an antipathy towards the nihilists, that led many to find a motive for murder. Vérod's new lover couldn't have thought about killing herself, but on the contrary, would have enjoyed her new relationship as much as possible. The prince and Natzichev must have killed her.

However, the discussions soon resumed. If the man from Geneva and the Italian woman didn't have a sincere and honest friendship, then the relationship between the two nihilists had to be even less so. As a consequence, if the prince and the student were lovers, neither of them would have been hurt by the love between Vérod and the countess, nor would they have wanted either of them to come to harm. Conversely, both must have been happy because such a relationship would have set them free to do what they pleased. The violent death of Fiorenza d'Arda, whether by suicide or murder, was inexplicable without some kind of disagreement, conflict or drama. The hypothesis of concord between the two couples was implausible given the presence of the bloody cadaver.

Few were as aware of the countess's internal struggle as Ferpierre. The poor woman's state of mind on the eve of the catastrophe was open to the imagination, and the judge recognized the possibility of suicide, that she had perhaps killed herself. But with regard to Vérod's accusation, the suspicions of the public at large and the attitude of the suspects, Ferpierre was prevented from definitively confirming these opinions by a kind of secret instinct and his own conscience as a judge. His long experience told him that the truth of a supposition when confronted by an unclear incident didn't exclude other possibilities. The love he had for his job was heightened by the idea that this case was intricate and difficult. He couldn't really remember encountering a more challenging one.

Beyond the countess's internal struggle, what other internal battles experienced by the accused could explain the catastrophe? Was it possible that, on falling in love with Natzichev, or rather, on starting a relationship with her in order to add another notch to his list of triumphs, the prince hadn't completely forgotten about the countess, or that, on seeing her close to falling into the arms of another, his love for her had been reawakened? Doesn't the secure possession of something good generate boredom such that the thing in question becomes undervalued and only becomes valued again when there is a threat that it might be lost? When we treat something with disdain, but someone else shows appreciation for it, that is often enough to make us change opinion and recognize its value. In order to maintain that Fiorenza d'Arda was killed, you would have to believe that this change had happened to the prince. Only could the events be construed as murder, if he had killed her knowing that her heart belonged to Vérod or if the nihilist had killed her knowing that Zakunin had started to love her again.

Nevertheless, if the resurrection of the prince's love was indispensable to explaining the crime, he couldn't be the killer, precisely because of such a resurrection! In fact, his jealousy couldn't have had much foundation since until recently, the countess had been faithful, and to keep her word, she had avoided Vérod. Was it realistic that the mere certainty of losing her heart and the conviction that he wouldn't be able to win it back could have caused the crime? Perhaps that wasn't completely unbelievable, given the violence of his nature. However, in order to consider this possibility, justifications, provocations and threats would have had to have passed between him and the countess. If he had pleaded with her to stay, to rekindle her love, but if she had replied that she no longer wanted to be with him, it would explain the murder. However, was it credible that she, who had remained faithful and submissive despite the mistreatment, would have rebelled on seeing him penitent and full of guilt? Taking the deceased's character into account, one had to believe, on the contrary, that the prince's change of heart and his insistent pleas would have increased her discomfort, added to her anguish and increased her scruples, thereby multiplying the heart-rendering difficulties she was struggling with.

On the one hand, Ferpierre had already confirmed this for himself through the reasoning he had previously undertaken. But, on the other, he was inclined to feel that Natzichev's position had gotten much worse. Realizing that Zakunin wasn't entirely hers and that through love, pity, respect or interest, he still belonged to the countess, the Russian woman could have started to hate her. It wasn't impossible that a scene had taken place between the two women, engineered by the nihilist, whose presence at the Villa Cyclamens wasn't easily explained. Although incapable of wishing to hurt anyone, the Italian woman could have injured Natzichev as she was counteracting her threats to take the prince from the villa after she had already been behind their separation. The result of a contretemps like this could have been bloody. But how could the prince not have intervened to stop the crime, given he must have been close by, if not actually present? And how had the nihilist, who had never entered the countess's room, known where to find her weapon?

These difficulties didn't overly concern the judge. Perhaps Zakunin hadn't intervened because he didn't think the conversation would end in tragedy and maybe the countess's gun wasn't shut away on that day or the young woman knew where to find it.

There was another issue, entirely moral and more serious, the same one that had made Ferpierre pause more than once: if the nihilist knew of Fiorenza d'Arda's love for Vérod, why would she wish anything bad to happen to her? The rivalry was only explained if Fiorenza had tried to keep hold of the prince, which wasn't the case. Perhaps Natzichev didn't know of her love for Vérod. A passion, which had suffocated the countess and been suppressed by the young man, could have remained hidden if no external factor or action had revealed it.

Therefore, although these suppositions weren't reinforced by proof and many things still needed clarification, the judge felt reaffirmed in his opinion that, dismissing suicide, the suspicion would most likely fall on Natzichev. The prince's repentance and return to his old lover, whether through lack of money or more refined sentiments, hindered the belief that Zakunin had wanted her dead. She was dear to him once more, which, at the same time, explained the hatred, if not the jealousy, of the student. If Zakunin seemed more capable of killing, it was also true that his position in the party, his feverish propaganda activities and his solemn responsibilities would have stopped him from a committing crime that would put him into the hands of justice. In Natzichev, however, less seriously committed, a conscience born of responsibility was almost non-existent. As a woman, political duty had to be less an obstacle to passion, and although she had no crimes weighing against her, police reports indicated that she would be capable of them. Wasn't this capacity for crime, the violence of her feelings, written all over her face and visible in her gaze? Wasn't there something hard and iron-like in her persona, in her words, a perpetual provocation, a silent threat and an implacable rebellion? The attitude she displayed before the dead body and during her spell in prison had turned Ferpierre against her. While Zakunin had appeared to be lost in anguish, she had remained cold and impenetrable. She had initially denied being his lover, then she had admitted it. These and other contradictions, such as the initiative she had taken during the last interrogation by answering for the prince, revealed, despite her indifference, a secret anxiety to save herself.

With regard to this, Ferpierre resolved to undertake some new investigations. If she was guilty, how could the prince, seeing the weight of accusation on her shoulders, not exonerate himself by revealing the truth?

It was evident that he was hoping to save them both by agreeing with all the arguments that pointed towards suicide. He wanted to save her because of love, compassion or rather through a feeling of comradeship engendered and fed by their ideals. If the prince had been the killer, wouldn't the nihilist have been motivated by the same feelings? It was very plausible. However, what would happen if the innocent party, whichever of the two, had lost all hope of being saved along with the guilty person? If both felt themselves to be irredeemably lost, wasn't it plausible that the innocent party would abandon heroism aimed at saving the guilty one, or that the guilty one wouldn't accept dragging the other one down?

Guided by this train of thought, Ferpierre wanted to try and prove something. He would call the two accused again and to Natzichev he would explain the suspicions falling on Zakunin and vice-versa. Their attitudes could reveal the truth.

Once more he renewed his interrogation of the nihilist. She had continued to occupy herself by reading and writing. Her disdainful indifference hadn't waned throughout the additional long prison days.

"I have come," said the judge in a light tone, "to complete a happy task. The forces of justice are convinced of your innocence. You are free to go. If you thought that we enjoyed accusing you, in being suspicious at any cost, I would hope you will leave here content in being wrong. Our task is to discover the truth. Despite how entirely worthy this duty is, we also suffer when misleading appearances prevent us from helping the innocent. But I repeat, the forces of law and order no longer have you under suspicion. The time you have spent here can't have been pleasant, but I guess it must have been useful to your sociological studies."

Without saying a word, without a single gesture of happiness, impassive, motionless, Natzichev fixed her gaze on Ferpierre. She didn't seem to understand his brief sermon. The judge almost expected to hear her say: "Have you finished?"

"No doubt," continued Ferpierre, "it would have been better for you to examine our penal system in liberty, but if we have had to detain you over these past few days, you must realize that the fault, in part, was yours. Your motivation was certainly respectable and does you great honor, but if by not accusing your lover, you gave us pause for thought, are we to be blamed for your prolonged prison stay?"

Natzichev continued to regard him fixedly. On hearing this question, she momentarily closed her eyes and said: "What are you trying to say?"

"Don't you understand?"

"No"

"Surely, it's not that difficult. Or were you still expecting to be freed along with him? Such an aim would be laudable, if it didn't run contrary to the truth that we are obliged to uncover, as you must recognize."

"What are you saying?" interrupted the young woman with a gesture of indifference.

"I'm not saying anything," answered Ferpierre, shrugging his shoulders and lowering his gaze to the papers on the table. "Your lover has confessed to being the killer."

By avoiding the young woman's gaze, the judge was driven by two different impulses. It damaged his sense of right and wrong to use a lie to discover the truth. Rarely had he fallen back on such a method: only in the desperate cases, like the one he was now dealing with and always with a feeling of repugnance, had he had recourse to this technique. Nevertheless, if a sense of shame had secretly grabbed hold of him and made him lower his gaze, his instinct and investigative habits had advised him to continue in this way so that the accused, unobserved, wouldn't try to repress her true feelings when confronted by the revelation.

Pretending to find something among the papers on the table, he continued: "Here is his signed statement. Do you still want to save him?"

Now he looked at her.

Her face had changed. It was as if the mask of proud disdain had dropped. Her cheeks went pale, her lips half-opened, her bewildered eyes showed the pain, fear, remorse and something that Ferpierre was, as yet, unable to detect, although it was without any doubt agonizing.

"Are you hurt by this? You must love him a lot!"

The sight of her sudden anxiety at first distracted the judge from the embarrassment he felt on continuing down a road he knew to be devious. But knowing that he was obliged to follow it to its end and noting the young woman's disquiet, his repugnance increased. Wasn't he inflicting a moral torture on this woman because of his love for the truth? Was there much difference between the horrible instruments of what was once the Holy Inquisition and the lies he was using to explore this woman's soul?

"I understand your pain, but you must be prepared to put up with it. You have done everything to divert our suspicion, and you can't feel tormented by the fact you have damaged the prince's case. But the truth always comes out. And I have to say that you could have been a little cleverer. How did you ever hope that I would believe the tall story you came up with about an argument when I last talked to you both? And is it really credible that the prince returned to the countess, as you would have me believe, in order to finally break with her and then take so much time to do it? If he delayed for so long, it was because he had changed his mind, because at the point of abandoning her, he noticed that she was no longer thinking about him, and then, his previous intentions were altered by his wounded pride. He didn't want the countess with someone else, he wanted her to be his as before, so he showed himself to be imploring and repentant. He hid this change from you, which was only natural, but how did you never suspect given his behavior? You must have been concerned about the delay in doing what he had promised. If compassion was stopping him from delivering the fatal blow, this would have seemed a dangerous precedent to your wounded heart. Passion, when it seems dead and buried, can suddenly surge more robustly than before. When you knew that he had been with her for longer than expected, didn't it hurt, didn't you suspect that memories of the past would overcome him once again, that he would seduce the countess, a woman who was almost new to him after such a long separation? Yes, you had guessed as much. Your painful silence tells me that now, but you have kept quiet because you still love him, because you understand that if we had known about Zakunin, the countess and your jealousy, the truth would have shone brightly. But your zealotry was never going to have a happy outcome. When I asked the prince why he was back by Fiorenza d'Arda's side, you, yourself, suggested it was compassion. He hadn't even used this pretext to hide the real reason, that it was love and jealousy! And you thought that I wouldn't notice your interruption and your friend's agitation; that I wouldn't finally discover why?"

Ferpierre, now caught up in the fervor of the investigation, forgot his remorse, realizing that he was very close to the truth. The young woman's silence, the growing dismay on her face, the trembling hands, the anxiety gripping her chest, demonstrated increasingly clearly that the judge had struck the right note, that Zakunin had truly felt a renewed affection for the countess, that the nihilist had suffered from jealousy, that this was the heart of the mystery. He had already deduced this by other means but had been distracted and sent down other blind alleys by differing motivations and a lack of proof. Now he was gathering all the pieces together, he pondered what was missing, so that his budding assertions could set off a kind of moral reaction that would gnaw at the young woman's heart, revealing what was inside.

"Your love for him must be really strong if you have accepted this role, if you have hidden the jealousy torturing you, if you have feigned ignorance and indifference! How badly you have been repaid! You haven't been able to create any illusions, not one. You have seen what has happened, and you foresaw what was to come, because Zakunin, once in a dispute over a woman, given the vehemence of his passions, wouldn't hesitate in committing a crime. You came to find him fearing that the catastrophe had already happened, and you arrived too late to stop it. Isn't that true?"

Hearing this question, the woman shuddered. She put her hands to her temples, almost as if the storm unleashed by the judge's words was threatening to overwhelm her. She then breathed heavily, which made the air whistle through her clenched teeth. Finally, with repugnance and impotent disdain, with the expression of someone who feels mistreated and oppressed, she exclaimed: "Have you finished? Do you want to carry on enjoying yourself by tormenting me? You're definitely relishing this too much. Enough now!"

"What are you trying to say?"

"What I must. I don't want your wicked contrivances to drag down someone who isn't responsible. Do you understand? Do you love the truth above all things? Is your sacred duty to discover the truth? Are you delegated by society to administer justice? Well then, tell this society,..." she had almost started to shout, "tell it that I killed that woman! Let your justice run its course, but know that I don't recognize it, that I despise it. Remember that I claim responsibility for this act not because it merits punishment but to gain praise!"

The impression of these words on the judge was enormous. His thoughts were bombarded by amusement and pleasure at the rapid success of his plan and the satisfaction of having his suspicions confirmed. A new feeling of curiosity also arose brought on by the offender's incredible boastfulness, in addition to a feeling of compassion, which secretly and almost unwillingly inclined him towards indulgence when the confession and conceit should have made him harsher.

"Ah, you confess?…" was the only thing he could say without thinking too much about what he had said in the first confusing moments. He soon recovered his composure: "You're also confessing?" he repeated, maintaining the artifice that had produced such good results. "Who should I believe?" Even now, are you two vying with each other for the generosity you can show? Are you both accusing yourselves to save the other? What a noble contest?"

The young woman replied harshly: "You're not capable of recognizing the truth!"

"Not always! When others try to hide it! Well, if you want me to believe you, I will believe you. However, I'm struggling to understand the vainglorious tone you used to accuse yourself. I know that you don't recognize the law, but in the ideal society you're working towards achieving, would you kill with impunity and would it be a stamp of glory to destroy a life in such a manner, just for pleasure?"

"Not for pleasure."

"What! So it's a duty for all jealous lovers to do away with the object of their jealousy?"

"You don't know."

"I don't, so it would seem! Is it true, yes or no, that the prince couldn't decide whether to leave the countess because he had fallen back in love with her?"

"It's true."

"And you weren't jealous?"

Natzichev answered with a glacial voice, clearly sounding out her words, one after the other: "My personal feelings don't matter. No sentiment, no interest, nothing is important when you have understood your duty. The life of others, your own life, honor, affection, all things vain must give way before it. This is the rule I live by, and it should also be his, but he had forgotten it!"

Now Ferpierre began to understand.

"You mean that he had stopped contributing to the success of your cause not because of his love for you, but for the countess?"

"Yes."

"Why, then, was he in Zurich with you and not with her?"

"Because he knew he had been unbearable to her, but he wanted to talk to somebody about her."

"And did he talk about her?"

"Yes."

"You told me, to begin with, that he hadn't said a word about this! But if he spoke to you of his life with the countess, was he in love with you or not?"

"He's never loved me."

Despite the cold impassiveness of her statue-like appearance, there was a painful echo in these words, and Ferpierre thought to himself: "Don't lie!"

"And did you love him? Do you still love him?"

"Why does that matter to you?" the nihilist responded with a renewed harshness that seemed false to Ferpierre. "Why would it be important to you if it doesn't matter to me? If I wanted to find extenuating circumstances for what I have done, if I wanted to find an excuse for you, for society, I ought to say that I loved him, that I killed her because of jealousy. Your society excuses, even glorifies, egotism and weakness like this. A lover who kills her rival to avoid her own pain and to assure her own pleasure is then forgiven. Such blind and lethal love is considered admirable and strong, even great. Whereas, the love that guides our conscious sacrifice and the beneficial work we undertake is condemned!"

"Strange work you undertake for the general good, going around spilling blood!"

"Do you think that one, ten, a hundred lives matter when all our destinies are in play? You, who fear blood, spill it in torrents through your wars. So great is your horror of blood, your governments' major preoccupation is purchasing weaponry. Here, in this country full of liberty, a display of deadly force is considered the most honorable of intentions, isn't it? And don't tell me that the only aim of such actions is to defend yourself against aggressors. Everybody always says the same thing! Does anybody ever admit to doing something bad? Decent motives are always on the lips of aggressors and those being attacked. Stupid ambition, underhand interests and pettiness propel countries to war. And in your wars, isn't it a guiding principle to allow the sacrifice of a soldier, a patrol or a vanguard for the good of everyone else? We are pursuing a different war, more just, the only just and holy war: a war for the redemption of mankind against all iniquity, all cowardice, against hunger, ignorance, the abuse of power, against the very war you advocate. When we come across an obstacle, we eliminate it: one, ten, a hundred lives, what does it matter?"

The Russian had spoken with poorly-concealed violence. The rigidity of her posture had changed, and her arm had stretched out in the manner of someone used to doing harm and causing destruction.

When she stopped, Ferpierre, who had been astonished and almost intimidated by what he had heard, said, with a cold and severe tone of his own: "We're not going to talk now about the morality of the principles you hold. It would be better if you told me why you thought the countess was an obstacle? What could you possibly fear from her?"

On seeing that she appeared to delay in answering, he added: "Do you want me to believe that, perhaps, she was going to denounce you, to reveal your conspiracies?"

"I don't want you to believe anything. Alexi Petrovich was lost to that woman."

"In what way?"

"Through love. Because he wanted her again, he had forgotten his duty. He had realized that she didn't love him anymore, that her heart lay elsewhere, but he still saw a way to pry her away from that other man. According to her, she went back to him, not so much out of love, but to take him away from us, to redeem him. He appeared a changed man, he showed her that she was his redemption and that if she abandoned him, he would slip into his old habits. This was the only way he could keep her: to tell her and to prove to her that he was different. Although she didn't love him, she couldn't let him return to us, therefore, she resisted Vérod's attentions. Many times, I confronted him with his foolishness, with the indignity of sacrificing his life's ideals for a woman. He refused to hear me. He was blinded by her. To begin with, he had come back to find me so he could cry over losing her, over losing her through his own actions, and he wanted me to help him. . . ."

The young woman's voice not only expressed disdain, but a secret anguish. Ferpierre could hear the hurt caused by the defection of her political co-conspirator, but also, deeper and more hidden, the torment of being a confidante to the man she loved, who had not even suspected her affection.

"And you?"

"I saw that it was all useless. I had little hope of changing him because I know what he's like. When an idea takes hold of him, nothing can stop him. He doesn't see anything anymore. He can't reason. However, I was hoping that the crisis would be solved somehow. One day, suddenly, I understood there was a new danger. He had seen Vérod; when he started to talk about him, his hands shook and his eyes lit up with violence. I realized that he would kill him, that he would end up hopelessly lost. The last few times I came here, I sought him out, foreseeing some sort of catastrophe. He asked for my help. I helped him."

"By killing the woman he loved?"

"By freeing him."

"And you really killed the woman like this, in cold blood, deliberately?"

"I came to see her. I came here on the last day to talk to her. Once everything else had been exhausted, given that he didn't hear the call of duty, she was the only means of saving him. I told her to abandon him and leave, to disappear. She didn't want to. I insisted: 'You love someone else. Go away with him, far away.' She didn't want to hear me talk like that. She wanted to know who I was. I answered: 'Someone who hates you!' From the first moment, I hated her because I realized she was different from me, from a different class, another cast, of a different soul. All her ideas and feelings were contrary to mine, and now she was arguing with me over him. No, it wasn't about Alexi's love for me, but putting him back on the right track, our common path. So, I hated her, I begged her, but even begging was useless.

"Then I said to her: 'You know why you don't want to leave? It's not because of him, but you, yourself. You're afraid that he'll think you have fled with your new lover. You want to show him a degree of faithfulness which, in reality, you don't feel. You want to play the part of a dutiful and faithful woman, as if fulfilling your obligations. After being his lover, you want to act like his wife, despite not loving him anymore. He thinks you're so kind and good, and I wanted to see why he praised your decency. But now I know that you're a hypocrite, false, an egotist, worse than all the others.' She let me speak. My attempts to scorn and offend her were all in vain. 'One day you'll end up breaking your hypocritical faithfulness,' I added, 'so you can run into the arms of your new lover, if you haven't already given yourself to him.' These words were equally useless. I only saw her shudder when I said: 'No! This isn't going to happen. Your lover will be dead. He'll kill him! You know that? You'll be responsible for the murder. You'll have brought it on. Every day, every hour, every minute that passes it's getting nearer. It's racing towards you inevitably!' It was then she exclaimed: 'Ah, death! I must, I want to die!' I felt nothing but disdain and contempt. Who says such things if they really feel them? If she had actually wanted to die, she would have already killed herself. I told her of my scorn and derision: 'It's not true! You're scared! You're a coward!' She agreed: 'Yes, I am a coward. The weapon's over there. I'm shaking.' I picked up the gun and held it out to her: 'Gather your courage, if you still have any, if you ever had any....' She joined her hands together, pleading with me: 'Kill me, free me from all of this....' My disdain grew before this display of cowardice. I promised her in a low voice, with the gun in my hand: 'I will kill you if you don't stop.' She joined her hands together again, pleading once more: 'Kill me! You don't want me to stop! Kill me! You don't!...' I heard his footsteps, her voice calling. I shot her."

Gasping for breath, she went quiet,

"And you don't regret it?"

"I don't. She'd been beaten by life. She wanted to die. She had to die. I had to free him to return to the work at hand. I've freed them both."

Ferpierre had finally uncovered the truth he had already suspected. Now everything became clear, everything was linked together logically. She didn't want to admit that it was more than sectarian zeal that had motivated her, that it was also jealousy. She had refused these extenuating circumstances, preferring to glory in the lack of such personal motives. There was a certain dark grandiosity in this refusal, which indicated the strength of her character. Without a doubt, though, her unrequited love must also have pushed her to shoot Fiorenza d'Arda. The prince's repentance, his ambiguous behavior in the last few months, his grief after the catastrophe, could all now be explained. In denying that he was the nihilist's lover, he had told the truth. He had only admitted it afterwards, when forced by her, in order to back her up, to save her, when the Russian woman had thought she could save herself in such a way. And even the countess's last words, her invocation of the freedom afforded by death, the words designed to incite her threatening rival, surely they were the natural outcome of the contrast between her inability to commit suicide and her wish to die, a wish that had really haunted her. Was Natzichev right? The forces of law and order had to hold her to account for the murder, but hadn't it almost become confused with the liberation of suicide.

The knot had been untangled, yet Ferpierre still needed to call Zakunin. On telling the nihilist that the prince had confessed, the judge had lied in his search for the truth. Now, a doubt came to mind. If, on hearing that Zakunin had blamed himself, the young woman had decided to admit she was guilty, what would the prince say on hearing about her confession? Was it possible that they would both admit to being guilty?

According to the governor of Eveché, the prince's behavior had changed radically since his previous interrogation. He no longer spent his time motionless and silent, indifferent to everything. The tedium of prison had started to make him angry. He had asked to speak to a lawyer, and not having managed to do so, had vented his spleen on the justice system. Several times a day he called for the guards to ask them if an order for his release had arrived. On hearing the negative response, he would arch his brow and let his anger show. He was constantly pacing up and down in his cell, his hands crossed behind his back, his head lowered and his gaze fixed and unforgiving. He waited impatiently for the daily exercise period in the yard, returning from it surlier than before. He had asked for books and refused the prison food, asking others to bring him some from the outside.

He had hardly found himself in front of Ferpierre before saying with badly disguised impatience: "More questions? Can't you finally see the truth?"

"The truth? Indeed, I know the truth now!" answered the judge with a degree of severity. "You may not be materially to blame, and I can't keep you here any longer...."

"So, then..."

"But your moral responsibility is much greater than you led me to believe at the outset, and your impatience is rather out of place at the moment, since you could've dispelled my doubts with a single word.

He stopped to give him time to answer, to say something, but the prince looked at him, remaining silent.

"It would seem, then, that the generosity that drove you before has subsided somewhat, and you're not worried whether you save her or not?"

"Save her?"

"Am I wrong then? Are you feigning astonishment and innocence? Enough! She has confessed."

"What?"

His tone of anxiety and amazement appeared to be sincere.

"Come, come! Are you really going to make me waste more time? Does it hurt to see her beyond help? Don't you know that she loved you? Surely the moral responsibility for all this chaos must weigh heavily on you. Are you pretending to be astonished after lying? You lied when you admitted you were her lover. At least that lie was motivated by the hope of saving her. But why hide your feelings about the countess?"

The prince was shaking, Natzichev had told the truth.

"And yet you spoke of the belated renewal of your love for Fiorenza d'Arda with someone who loved you; an accomplice in your rebellion whose jealousy and fanaticism were stirred at the same time, prompting her to act against that unfortunate woman! Now you're moved, you shake, after creating two victims. So why did you hide all of this? It can't, then, be generosity towards the accused. It was altogether another feeling. One of fear. If I had known what impetus had prompted your belated passion, I would have, and indeed, should have found more basis for suspecting you."

The prince then resolutely raised his head and looked the judge right in the eye, answering him in a muffled voice: "I won't say why I remained quiet. You already know the truth, why don't you just let me go? What more do you want from me?"

VIII

The Letter

When the papers published news that the case had been closed and a jury trial would ensue, owing to Natzichev and Zakunin's confessions admitting to the countess's murder at the hands of the nihilist, public curiosity, which had greatly increased in the last few days, finally began to wane. Those who had not believed in the suicide, seeing their reasoning confirmed, felt vindicated in their opposition to such an unbelievable theory. On the other hand, those who had supported the theory didn't feel too deflated because, despite the supposedly secret investigation, it was generally known that Alexandra Natzichev, on killing the countess, had done nothing more than obey her wishes, almost acting at the command of her desperate victim.

This didn't lessen the judgment of Natzichev. The motive she had given was only partly believed: that she had killed the unfortunate Italian woman simply to liberate Zakunin and return him to the party. It seemed credible to those who had a greater understanding of sectarian zeal, but the majority thought that a lover's jealousy also had to bear some of the blame. Her rebellious ferocity inspired a certain fear, however, nobody could pardon the woman's jealousy. Even those who looked indulgently at crimes of passion thought the nihilist and her actions lacked any decent qualities. They judged her as cold, hard and savage.

While the nihilist appeared in such a sad light, Zakunin's detractors, without fully accepting everything, were forced to recognize his innocence. Since he was seen as the source of all the damage, they only relieved him of the material responsibility for the crime, refusing to completely retract their judgments. The most indulgent credited him with trying to save Natzichev, but his harshest critics, on the contrary, accused him of running the risk of being condemned alongside her precisely because he had tried to save her. Hadn't he, himself, actually admitted in the clearest possible terms that they were both liable to identical treatment? Finally, though, everyone sided with Robert Vérod, who against all appearances, had insisted on believing it had been a crime and who, in the end, had managed to avenge his beloved.

As the curious onlookers, chatting away in public, waited more calmly to see the final moments of the drama, Vérod was the only one who remained in an anguished state.

If, standing before the body of Fiorenza, his heart had broken; if the unbelievable idea of not seeing her anymore had almost driven him mad; if the impotence of trying to avenge her had gnawed away at him; if the fear of causing her death had added terrible remorse to his already overwhelming grief; he could finally see the end of his cruel ordeal. However, a new horror had begun to assail him. At the moment of accusing the two Russians, he had felt a hidden embarrassment, a fear of revealing his friendship with the countess, but this feeling of shame, which had stopped him from telling their intimate story, had been suppressed and quashed by his desire for vengeance. When he eventually opened up, he had feared that the judge wouldn't believe in the purity of his love for the unfortunate Fiorenza. Although his good intentions had been demonstrated, he still felt as if he had somehow tainted her. Did he have the right to reveal her innermost thoughts? If she had hidden her secret not only from others but almost from herself, was it up to him to reveal it? And he, he who knew his beloved's scruples, who had understood and respected them, had now ended up in this position, where everybody pointed him out as the dead woman's new lover…

On making his accusation, he hadn't thought that what he was going to say to the judge would, one day, become known by the public at large; that even he would have to repeat it in front of a crowd gripped by an unhealthy curiosity; that the name of the woman he loved would be on everyone's lips; that the demonstrable innocence of their love wouldn't be believed; and that, after causing his beloved so much sadness in life, he was now contributing to the denigration of her memory. In his need for revenge, in his hatred for the two protagonists, he hadn't foreseen these natural consequences of his behavior, and on seeing the results, his torment had increased beyond all measure. The innocent victim, according to many, was so linked to the contempt they held for the perpetrators that some even said if she had been killed, she had warranted such a sad death because of the disordered life she had lived!

What would it all matter if the truth is known in the end? How to vindicate the memory of an innocent woman who has been profaned and vilified? Above all, on the day of the hearing, didn't he have to swear on the bible her innocence? Or was it better to hope that the trial didn't go ahead and to declare that he had been deceived, and to recognize that the innocent woman had killed herself, thereby avoiding the obligation of revealing the poor woman's secrets before the curious masses?

The contrast in the two duties weighing on his conscience, that of avenging her death and insisting on his accusation or that of respecting her memory by remaining silent, should have been wiped away when Natzichev's confession was announced, however, it only continued to grow.

His moral certainty that suicide was impossible had pushed him to accuse the two Russians, but he hadn't known which of the two suspects should take the full responsibility. On hearing that the nihilist had confessed to the crime, he was left as troubled as he would have been had suicide been confirmed. Seeing Zakunin proven innocent, he realized that his hatred of the prince had prompted the accusation, and he had been guided by a secret internal voice that told him he had to be the killer: this man, not Natzichev, had to pay for the unfortunate woman's death. Finally now that his ambiguous suspicions had been confirmed, he realized that he had been wrong in not directing the magistrate towards Zakunin alone from the very beginning.

Could he still make amends for this error? If, for some secret reason, in order to save her political accomplice, the nihilist had confessed to a crime she hadn't committed, shouldn't he persist in his accusation against Zakunin?

Now that the forces of justice and public opinion had been appeased, seeing the mystery logically explained, could he openly refute the explanation so he could denounce the young woman's supposed heroism and the supposed infamy of the killer, who would let an innocent pay for his crime just so he could save himself? If he were to do this, he would have to give good reason to those who believed him to be Countess d'Arda's fortunate lover and the prince's jealous rival! How much more jealous he would seem in accusing Zakunin when the Russian's innocence already appeared to be assured. It would only be natural to believe that he was motivated by blind hate, and his love for the countess would be the explanation for this hate, for his desire to see some form of vengeance! Although Natzichev's confession had made him forget the heights of his passion and even allowed him to avoid further testimony, he had to intervene more actively, by declaring her a liar, to insist on the sentiments that had united him with the countess, to protect her from any profane suspicions! However, to avoid intolerable damage, he also had to admit to himself that Zakunin was innocent. It was this idea that consumed him: no, if anyone was guilty, it was him! It couldn't be anybody else but him!

If anyone was guilty!... Even supposing that Vérod could go ahead and denounce Natzichev's lie to the judge, how could he convince him of Zakunin's guilt? If she had accused herself to save him, how could he be persuaded to confess? Because of the lack of testimony, it was only the confession of one of the accused that had eliminated the idea of suicide. With the nihilist's statement in doubt and with no prospect of Zakunin incriminating himself, the inevitable result would be the judge's reconsideration of suicide as the likely explanation.

Therefore, whichever way the young man looked, whichever turn he thought to take, damage would be inevitable. That his instinct was deceiving him, and it was only hate pushing him to act against Zakunin was something he denied to himself. If he had been able to inspire in the judge the same certainty that he felt, then the prince's sentencing would have been inevitable. The events were too serious and too sad for the murder to go unpunished. Furthermore, it's now sadder still and even more serious that someone else will pay for his crime.

A love of justice and need for the truth had driven the poor victim. Wouldn't these things remain unsatisfied and offended by the triumph of such a lie? Wasn't it his duty to counter this lie? And even if he hadn't idolized the countess sufficiently in life and had still wished to avenge her, shouldn't her inspirational love of justice and truth be enough to move him to save the innocent woman and unmask the guilty person?

At this point, from the depths of his heart, from the hidden folds of his soul, another memory surged clearly to the surface. She hadn't only inspired truth and justice, but other stronger, more potent sentiments: Christian feelings of forgiveness and compassion. The young man's anxiety increased further, seemingly without end.

His pleasure and pride had been to think, believe and act as his beloved would have thought, believed and acted. Her approval and praise had mattered more than anything to him. Her thoughts had been his guardian and his protection. Now she was dead, shouldn't he continue to be inspired by her life and follow her example? Surely this was the best way of keeping her memory alive. What would her advice have been, if he had been able to ask for it and she had been able to give it? How would she have behaved in a similar situation to the one he now found himself in?

Yes! He was being driven by hate, which was making him greedy for vengeance. Confronted by the idea of not being able to hear her voice, of having to be happy with an elusive memory, to the exclusion of any other feelings, he was dominated by hate for the man who had fought with her and taken her away. If she could no longer remind him of the idea of forgiveness, if her memory was ineffective, the blame belonged completely to that man.

In the first few days, Vérod hadn't even considered the moral issue that was now adding to his torment. But when the first phase of grief naturally began to subside, as he inevitably had to become accustomed to her death and as all his strength was intent on gathering, keeping and preserving her memory, he began to think that she wouldn't sympathize with his blind hate and sense of vendetta. At the moment when the bullet pierced her skin, when her eyes lost their light, wouldn't she have been full of reproach? Wouldn't her last thoughts have been ridden with rage?

When Vérod asked himself these questions, he didn't doubt the answer: she would have thought of forgiveness.

Shouldn't he, in turn, act like this? If he wanted to be worthy of her, shouldn't he follow such an example?

Occasionally, Vérod closed his eyes and tilted his head. He was assailed by memories of her decency and was almost ashamed of having forgotten it. In other moments, he felt able to protest and rebel. Life can't only be filled with love! If evil is countered by forgiveness, what reward is there for being good? But then her words would come to mind: "If one doesn't forgive wickedness, if it's countered with further evil, what happens to good intentions?" She also said that people should love justice, but that it alone wasn't enough in life. Given that human beings are too weak and prone to sin, when they are confronted with their sins, in the face of the overwhelming sum total of their errors, a degree of leniency should be conceded. "Lenient justice isn't just!" had been his answer. She had replied with: "Strict justice is impotent; only kindness can defeat evil."

He had agreed. Why had he agreed? Was he being sincere? If he had sincerely believed her, if he had candidly come around to her way of thinking, shouldn't he now think of forgiveness? If he was now incapable of forgiveness, was it due to his insincerity? Had he feigned his feelings to win her over, to overcome her defenses? Should he accuse himself of past hypocrisy or present weakness?

From such doubt sprang the thought that truth is not always the same; that the disparities of life put man in opposition to himself without any accusation of bad faith. No, he hadn't lied when he recognized that goodness was necessary. Hadn't he demonstrated that he had understood her simply by recalling her call to forgiveness? But how could he accommodate these feelings now when his reason, his passion, his entire being wanted, and by necessity, demanded punishment? Then he heard more words, as clearly and strongly as the day she had proffered them: "The truth is but one thing: to recognize it as an abstract concept is worth little, and there is no merit in it if we don't uphold it against our own interests."

One evening he had a vision of her coming to him with her arms outstretched, her hands open, her face lifted to the heavens. He heard her utter one word: "Forgive." The illusion was so intense, he woke with his eyes bathed in tears.

Now awake, thinking that he had to be content with the empty visitations of his dreams, he was, once again, assailed by the impetus of vengeful passion. Wandering through the places he had been with her, still looking for something of her that remained, he heard her subdued voice once more advise: "Forgive." His answer: "I can't."

He wasn't able to do it. To sincerely pardon, from the heart, he couldn't, he would never be able to do it. However, should he let justice proceed in its own way and not get involved anymore? If he was sure of some new deception, wasn't it his duty to reveal it?

The fear of profaning the memory of her love stopped him. Hadn't he already let it be profaned? Shouldn't he listen to the voice of forgiveness and let the deceased woman forgive him? In order to support his accusation against Zakunin, he needed to explain that the Russian had been jealous of him and had believed his jealousy was founded. This would be impossible for him to do. What next?

"Forgive," the voice kept on saying.

He heard it and not just in secret or in his dreams, but clearly, in the light of day. One day, wandering around the mountain where he had acted as a guide for Fiorenza, he found himself in front of the little chapel that her delicate hand hadn't been able to open. The door was closed as it had been before. Vérod stopped, trembling, his blazing eyes furiously blinking. She had placed her pale hand on this rusty key. He had wanted to turn the lock and open the door, but he held back fearing he would erase any trace of her touch. He extended his arm again, and the door groaned on its hinges. He felt a creeping fear. Inside the chapel he saw her kneeling, with head lowered and hands together, facing the altar, wearing a flame-colored dress....

Vérod fell to his knees, bursting into tears. As he was crying, he clearly heard her voice say to him: "Forgive..."

The following day he was called by the judge. It was the first time he had been before Ferpierre since the day when the judge had triumphed over Vérod's arguments and told him that he believed it was suicide. The young man was feeling extremely confused, not knowing what they could still want from him.

"I need you, above all," Ferpierre told him, "to realize that I recognize my mistake and that you were right. It was a godsend that you insisted on your accusation, irrespective of the evidence. Without your insistence, without the conviction that I saw was driving you, I would probably have stopped the final investigations that led me to discover the truth. No doubt, by now, you already know what happened, but I wanted to confirm personally that your friend was killed. Natzichev has confessed to the crime and the prince, who had remained silent in the hope of saving her, has confirmed her confession."

Robert Vérod kept quiet, still confused.

"Are you satisfied?"

He still didn't answer.

"You have done a service to the forces of law and order. Without you, the killer would have gone unpunished, or worse still, an innocent would have paid the price for the guilty party. There was someone to blame and the instinct that drove you didn't deceive you. It was only your suspicions of the prince that were unfounded."

Once more, Ferpierre fell silent for a moment in order to give Vérod time to say something, but as he remained mute, the judge continued: "The prince couldn't have wanted the countess to die because he had started to love her again, a love both fervent and timid, which forced a rebel like him to refrain from his propaganda activities, to renounce his past, his political faith and his accomplices. And this was because he knew that you now held the countess in esteem and had gained her affections, affections that he had previously scorned. Such is the reasoning of the human heart! It was at this point his accomplice realized he was lost, not only to the party, but also to her, because she loved him and was suffering thinking that he belonged to another, especially since she had become a confidante to their resurrected love. She went in search of her rival so she could persuade her to leave him. She had a tempestuous altercation with the countess that led to the crime. She has confessed everything to me."

The judge made another pause, which Vérod continued to greet with silence.

"Are you satisfied?" repeated the judge.

"Why are you asking me that?"

The two men stared fixedly at each other.

"You ought to be satisfied, I think, having avenged the death of your friend, helped to confirm the perpetrator and seen the triumph of truth and justice."

Both men continued to look at each other in silence.

"And you, aren't you happy?" Vérod finally said.

The judge saw a hint of provocation in the question, almost a provocation to spill his secret thoughts, as if the young man's secret thoughts were those of the judge.

"I have no passions to satisfy," he responded. "I am guided by one love, the love of justice...."

"If justice has been done...."

"Do you doubt it?"

"It's not for me to be doubtful."

"What do you mean then, that I should be? And why? You made an accusation: the accusation has been proven to be correct. You didn't know which of the two possible perpetrators was really responsible since both were capable of committing crimes. The guilty woman accused herself! Perhaps you're going to tell me that a single confession isn't enough? I already know that! That might well be the case, but only when the confession isn't corroborated. A madman can declare himself guilty of a crime, but he won't be able to give a motive for his actions or to explain the circumstances. But in this case, doesn't everything have an explanation? Doesn't the other testimony confirm it? Or do you have little faith in this?

"Indeed," said Vérod, jumping in. His doubts had been growing to the point of showing them with an such attitude that made the judge's questions more pressing. "Indeed, I have little faith in such proof, and you also have doubts! A testimony like this isn't impartial, and the person who provided it to you has his liberty at stake! It's not only a madman who can declare himself guilty of a crime he hasn't committed, but also someone who is prepared to sacrifice themselves."

"In which case, what are you saying?"

"I'm saying," added the young man quickly, as if he didn't want to give himself time to think about the words, as if he was overcoming his thoughts, "I'm saying that the woman sacrificed herself for love, for secular zeal; that the killer took advantage of her sacrifice to get away unpunished. I'm telling you that he is the killer, that it can't be anyone else but him."

Yes, Vérod had said that. The voice of forgiveness had been silent; the voice had never spoken. He had dreamt it all. It had been a figment of his imagination. The truth was something else altogether: his beloved lay underground, her blood stains still hadn't been cleaned away. Her blood was asking for vengeance, and he had to get it.

"Why didn't you say this before? Why did you hesitate at the beginning?"

"Because I still didn't know. Because I still hadn't thought about it in sufficient detail. Because you didn't believe it had been murder, and all my strength went into refuting the notion of suicide."

"Therefore, this man wouldn't only be a killer but would also be ignominiously responsible for letting an innocent woman take the blame for the crime?"

"Are you surprised? Don't you think he must be rejoicing now?"

"What a horrible thought! I see that you've been blinded by hate, but I haven't. He is not as perverse as you think. There are acts of valor in his life, and his attitude when he saw her body and during the first days he spent in prison had nothing to do with rejoicing."

"During the first days.... And what about the rest?"

On the hearing the question, the judge reflected for a moment before continuing.

It was true. When the nihilist had confessed, he immediately had faith in her statement. Doubts now began to occupy him once again. If the young woman had sacrificed herself, what value should he put on her confession and the prince's confirmation? He had, though, interrogated them both once more, separately and together, and they had remained firm in their statements.

When comparing them, he had come across a few contradictions. Natzichev assured him that in the final moments of her argument with the countess, hearing the agitated voice of the prince call out, she had fired the shot fearing that his sudden arrival would prevent further opportunity to do away with her rival. The prince, however, stated that he had hurried to the scene after hearing the shot from a distance. When the two had been put in the same room once more, Natzichev corrected herself, declaring that she thought she heard his voice, but that in her agitation, she had perhaps been deceived. Other small details had, though, confirmed the judge's suspicions that, as in the previous interrogations, the young woman, to a certain extent, had taken the initiative when explaining the drama and had incited the prince to back her up. Nevertheless, he had decided to put her before a panel of judges because he felt that a public debate would finally throw some light on the mystery.

Before doing so, however, he had wanted to call Vérod to see if he also had doubts and to discuss any new suspicions.

"During the first days, he was overcome by grief," the judge answered, after running through things in his head yet again; "but then it was obvious that prison was making him suffer."

"There you are!" exclaimed Vérod. "At the beginning, he realized the horror of his actions. He then became eager to gain his freedom. The way for him to do it was too easy!"

Ferpierre had also been thinking along these lines. Such a man, prone to sudden diverse and contradictory impulses, who was not completely incapable of decent action, but who was drawn more quickly to the siren call of malicious deeds, had perhaps been on the point of confessing. However, his mood, eager for freedom, had changed from one minute to the next, and he had little scruple in grabbing for any life jacket capable of providing salvation.

"Yes, he is that wicked. Are you saying that Natzichev acted heroically?"

"What would stop you from admitting it?"

The judge had, on the contrary, expressly recognized that owing to her zeal and the tenacity of her feelings, the young woman was capable of heroism.

"But how can we get to her? She explained the crime very well! She had two reasons: love and fanaticism."

"Both things must have prompted her to save her beloved and her fellow believer."

This was also right. If the prince had killed the countess, the young woman must have tried to save him, as much for her love of the man as of the party.

"Ok, but, what about proof?"

"Ah! Proof! We've still got to find some!"

"Right then, while we find this proof, as much as you have the right to insist on your suspicions, I also have that right to go back to my own original opinion."

"Why?"

"Well, yes! I'm starting to believe once more that the countess killed herself!"

"After they've already admitted to the crime?"

"And how did they admit to it? You don't know how, in what circumstances Natzichev admitted her guilt! She confessed when I told her that the prince had confessed! She thought he was lost, and she wanted to save him!"

"And this doesn't clearly show you that he alone is the killer?"

"But he confessed to nothing! I used that ploy as a desperate measure!"

"And you don't see that you told the truth?" urged Vérod. "If that woman had known that Zakunin was innocent, she would have laughed at hearing this! She wouldn't have believed it! She would have uncovered your deception. How could she believe that her friend had confessed to something that he had never committed? If

Natzichev did believe what you told her, it would mean you had unconsciously told the truth. And she had wanted to save him because she really thought he was lost!"

Ferpierre didn't answer.

He was amazed that he had never thought of this obvious motive after mulling over so many others. And he now felt the full weight of this understandable argument, and furthermore, he saw that, if it was true, he had followed a blind alley.

"Hypothesis or presumption like everything else!" he exclaimed brusquely, wishing to deny through confusion the importance his thoughts had placed on Vérod's words. "The only thing we're doing is going from one hypothesis to another. If the countess didn't kill herself, she was murdered. If she wasn't murdered, she killed herself! The crime was committed by the nihilist, if it wasn't committed by Zakunin. If the nihilist is innocent, Zakunin is the culprit! Your passionate suspicions aren't proof! As long as you haven't brought me any proof beyond your fervent declarations, however harsh we would like to be with the accused, we'll have no choice but to acquit them through lack of evidence!"

And almost abruptly, he dismissed Vérod.

When he was alone, he gave an order to stop anyone else entering the room. The seriousness of his thoughts at that moment and the irritation he felt with himself stopped him from being concerned with anything else.

The observation made by Vérod held weight: how could he deny its value? If he had already felt many doubts about Natzichev's confession, how could he not admit this one? It was the greatest of them all. Given Vérod was seeing things with more clarity, the young man's passion was worth something, while the cold-blooded analysis he was obliged to employ was going nowhere.

It's certain that, without the deception he had used on the nihilist, she and the prince would have kept on denying things, hiding behind the shield of suicide. It was also evident from the beginning that, of the two, Natzichev had been the most keen to ensure their mutual freedom. In all the interrogations, she had visibly been pushing the prince to defend himself. She had admitted to being his lover and had implored him to confirm it, hoping to stop the discovery of his reignited affair with the countess, a reignited flame that could lead to suspicions of jealousy as the motive for the crime. Afterwards, believing that Zakunin had confessed to being the jealous culprit, she had devised her own intervention between the two actors in this drama! Couldn't Zakunin's silence and sadness be a guilty man's remorse? Weren't they just that? Whichever way you looked at it, for the first days, faced by the grief, he had seemed indifferent to his fate.

All this made Ferpierre think that he had succumbed to an error of judgment in using the tactics of deception against the young woman. Instead he should have said to the prince that Natzichev had confessed. He should have said it when Zakunin was still feeling the weight of grief and pain. Then, probably, he wouldn't have let someone else shoulder his guilt and would have confessed the truth.

The truth! If this was really the truth. How could he ever be sure? Given that Natzichev wanted to save the prince, after hearing about his confession, wouldn't she have done what she, in fact, ended up doing just after hearing the judge's specious story? Then, with them both taking the blame, the confusion would have been greater! Or, on the contrary, their confrontation might have proved more fruitful.

Any such actions were now useless. In deciding to take advantage of Natzichev's generosity, Zakunin had recognized her guilt, and given she was insisting on her confession, how could he refute them both? Ferpierre thought about calling Natzichev again and telling her, with the force of conviction, about his new theory: "You think you've saved him? Instead, you've lost him! Because you confessed? Because I told you that he had confessed to the murder of the countess? Well, that's not true, he confessed to nothing! I told you a lie. But now I see that what I thought to be a lie was the truth and you, yourself, without wanting to, or rather wanting the reverse, have proved that to me! If it had been a lie, you would have simply laughed at me. Instead, you were afraid for him and in vain tried to save him!"

However, Ferpierre stopped himself abruptly, foreseeing that the young woman wouldn't be left without an answer: "I didn't laugh at your lie, because it didn't provoke laughter, but rather, pain. Believing that you had told me the truth, I thought that Zakunin had accused himself in order to save me, and as he's innocent and I'm guilty, I couldn't laugh, only tremble, so I told you the truth!"

What could he answer to that? And how could he prove to her it was a lie? And if what she had said was true? If she really was guilty? If her behavior wasn't that of a heroic savior but of a self-confessed perpetrator, what reason was there to consider her not guilty? Was it possible that she had the ability to reconstruct a false solution to the events in question that was so vivid and that she was capable of telling such an accumulation of lies with an anxious voice and sincere expression?

Once more Ferpierre weighed up the probability, sifting through the presumptions, going over the work undertaken in the previous days. He paused, considering first one hypothesis, then another, recognizing as he had before, the difficulties of the case.

Should he really discard his investigations up to this point? Was the chance of getting irrefutable proof totally lost? And how could he conclude these long and perhaps fruitless hearings? Did he really need to accept the last statements of the accused? Or should he refute them and reaffirm that the countess had killed herself and that Natzichev had incriminated herself solely because she feared the prince would be found guilty, although she was as innocent as he was, and therefore, their version of events hadn't coincided? Or should he return to the hypothesis, already discarded as the most improbable, that they were both guilty, that Natzichev had helped her lover to carry out the crime with robbery as its motive and that trying to save him she had accused herself?

The judge was repelled by every one of these conclusions, but he needed to decide on one. He was already thinking of trying again with the two Russians when, in spite of the order he had given, he heard a knock on the door. The attendant, excusing himself for disturbing Ferpierre, handed over a communication from the Attorney General: two underlined characters on a corner of the document indicated that the item was urgent.

Ferpierre distractedly ripped open the envelope. Nothing seemed urgent if it couldn't lift the longstanding ambiguity of this situation. Inside, there were two pieces of paper: a telegram and a note from the Attorney General who had written the following: "I am immediately sending you the dispatch that has just been received by the Swiss Consul General in Edinburgh. Finally, we can now know with some degree of certainty about the Ouchy mystery."

And with a trembling hand, Ferpierre unfolded the other sheet of paper, which said: "Sister Anna Brighton lives in Stonehaven, in Kincardine County, Scotland. It has already been agreed that the English judiciary will take her statement."

Public curiosity was, once again, awakened. It was more clamorous than ever when it became clear that the judicial process hadn't finished, that the judge distrusted Alexandra Nazichev's confession and that everything was again thrown into doubt at the very moment when the mystery seemed to have been solved. Discussions worsened, ever more heated and useless, between those who believed the nihilist's sincerity, those who saw her conduct as proof of the prince's guilt and those who had renewed faith in the verdict of suicide, accusing the judge of dragging a confession from an innocent woman via his inquisitorial methods. However, most recognized that he was in the middle of one of those cases where doubt prevailed, the solution of which would have to wait until some unexpected circumstance rose to clarify matters or that it would, more often than not, remain unsolved forever.

The news that Sister Anna had finally been found brought expectation to fever pitch. Her statement and the last letter written to her by the countess hours before her death were going to explain everything.

Such faith, though, wasn't generally felt and Ferpierre, despite his first feelings of astonishment and pleasure on receiving the telegram, feared he would still be left with doubts. If the dead woman had confessed she was going to kill herself, if she had sent her final farewell to the nun, wouldn't Sister Anna, on receiving the card, on reading this news, have rushed to her, or at least, have answered or tried to get further news to see if Fiorenza had put her fatal plan into action? And, given that newspapers worldwide had written about the tragedy, about the accusation, the arrests and the investigation, surely wouldn't it have been a matter of conscience for the nun to write to the judiciary? Nothing had been received; therefore, the letter couldn't have forewarned of her suicide.

In which case, it was only natural to think that the situation of the defendants had singularly worsened. If the letter lacked an explicit allusion to the author's desperate plan, it had to be less probable than ever that, just over an hour later, she had killed herself. However, which of the two should carry the blame for the crime? Could one hope that the countess had expressed the fear she felt from the threatening attitude of one or other of the accused? Wasn't it more likely that the letter would lack detail and that, although revealing the anxiety she felt, it wouldn't reveal her determination to end her life? If so, the ambiguity would still be there.

Initial news from the British press announcing that Sister Anna had been found, did away with any of the judge's doubts. According to reports, the nun had been suffering from a serious paralysis and had lost the use of her body and speech.

A telegram from London to the *Journal de Genève* sent on the following day, stated that her illness had started a month ago and that her seizure, according to Sister Anna's cousin, her only relative, had been provoked by reading some desperate news in a letter.

And when, a week later, Ferpierre received confirmation of these rumors in the report from the Scottish magistrate, he understood that he had again erred in his predictions. Sister Anna hadn't been able to respond to the countess or to aid the forces of justice because the letter from her favorite ex-pupil had caused her to fall into a comatose state.

The letter, found by her side and attached to the report along with others of no significance, said: "Sister Anna, pray for me. Pray a lot, with all the fervor of your kindly soul, because I'm in great need of forgiveness.

"This is the last letter you'll receive from me. If, one day, you hear what I have done, remember the name you always gave me, from the first time that I felt your caress. Remember that you called me your daughter and that you loved me as such. To a daughter you'll be indulgent.

"God reads my heart. I can't and don't want to tell you what storms are destroying me. You're in blissful ignorance not knowing my mistakes. Why tell you of the things I have fought against? Only think of this: that if I have sinned too much, I now want to flee from further sin. I am reduced to such a condition that everything is full of guilt and horror. Only death can free me. I have to wait for it, though it won't be long. But evil, no, evil won't wait.

"If I'm causing you pain, forgive me. Remember, I have nobody else in the world to whom I can say these words in this desperate hour. I would like to make one further plea to you: take with happiness the memories I leave for you. I'm sure that you'll keep them with the kind of love you have always shown me.

"Sister Anna, pray for me."

IX

Agony

The years passed and Countess Fiorenza d'Arda, Prince Alexi Zakunin and Alexandra Natzichev were slowly erased from the collective memory. The owners of the Villa Cyclamens had initially thought about changing the name of the villa, fearing that sad memories would stop others from wanting to live there, but the following season, an Englishman expressly asked for it, moved by a curiosity instigated by the drama at Ouchy. Two years later it was rented by an American family who knew nothing of the dead woman or the subsequent proceedings, and so the name remained.

Baroness Börne, a frequent figure at the doctor's office, told the story to all the new arrivals in great deal detail, and they stood listening to her, indifferent to these events from the past that they had not been around to witness, even to the point of boredom with her monotonous drone. And it didn't even take that long for the baroness to forget.

Sister Anna Brighton must have died in Stonehaven. The name of Countess d'Arda was erased from the cross in Sallaz cemetery. With regard to the prince and the young nihilist, nobody knew anything more of them once they had been set free. They must have returned to their propaganda activities. And what about their relationship? It was likely that after her heroic attempt to save him, Alexandra Natzichev would have seen Zakunin reciprocate the love that she felt for him. The newspapers, once full of news relating to the accused, no longer wrote about them. Other stories and other passions occupied the space formerly given to the events at Ouchy.

Judge Ferpierre, notwithstanding new proceedings and cases occupying his investigative skills, was, more than anyone else, the person who remembered the drama. His preoccupations had been too profound, his vexations too troublesome as he had not been able to see a clear way through the tangle. Trying to justify his own behavior, he thought that, after reading the countess's diary and interrogating Vérod, he had seen and confirmed the truth, but the memory of his hesitation and suspicion, as well as his ambiguous and unfortunate actions, continued to embarrass him. Why hadn't he kept to the opinion that the accusation was all due to Vérod's hatred of Zakunin? A kind of mute and pernicious remorse stayed with him for a long time because of the thought that he had pushed an innocent woman towards a terrible sacrifice. Although his error had been confused with others, he realized that there had been no blame he could attach to himself other than that of an excessive zeal to uncover the heart of the matter. Therefore, over time, even he started to lose his detailed memory of the events.

Robert Vérod also told himself that he would be able to forget, but this hoped-for goal was a long time in coming.

On occasion, when a new idea presented him with a painful memory, he would shudder, as the new train of seemingly endless thought was even more somber. In face of the evidence, he was given no choice but to recognize his error, admit the injustice of his accusation and agree that it had been hate motivating it. Seeing that the proof backed up the judge's stark opinion, he felt that he had contributed to the poor woman's death. He now bore lightly the remorse that had once seemed dreadful. Not only did he make no attempt to excuse himself, but he insisted with a certain dark efficacy on confessing his mistake. He made caustic accusations, increasing the weight of his own responsibility in order to try and avoid a more troublesome conclusion. It was all in vain. He wanted to think that his love had been responsible for her death, thereby evading the thought that she hadn't been worthy of it.

All the reasons he had adopted to combat the hypothesis of suicide were indelibly imprinted on his brain. Was it believable that the countess had killed herself without leaving him a final farewell? Given her faith in God, could she have taken her own life? Whatever the anxiety that had taken hold of her, despite her deadly intentions, wouldn't her hand have trembled at the point of putting her plan into action? Wouldn't her arm have fallen, motionless, at the idea of leaving behind such a sad example for him, the man who had reconciled her to the idea of life? By killing herself, wouldn't she also be killing him?

"This is serious: when in love a lover isn't only responsible for his or her actions, but also those of the partner."

Those were her words. In order to kill herself, she must have forgotten them. And she had forgotten them! Her faith in God wasn't as firm as it had seemed given she had succumbed to taking her own life! She had killed herself thinking him a relative stranger, without leaving him one word of goodbye, instead, throwing in his face the doubts he had wanted to shake.

This was the truth: he had been a victim of an illusion, of love's eternal deception, attributing to the countess sublime virtues that she had never possessed, exaggerating the beauty of her soul until he had wrapped it in superhuman perfection.

"I ought to have known," he said to himself, trying to overcome the sadness of disillusion, "that perfection is beyond human reach, that humankind can think about it, look for it, but never obtain it. This certainty would have stopped me praising everything about her. It should now temper my mistrust and stop me maligning her memory beyond measure."

Effectively, changing the nature of her character in his memory, he now not only accused her of weakness, but of lies and almost a certain unworthiness. Before she had killed herself, she had told him that she loved him, and it was evident that she had lied to him. Who could then be sure that she hadn't lied on other occasions? As happens with all virulent yet dormant humors in infected blood, they are awoken by the lightest wound. They are exacerbated and become gangrenous. Thinking in such a way fed an increasing number of thoughts which gnawed away at the young man, thoughts that had never previously come to mind. He almost reached the point of despising and mocking himself for having made a woman who lived in sin the ideal of perfection.

Hadn't she, indeed, lived beyond the norms of society? Wasn't her relationship with the prince shameful? What value could be given to the promise she claimed to have secretly made to herself? Was it believable that she was sincere in making it, or was she trying to redeem herself in her own and others' eyes with such an assertion after realizing the seriousness of her sin? Was it credible that she had given herself to Zakunin so she could play the part of the redeemer? If only she had loved him with a simple love, rather than the chimera of redemption or faith as part of her lasting pact!

However, Vérod even denied this. He couldn't bring himself to think that a man like Zakunin could inspire any sincere feelings. Bloodthirsty and tyrannical even when he preached peace and liberty, intent on avidly enjoying himself as he claimed to cry for the sufferings of others, lustful, a squanderer, unfaithful, a liar, Zakunin couldn't be the object of noble affection. He could only inspire a perverse fascination, an unhealthy curiosity, a submissive yearning. That woman's passion had been submissive, unhealthy, perverse.

Impotent jealousy and his lack of self-esteem made Vérod come to these conclusions. When Fiorenza d'Arda was alive, he hadn't thought of them. While he had been able to see her death as the work of a murderer, while she had appeared to be surrounded by the halo of a martyr, no suspicion could have touched her. While he felt loved by her, by a pure and faithful love, he had repaid it, but he had discovered that it wasn't true. If she had really loved him, how could she leave him like this? If her relationship with Zakunin was such a block to her happiness, she must have felt something for him? Had she killed herself to avoid being unfaithful? Could the notion of abstract duty have had such force if it didn't chime with concrete feelings, with an entirely personal and existing interest? The deceitful repentance shown by Zakunin, the false resurrection of his love, which had never been believable, had awoken her former submissive nature, but it never took her over since she had taken her own life.

With thoughts like these, the figure he had once placed on a pedestal was corrupted and little by little began to rot away. And then these prophetic words from long ago came to his mind: "I have lived outside the rules for so long that I can hardly now expect to return to the fold. You don't want to believe it now and you're sincere, but you'll be equally sincere later on when you will believe it. I don't make myself out to be worse than I am, but even if everyone else isn't aware of my decadence, I am, indestructibly so. This feeling makes life compete with faith.... It ought to make me give my life to religion, later on it should make you too."

Vérod felt overcome by an immense anguished astonishment on finally seeing the prophecy realized, on understanding that he no longer had the right to withhold his respect for the dead woman, given that she had humbly recognized her own unworthiness while painfully combatting his fervent trust.

He had rebelled, but now his heart filled with reverence. He had to recognize that she hadn't been wrong. She had foreseen the inevitable future, which logically and inescapably had to produce this result: "The day will come when you judge me as I now judge myself." Hadn't that almost happened while she had still been alive? Wasn't it true that on the last day they had met, when she told him of Zakunin's wish to return to her, his hatred for the man and his lovelorn feeling of powerlessness had almost caused him to turn against her?

"Behave as you must," he had said to her, "but the man will leave you again." Hadn't he pursued the thought further? Hadn't the fear of being scorned almost prompted him to press her hand and say firmly: "And for a man like him, you're rejecting me? And losing yourself because of him…him, you refuse to be rescued?"

In the shadow of such thoughts, he rounded on himself doubtfully and posed another more anxious question: "Was she right in killing herself?"

If a poisonous seed had worked its way into their new liaison, was it better that she had died? If she had thought that his actions were prompted by the idea of rescue or an act of generosity, wouldn't she have resisted and killed herself, not out of faithfulness to Zakunin, but because of a fatal misunderstanding about their new relationship? Dead thanks to him, how could he still presume to judge her? If, believing her to be the victim of another's cruelty, he had given her all the compassion his heart could muster, shouldn't he now show her greater compassion, one fed by remorse, given that she had rehabilitated herself with a voluntary sacrifice?

The full severity of his judgment was subsequently directed against his own opinions. Who was he to pretend that he could begin to judge her?

And why had he condemned her if not for the fact that she had escaped him? What besides egotistical passion, that most voracious and insatiable of passions, had made him so harsh when thinking of her memory? It was simply the dishonesty of these feelings that had made him believe the commitment she had taken wasn't valid and that by forgetting it and getting involved with him, she would have been behaving honestly and justly! He wanted her to be perfect, but like all human beings and perhaps more so, he had his weaknesses and faults.

He emerged from all his opposing thoughts finally resigned to the inexorable truth, prepared to recognize that although Fiorenza hadn't been as beautiful as he had painted her in his amorous fantasies, neither had she been as bad as he had seen her in the depths of his abandon. Nevertheless, he felt uncomfortable and sorrowful. It was hard for him to reject her imagined perfection. He told himself that nobody in the world was perfect, but he still wanted to believe that she fulfilled this ideal. All his efforts to glorify, or at least, legitimize her voluntary sacrifice were in vain.

It wasn't true that she had been redeemed by killing herself. Redemption is to be found in life, not in death. Death doesn't resolve a moral dilemma, it only avoids it. If she couldn't or didn't want to be his woman, as he had wanted, there was another way out: to flee, to disappear, but without giving up on life.

Wasn't this the way it should have been?

Vérod felt hesitant, doubtful and anxious, but his judgments on humanity's most serious problems had been illuminated and given a degree of certainty by the valuable example of her virtue. This miracle was of her doing, making him leave behind the doubt, uncertainty and skepticism that had been part of his life. She had been his religion, the light of her ideas had dazzled him. She had guided him with a firm hand through life's contradictions, deceptions and mistakes. She had known what to believe and what to discard. However, he was soon assailed once again by further indecision. She should have lived! She had to die! How to resolve the formidable dilemma of either living in error or dying to avoid it! Did human beings have the right to do away with their own existence? If this right was in doubt, who could stop someone from doing it? Turning his eyes trustingly to the heavens, where once he would have looked only to find emptiness and an impenetrable desert, he had felt her gaze on him. Yet he knew, or worst still, he feared that he knew too much. She had taken her own life! She hadn't feared the judgment of God! She hadn't thought about the salvation of her soul. She hadn't believed in the life to come. She had killed herself because everything ends with death.

"So, there's nothing then, nothing at all?"

The question hung in the air, unheard.

By the sole virtue of being in her company, he had heard, understood and looked upon the soul of the world. Mysterious voices had told him memorable things. Everything had throbbed with life, had been brilliant with light. Now silence and darkness pressed in from every side. What had first possessed a palpable or secret meaning remained mute.

So profound and sincere had been his conversion that at times he had felt lit by lamps of the old faith. Then the shadows had closed in, thicker than ever. In his doubts he found a silent and desperate terror that he thought his old self had managed to bury deep inside. His thoughts were dark, confused and lost, as they were before he knew the countess. The miraculous flowering that had entered every crevice of his soul had withered and thinned out. Previously, his closed heart had been satisfied with its own greed, then her seed had been sown, but it was now just embittered by endless resentment.

He decided to travel. He saw other lands, other men, hoping to leave his grief behind on the world's roads, but nothing was able to mollify him. In Nice, before his sister's grave, he cried bitter tears which, far from assuaging him, simply led to further rancor. He didn't return to the lake. He was consumed by a toxic fear that plagued him when he thought of seeing again the only places he could truly say had brought him to life. He feared dying by the weight of suffocation on revisiting the lakeside at Ouchy, the hills of Lausanne, the Villa Cyclamens, the forest at Comte, the humble chapels, the panorama of Leman veiled by clouds or smiling in the sun. Yet one day, he did return.

He found the places just as he had left them. The impassiveness of nature's eternal face upset him like an insult: if only something had been destroyed in the landscape; if only he had discovered in his surroundings a devastation equal to what he felt inside.

The secular mountains, the everlasting lakes, those voracious graves for the unwitting living, remained immutable. He came to recognize every step of the way, every nuance of the view. With the desperate certainty that no power could give him back what he had lost, he, nonetheless, fixed his gaze and sharpened his hearing, as if an apparition or a voice could suddenly evoke his lost wellbeing.

And one afternoon, as he was contemplating the summits of the Dôle from the window of his room, as the radiant sun began to descend, he was startled on hearing a voice speaking behind him.

Was it a hallucination, a waking dream?

Prince Alexi Zakunin was there in the room.

"Robert Vérod," said the voice, "don't you recognize me?"

A shudder of horror took hold of him as it would on seeing a ghost. What did this man want with him? Why had he come to seek him out?

"You know who I am, don't you? But you're not expecting me? I have come to see you because I have something to tell you."

He spoke with his head lowered, almost submissively. Seen from above, from his ample forehead to the point of his beard, his face appeared to be scored with deep lines. His hair, already scarce, had whitened at the temples. His entire person wore the signs of a rapid decline.

Vérod looked at him, fascinated, incapable of answering as he tried to make clear the tumult of feelings that had been unleashed.

"I have to tell you something. I had wanted to tell Judge Ferpierre, but I thought that it would be better to approach you first...."

After a pause, he added: "Listen Vérod, Fiorenza d'Arda didn't kill herself. I killed her."

Vérod passed a hand across his forehead and his eyes. Once more, he had the sensation of being in a waking dream, but even more so than before.

"You don't believe me? And yet you were so close to the truth! I know that you asserted as much despite everything and everyone, and there wasn't much more you needed in order to prove it. It's true that many circumstances were against you, one in particular. Sister Anna's letter seemed to pronounce the last word on the countess's fate. This deceived the forces of law and order. She really was on the point of killing herself when I killed her. I'll tell you how I did it."

Vérod shook as if taken by some fever.

"I have to tell you of my infamy. It will be the start of my punishment. Never when she was alive did I understand the beauty of her soul. I didn't understand beauty at all: the world and life itself seemed devoid of such a quality. I carried a sort of hell within me, and nothing could put out the flames consuming me. Everything I touched was reduced to ashes. She loved me out of compassion: instinct, need and the voluptuousness of her sacrifice gave me to her. Although I didn't understand it, I was, for a moment, bathed in her light. I couldn't bear its clarity, and I turned away. I derided her. I offended her."

He remained quiet for a moment, he eyes fixed on a spot before him as if blind, then he continued: "Listen, when I've told you everything, you will know that my words hold weight. During my initial happiness, I felt like another man. Nature and life itself drove me from one sensation to completely the opposite with a swift ferocity of feeling. Those who know what I've done in the world might think that at times, I've been driven by the voice of decency, but I've got no conscience. If I internally judged my actions and those of others, it was all reduced to a mechanism, a game of blind and fatal impulses. I couldn't, therefore, believe in the change brought on by her virtue. I didn't only deride her, I was also laughing at myself....

"I must also tell you about my shocking behavior: how day by day, hour by hour, to her face, I countered her constant, tireless, divine preaching of love and decency with scorn, insult and betrayal. But you know all that. And yet, and yet...

"All that your hatred of me suggested was too little. What I did to her was unbelievable. At times, I destroyed her faith when I used poisonous and corrosive words to vilify and despise her, showing her that nothing existed except evil, with the only remedies being iron, fire and death. When I encouraged her to leave me, to betray me, to lose herself, I felt a violent reaction building inside and tears came to my eyes, but I hid them.

"When you got to know her, I realized that she had started to fall in love with you, and I was filled with joy. I was filled with *schadenfreude* on seeing that her much vaunted eternal feelings were proving deceitful; on foreseeing that she would fall as we all fall; on being able to say to her, 'You see? Where are your moral codes now? You're like all the rest, doing what pleases you!'

"After a while, I completely gave myself over to the work of undermining this decayed society in both my own country and others. Our last attempt seemed destined to be successful. I was already beginning to savor its triumph. Everything had been prepared in detail, and I had incited to action the idle, the irresolute and the fearful. I had handed over almost all of my resources without thinking of the difficulties I would encounter later.

"My duty was also to take action, and being a part was my objective, if I hadn't been obliged to stay behind and prepare a new offensive in case we suffered a reverse. One day, I heard that my brothers in arms had been killed, swinging from ropes on gallows found on the road to exile where they had suffered the lash of prison guards. I knew that the women, the children and the innocents who stepped up to the scaffold were paying for me; that terror was reigning over all those of my ilk. On that day, in the face of this loss and doubting whether I had taken the right turn, I found myself alone and almost poor. Then all of a sudden, something surged from within, like a need, anxiety or a burning thirst for assistance. It was as if I had held out my hand to find help by my side. I almost prostrated myself when I heard a word of consolation.

"There was someone who could console me. I didn't need to do anything but go in search of her and open my heart. Perhaps there would still be time. Or perhaps not, perhaps it was already too late.

"Too late! Do you know what these words mean? Notions of pride stopped me. Would I have to beg? However, I realized that nothing in this crisis would be able to cure me like the love of a woman such as her.

"I came back to her. I said nothing. My attitude, though, must have shown her what I was going through. Too late! We can suffer and accept the suffering, we can despair and live in desperation, but when confronted with the idea that we only have to hold out our hand and say a word to achieve happiness, that it's possible, but that fortune has passed us by because we have proffered our hand and spoken too late, it's that idea that will stop our heart from beating.

"She was no longer mine. She was yours. When I discovered this, once again I began to mock and laugh at myself. I fled from her, but I had to return. By her side, however much I tried to be repentant and a convert, I felt insufferable subjugation, but I couldn't live apart from her. So passed the final few months in bouts of departure and shorter return visits. In Zurich I lived for the moments when I talked about her to another equally unhappy woman, Alexandra. Alexandra Natzichev is dead. . . ."

Vérod was stunned. No, it wasn't a dream, but reality had every appearance of being one. The man who was speaking in front of him looked like the proud revolutionary in the same way that pallid images from a nightmare seem to represent living people. Natzichev was dead? How, why was she dead? Even the hour of day and the light were unnatural. The yellowing glow of dusk lit up the room in a strange manner along with the ornaments and the squalid face of the prince.

"I confided my inner torment to Alexandra. She fell in love with me, and I didn't even notice. Life had wanted it that way: that these four human beings had found each other only to suffer indescribable agony. And none had known what the other was suffering or that it was always too late! When I showed Alexandra brotherly love, I tried to protect her and aid her like a sister or a daughter, given the loneliness she was experiencing and the strength that made her capable of enduring and beating life's difficulties. But she loved me with a more burning passion! If I'd been aware of her love, would I have made her happy? It was only with her that I could divulge my passion for another.

"Alexandra tried to refocus me by calling me back to serve the cause. I wanted to listen to her, but it was in vain. The idea of recapturing a love I had previously scorned, occupied and directed my entire life. After belittling it, it now seemed that my love for the countess had an incalculable price. This was indeed justice!

"I said nothing of this to Fiorenza. When I came to see her, I spent my days fearing that I would discover, given her heart was no longer mine, that she had already given herself to you. To avoid thinking about this horrible eventuality, I told myself that: 'She has such lofty ideals, she would never do it!' Inside me, a voice would respond: 'So now do you believe in the dignified morals you previously scoffed at?' Yes, I had laughed at her before. And now I still didn't believe in her!

"My confidence that she wouldn't betray me wasn't so much founded in the esteem I had for her character as it was in the impossibility of believing that everything had irredeemably finished between us. I felt that my return and the mending of my ways had made her really anxious, and I was enjoying the experience of getting her back.

"Being by her side and not being able to take her hand! Oh, to remember the past and be desperate to relive just one hour of it! All that I felt but couldn't mention. Pride still held me back, and another reason, no less sad. I was now poor, and she was rich. Could talking about love seem like a lie suggested by cold hard calculation?

"One day, I did speak to her. I told her this: 'I know I left you. I wanted to leave you. I feel like my guilt is irreparable. But you know what I feel inside! I ask you please not to abandon me at this moment when it's all crumbling around me. Later, you must do what you want....'

"That same day, the day of the storm, you also spoke to her. She was caught between the two of us. She decided to end it all. She answered me with this: 'I'll never abandon you because I'm your wife but realize that our love is dead.'

"Her voice was cold, her eyes avoided mine.

"When I knew that you had also spoken to her, it occurred to me that she hadn't been sincere, that she was hiding something. I feared that she was thinking about leaving. I didn't know, I didn't believe that she had resolved to die. I still didn't truly know her.

"It was an awful night. She also spent most of it awake. One hundred, maybe a thousand times, I had wanted to go to her, but her door was always locked. In the morning, Alexandra came to find me, to call for me, foreseeing a catastrophe. I promised to leave with her, but I first wanted to see Fiorenza for the last time.

"On hearing me enter her room, she quickly hid something. I saw that it was a gun.

"Stuck between two opposing passions, she had decided to be free by killing herself. I realized that having invaded her space, I had no right to speak. I had to leave her to her fate, to freedom and to death, but I couldn't. The idea that nothing more existed between two people who had once been united, that I was little more than a stranger to her, never entered my mind. My secret voice uttered once more: 'Before, you believed that love was the fleeting meeting of two impulses, before, you laughed at the notion of an unbreakable link....'

"I couldn't concede that she was someone else's, even when it was no more than a thought. I, who had betrayed her, couldn't admit that I had been betrayed in return. My pride was limitless. I couldn't tolerate anyone valuing her more than I did. And as I began to understand that you would know how to make her happy, pride, love, jealousy, all the feelings, all the savage instincts in my blood, in my nature, rose up threateningly within me.

"'You promised me yesterday that you wouldn't leave me,' I said to her with bitterness, 'because you were my wife, and now you want to kill yourself!'

"She didn't deny it. 'Let me die,' was her response, 'it will be better for everyone.'

"There was something in her voice that I didn't recognize: her love for you, the rancor of having to leave behind the happiness that beckoned with you.

"'You can't tolerate the sight of me then? Do I horrify you that much?'

"I said these words and many, many others.

"She only made this one response: 'Who's to blame then?'

"Listen, this was the first time she had reproached me after so many months of anguish.

"'Right,' I replied, 'I'll disappear, I'll leave this very day, and you'll never see me again. Do you still want to die?'

"'Yes,' was her answer.

"I was afraid that I understood, nonetheless, I asked: 'Why?'

"Her words told me nothing that I didn't know already: 'Because if I live I will be his.'

"His, yours, belonging to another!

"A burning heat came to my eyes and face.

"'That's not possible, it won't happen!'

"She shook her head.

"'Don't say no!' I insisted. 'Don't say no! I already know that you don't love me anymore, that you hate me, that you loathe me; but don't tell me that you love somebody else, because...because...'

"'I love him,' she said.

"I implored her. I even cried, but she said it again: 'I love him. I can't lie. I don't know how to pretend otherwise. I love him, but because this love is forbidden to me, I must die.'

"Then I laughed at her, I mocked her: 'A person who wants to die never says so! However, as you've got this far, you should play your part!'

"I saw her eyes widened in astonishment.

"'You don't believe me? Don't you realize that I've already said goodbye to the only person who will sincerely cry for me?'

"'Him?' I said to her.

"It was Sister Anna that she had written to. In the face of my suspicions and the ironic tone I had used to express them, she didn't reply with scorn, she simply corrected me: 'Sister Anna.'

"I added with a mocking smile: 'And what about your soul?'

"On hearing these words, she hid her head in her hands. I suddenly took hold of them and tried to draw her to me.

"'No, you won't die, you'll live for me, with me...'

"She jumped back, moving away: 'Don't touch me!'

"I felt my overwhelming love clash with an implacable hatred.

"'I see, this horrific pain is my doing,' I told her. 'And you love him! And, even if you want to, you can't take your own life because you fear the wrath of your God. I want to free you from this pain!'

"And before she had time to suspect what I was doing, I grabbed hold of the weapon she had hidden inside her books.

"'You won't really be able to kill yourself. You won't provoke the anger of your God, and you'll also be able to go in search of caresses elsewhere.'

"From that moment on, I didn't recognize her anymore. She looked around, bewildered, as if she was lost, as if pursued by a voracious, howling whirlwind.

"Then she looked at me. Her eyes were lit by a flash of delight, something akin to a contemptuous smile.

"'Ah! You believe me. Even you believe that I want to die. Why? You've taken the gun away. It's not death waiting for me, but life and joy. Go, leave me alone: he will come to me now!'

"I also looked around me, alarmed. My hand trembled on the weapon. There was a question in my eyes that she understood.

"'He's going to come, I'm his!'

"The burning sensation returned to my eyes and face, more acrid than before.

"'Shut up!' I shouted at her.

"'No, I won't, I can't! I love him, I'm his!'

"'Shut up!' I yelled once more.

"'No, I won't be quiet! I love him, and I hate you, I despise you! You have caused me so much pain that I have the right to leave you for good! Nobody could blame me!'

"'Shut up!' I ordered for the third time.

"'No, I won't! Although I might be blamed, what does it matter? My whole being needs to feel the joy that is finally trying to enter my life. I want to shout to everyone and show them the happiness washing over me.'

"'You're mad!' I shouted.

"'Yes, ever since I've been yours!'

"No, this wasn't possible. If it had been true, if I truly believed it, I would also have gone mad.

"'It's not true! I don't believe you!' I told her.

"She answered me, astonished, laughing: 'You don't believe it? How can I make you believe it? Listen, if it weren't true, would I have wanted to die? You found me with a gun in my hand. I have sent a letter with a last goodbye. I was on the point of writing my will, then afterwards I would have written to him. Do you think that I want to leave it all like this, that I could? Without remorse triggered by guilt, would I have thought about death? If it hadn't been for my fall from grace, would I have carried on living like I have up to now? I wished to die because I used to believe I had committed sins, but now, no longer…no longer!'

"'But haven't you?'

"'I have, and I will do it again. I love him, he's mine, always. Do you want to know when? Do you want to know how?'

"'Shut up, you're trying to provoke me!'

"'I'm not provoking you. What do you matter to me? Who are you? What are you doing here? Who gave you the right to enter these rooms? Go! Leave me! He's waiting for me, I tell you. Are you trying to scare me? Eh!'

"My eyes must have been truly frightening, but she laughed and insisted: 'I'm not scared of you! What can you possibly do to me?'

"I interrupted her: 'Kill you!'

"She opened her arms, raised her chin and pushed her chest forward.

"'Do it, kill me! I will still be his, even in the grave!'

"'Shut up, or I will do it!'

"'Even in the grave. There isn't a single thought, a beat of my heart, a movement of my soul, a fiber of my being that isn't his.'

"I lifted the gun. Her eyes blazed with intensity, her voice rang out: 'In life, even in death, his alone...'

"I fired...."

Robert Vérod had been shaking as Zakunin related the story, shaking from grief, from horror, from pity, from impotent remorse and badly contained hatred. On hearing these last words, he took a step forward and lifting his fist, shouted: "Murderer!"

The prince held his gaze and said: "Hit me."

The two stayed like this for a while, face to face, without noticing the time. Finally, Vérod let his arm fall and, with a quaking, hoarse voice, repeated: "Murderer!"

"I came here so that you can finally have justice. What you do will be right and proper, but just listen to me for a moment. When I saw her fall, when I saw the blood spill from her horrendous wound, I shrieked from deep within. She was still alive. She lived to tell me her last words: 'I have lied, to die. I couldn't.... Thank.... Forgiveness....'

"These were her last words. I wanted to die with her. I had the gun in my hand, and I turned it on myself, but somebody grabbed my arm with a vice-like grip. Alexandra was in front of me: 'You have to live! You must live! You must save yourself! Let me do it!'

"I didn't understand.

"Alexandra put the weapon next to the body, studying the best way to place it. She took a cartridge from it.

"'She killed herself, just like she said she would. Everyone will believe that....'

"The noises and voices from the passageway were already getting closer.

"'Do you understand? If they suspect anything, let me answer. Whatever happens, just confirm my replies. Think about your obligations! Think about the cause! Think about me, that I love you, that I want to be with you, that I'll know how to make you happy!'

"I didn't understand. I ran to ask for help, hoping that she was still alive. Why hide the truth? My first impulse was to admit to everything. If I didn't immediately say that, it was because I still didn't understand anything. I didn't hear the questions they asked me. I responded mechanically, as if in a dream. Though, later on, when you threw the accusation in my face, I rebelled against it. I remained like this. My thoughts, my feelings were governed by this sudden reaction. Accused by you, I defended myself. I said all I could against myself. I recognized that I was the one who had pushed her towards death, but I denied being the perpetrator. More than once during the interrogations I was about to confess, but on hearing your name, on seeing the judge's harshness, I flared up again. From the desire to destroy myself, to die, to clear my guilt, which I felt at first, I moved on to wish for freedom like a caged beast who had no other task than breaking his chains, running free and being his own master. I backed up Alexandra's statements without completely understanding them, and when she accused herself, when I finally understood her, that she was handing herself over because she loved me, I, naturally, accepted the sacrifice.... We were both set free. At the point when I was given my liberty, when the lie had triumphed, I resolved to tell the truth. Yet I still kept quiet, because inside, during the long night of my soul, the dawn of a new day was beginning to emerge. Alexandra thought she was watching over me given that we were together and that she talked to me. I didn't see her. I didn't hear her. A silent and invisible spirit was already ruling my life."

He stopped himself for a moment, lifting his eyes to the heavens. The sky had grown calm, the yellowish clouds had disappeared. Pure pink and green tones lit up the western horizon.

The prince continued: "Rancor, hate, envy, greed, the miseries that had been part of my life, all finally appeared in their somber light. The blood that I had previously spilt still said nothing to me. I had needed to spill the blood of a victim, of a martyr, in order to understand the law of love. All of Fiorenza's lessons, which I had once scorned and derided, came back to mind. The seed that had seemed lost now bore fruit. Do you believe that she's dead?"

The penitent prince's voice was so sweetly sincere that Robert Vérod felt deeply moved.

"She's still alive, in everything that's beautiful, everything that's good. Through these things her voice speaks, advising us. She told me to come to you, you who loved her and had that love reciprocated. She said that you would know what to do with me."

He waited for Vérod to answer, but as he seemed incapable of saying anything, Zakunin continued: "You can't kill me as you know all about her belief in forgiveness. But should I still live my life in freedom? Is my return to the faith enough? Is it enough that in all this time I have tried to repair the harm that I have done? Should I not give the world proof of conversion and my sincerity? And to truly merit a pardon, shouldn't I atone for my sins? There are two paths before me. I can hand myself over to the forces of law and order in this country and pay for my crime where I committed it, or I can go to face justice in my own country, where I'm also responsible for other offences. Would you like to tell me which of the two seems the better path?"

Robert Vérod didn't answer. What could he advise him to do? What right did he have? Grief overcame him to such a degree that his judgment was completely shattered.

"Right, I think I'm not wrong in following what seems to me like an exemplary lesson: I will leave for Russia. Perhaps here they will judge my crime with too much indulgence, as it was a crime of passion. I will await the death penalty in Russia. And then I must confess to the world that I deceived myself. If the laws that govern societies don't make them happy, the blame doesn't lie with the men who wrote them. Others can't come up with anything more than human laws, in other words, those that are deficient and ineffectual. To hate each other and to fight each other for a rigid change in the way humanity feels, a pain to which it's condemned, is a mad proposal. The fight against injustice and evil is necessary, but except for love, there is no useful weapon. We need to love each other, to sympathize with each other, to help each other. I want to proclaim at the top of my voice that I was wrong, I want to ask for forgiveness for all the damage I have inflicted on so many, so very many...."

He hid his face in his hands, remaining in this ponderous state for a while. Eventually, turning his face to Vérod, he continued: "And to you, whom I have deeply hurt, I humbly want to ask for forgiveness. No doubt, it's too soon for you to be able to stand the sight of me. But I know that your heart is full of decency. If you were worthy of her love, you must be the best of men. Before I leave here and never return, before I complete my atonement, I ask you, out of mercy, to just give me a few words. Remember that I will soon die. Her last words were of forgiveness, she asked me to forgive her, I, who had killed her! Tell me that you won't hate my memory."

Robert Vérod was still silent, but it was now a powerful feeling full of emotion that stopped him from speaking.

"It will have a serious impact on me if I feel dogged by your hatred. You were such a part of her life that one word of kindness from you will keep me going until I fulfil the obligation I have set myself...."

He took the young man's hand and begged him: "Robert, will you forgive me?"

Vérod made a gesture of agreement with a slight nod of his head.

Seeing Zakunin's eyes begin to fill with tears, seeing this man with a heart of iron begin to cry, he also ended up in tears.

"Fiorenza's soul is here in this room," said the prince.

The crying hadn't broken his voice. His tears were gentle and quiet.

He then added: "May she always be happy and blessed."

Vérod's tears were wild.

"Robert, you are a decent man, thank you.... Goodbye!"

On saying this, he bent to kiss the young man's hand, but Robert Vérod withdrew it and opened his arms. The two men remained momentarily locked in an embrace.

The prince asked in a subdued voice: "Brother, do you forgive me?"

"I forgive you, brother."

Loosening from the embrace, Zakunin passed a hand over his eyes and immediately retreated from the room. At the door, before disappearing into the shadows, he turned and said: "Goodbye!"

A month later, the papers were full of an extraordinary turn of events: Prince Alexi Petrovich Zakunin, the fearsome nihilist, the implacable revolutionary, who had not been heard of for quite some time, had returned to Russia, to Odessa, on a steamer. On board the vessel, he had sought out police agents in order to hand himself over to the forces of justice. In addition to admitting to his political crimes, which he solemnly regretted, he also revealed that he had committed a *crime passionel* in

Switzerland. This new version of the Ouchy drama greatly excited a curious public. The commotion was greater still when the death sentence hanging over his head was commuted by royal decree to permanent exile in Siberia owing to the heretical rebel's conversion.

Robert Vérod stayed in Lausanne among the places he now couldn't bear to leave. One day, after reading this latest news, he met Judge Ferpierre. He hadn't seen him since the judicial proceedings. He approached him with trepidation and anxiety, as the judge was the only person he could talk to about Countess d'Arda, Zakunin, and indeed, about himself.

Ferpierre, who had discovered everything through the newspapers, said to him: "I'm pleased I bumped into you. Your gut reaction didn't deceive you. What you held to be the truth right up until the end was right. You only had your passionate belief, but that was enough to make you see clearly. Fiorenza d'Arda hadn't been able to kill herself, she couldn't die by her own hand, leaving such a sad example and without any words of comfort. However great the anguish in her soul, however much she had intended to die and had forewarned that she would do it, at the last moment her Christian faith had stopped her. Yet, as she couldn't carry on living either, given Zakunin's jealous fury, she provoked him so that he, himself, would free her. Appearances deceived me. What strange things happen in life! All of you could have been happy if fate hadn't made you meet only to put you through indescribable suffering. The countess was caught between respect for herself, for her word, for her faith and for her love for you. You were desperately in love with her and jealous of Zakunin. Zakunin was lost because of his jealousy of you, his belated love for her and his fruitless self-loathing. Natzichev, the taciturn lover, was ignored and disdained.... What became of her?"

Then Vérod remembered the prince's words.

"She's dead."

But how, where and when? Zakunin hadn't explained it, and he hadn't thought to ask. Had she succumbed to a natural or violent death? Had she been killed, or before Alexi Petrovich, had she returned to Russia and let herself be condemned? When the prince had said that he wanted to follow an example that had been like a lesson, had he alluded to her? Nobody could tell. Perhaps Vérod would never know.

"How mysteriously she lived her life!" said the judge. "And she had a great heart."

"Indeed," agreed Vérod.

"Nor was the unfortunate prince totally immoral. The Tsar did well to commute his sentence. Death should remain in the hands of God. Alive, the murderer can still hope for redemption."

"He is redeemed."

As the judge met his eye with a quizzical gaze, Robert Vérod told him of his meeting with Zakunin.

"I forgave him. I felt that Fiorenza wanted him to do it. She wouldn't have wanted me to continue resenting him so much, given she had changed him, and on dying by his hand, had fulfilled the work of salvation she had set herself when she went to live by his side. He has yielded. His haughty, ferocious spirit is now a loving one. I began to doubt things again, having initially believed it, then I finally turned to the faith that she inspired in me. It's true: on that day you were right to marvel at the hatred I felt for him. Our natures were different, but we were both in agreement on life's despair. We both saw an unconscious mechanism, an empty game of blind overwhelming forces in this world. She united us in decency of sentiment, she showed us love and human fellowship. After he told me, we embraced like brothers. His behavior, his acceptance of punishment should serve as an example to the world. Even I realize I must renounce the desperate ideas that I once held, that I must adopt the things she showed me. . . ."

They had walked down to Ouchy. Both remained silent as they passed along a stretch of the lakeside, with its smooth, azure waters like a piece of sky fallen to earth.

The judge then said: "There are people like that, sent to earth to make us believe in the things that life makes us doubt too much. Their hearts are like a well of health-giving water. Be happy that you knew her, that you loved her, that you jealously guard her everlasting memory."

This Book Was Completed on 8 September 2020

At Italica Press in Bristol, UK.

It Was Set in Garamond

and Garamond

Expert.

Ingram Content Group UK Ltd.
Milton Keynes UK
UKHW012122060323
418148UK00013B/466/J

9 781599 103938